EDDIE MANN

The Nameless Ones

First published by Dark Heart Books 2019

A CIP catalogue record for this title is available from the British Library.

First edition

ISBN: 978-1-9160330-0-9

Editing by Hillary Crawford
Cover art by Fraser Price

This book was professionally typeset on Reedsy.
Find out more at reedsy.com

Dedicated, as always, to Dawn. My friend, my wife and the original author's widow.

Contents

Foreword

Brotherhood is not merely a word, it is a total dedication to each other, not just when it is convenient. My brothers are from different mothers but still I am at ease with trusting them with my life.
We are nothing without brotherhood, but the price for being something is making the promise that we will do everything humanly possible to protect and defend the people that matter.

"To lose love once is heart-wrenching
To twice lose love deadens the heart completely."

Preface

The beaten man's life had been shit for years, from the day he had left school, if the truth be known. He had done his best with the cards he had been dealt, but life had not been kind to him.

To his credit, he could have taken the easier path toward crime and prison like many of his so-called friends, but instead, he took inspiration from the one friend who had broken away from a town that offered nothing, but a life down the pits or working a china-dust covered existence in the pottery factories. That friend had been heading rapidly toward a life in prison, hanging around with a gang of youths, whose method of operation involved carrying Stanley knives and marking their victims' faces with the said weapon. Their friendship had been stretched, because of this behaviour, but even this could not break a link that had been forged many years ago in junior school.

It had hurt when his friend left the town where they had both grown up together, boarding a train that would take him to a military life in the Army. The two boys had met up a few times during the following two years when, because of periods of annual leave, his friend returned to spend time with his parents and his slowly dwindling friendship connections with the boys he once knew.

David remembered these visits with fondness and jealousy,

his friend always looked happy and was loaded with cash every time he came home. He was smartly dressed, as fit as a butcher's dog, and together with his level of confidence, it was so easy to see how he was growing and maturing. It was also obvious that his friend's future was not going to have anything to do with this shithole of a town. He vaguely recalled being told that his friend had completed his Army training and had been posted somewhere. The two weeks leave that preceded that posting was the last time David had seen his friend; he was alone, and for some reason felt nothing but hatred for a young man who had been his best friend for years.

Over the next few years, David staggered from one job to another, each one failing, until eventually an apprenticeship in carpentry led to a full-time job offer, which he accepted, because it wasn't working in one of the few working mines left or in the life-sapping pottery factories. He hated wood, he hated the job, but it allowed him to exist outside of the criminal lives being led by many of the people he had gone to school with. Eventually, he had met a lovely girl, dated her for a few years, and then inevitably married her to the joy of both his parents and sisters. *Any opportunity for a party and to get glammed up*, he had thought to himself. They were lucky enough to qualify for a council house, which they were later allowed to buy at a massively discounted price. In that house, they produced and raised three beautiful girls, who were little miracles in their own right, due to the fact that, despite trying every night for many years to have children, it was IVF treatment that eventually made his wife pregnant. So, because of the time it had taken, he was an elderly parent with three young children.

Just before the birth of his third daughter, his first two being three years old and two years old respectively, a new family moved into the house next door, and from that day forth his life and the lives of his family members, became hell.

The Armstrongs were a family of career criminals, who took no shit from anyone and gave shit to everyone. The ironic thing was that if David had not purchased his home from the council, it would have been easy to move to another house. The council would have willingly moved them, but he had followed his father's advice. *"Invest your money in brick, lad,"* he recalled his dad saying to him at the time. The day his wife lovingly carried their third baby down the short path to their front door, a leering Kelvin Armstrong had been leaning against the small fence that divided the two properties.

He had looked at the newborn wrapped in a thin blanket and wearing a new pink all-in-one baby outfit and said, "She looks like you darling, an ugly little pig."

His wife, Rachel, hurried into the house and he slammed the door behind them as his wife burst out crying.

"Fucking wanker, I will kill him one day," he said to his distraught wife.

"When?" Rachel asked between her sobs. "When will you do that, Dave? Never, that is the answer you are looking for, because you have never done anything and you never will, you spineless bastard."

She raced up the stairs, clinging tightly onto her newborn. David heard the bedroom door bang shut. He hung his head in shame, because he knew that his wife was right.

Over the next few years, they continued to face verbal abuse, threats, and cruel words on a daily basis. Their property was vandalised regularly, the content of rubbish bins emptied into their small front garden. His wife was a victim of it all more than he was, his hated job becoming his saviour—the one thing that got him away from his home. His three daughters were constantly harassed and bullied by every member of the Armstrong family, as well as their extended family and friends. Drug dealers and other criminals were constant visitors to the Armstrong household, but despite the involvement of the police and social services, nothing ever changed, and through it all, David did and said nothing.

For his fiftieth birthday, eight members of the Armstrong gang decided to give him a gift. They all defecated into a plastic carrier bag and emptied the contents onto the front doorstep of David's house. He had found it when he stepped into the huge pile of human shit, after going outside to have a smoke. His only reaction was to throw his shit covered slippers into the bin.

Two weeks later, he learned how terrible his wife's life had been, when he came home from work and found her letter. In it, she described the effects the Armstrongs' behaviour had had on the lives of both her and their daughters. The letter had ended with the words:

> **And through it all, you did nothing for us. Your job as a man, a father, and a husband should have been to protect your family. I am better off dead than living this life with you.**

He found her body lying on their bed, empty bottles of pills were strewn around the bed and floor.

On the day of Rachel's funeral, the Armstrongs invited family and friends to a barbeque, which they held in their front garden, blasting out rap music, it's vile and threatening language accompanying the carrying of her coffin to the hearse, as the Armstrongs laughed and raised glasses and bottles of beer in the direction of the coffin.

David had no other choice, but to give up his job to look after his children. Life on benefits was impossible and slowly, he began to fall behind on his mortgage payments and other important bills. The most that the Armstrongs did was to offer him a chance to sell drugs for them to earn a bit of money. Well, that and increase their anti-social behaviour toward him and his daughters.

Following eleven months of threatening letters from his bank and mortgage lender, which eventually culminated in visits from bailiffs and then, finally, notices to evict, David knew he had no choice, but to seek help. He asked a friend's daughter to look after his children so that he could attend an appointment at the towns' advice centre. His daughters rarely attended school these days, because of the bullying they received from the Armstrong children.

Just four hours after leaving the house, he returned to find the front door wide open. He raced into the house, searching every room downstairs and calling for the babysitter. Eventually, he went upstairs and lying face down on his bed, fully naked, he found the dead bodies of his three girls. Each had a black-handled hunting knife embedded into the base of their necks, cut into each of their backs were the words, *Slut, Whore,* and *Tramp.* Debbie was nine, Karen was eight, and his gorgeous little Amy was six. David did not say a word.

Walking out of the house and casually closing the front door behind him, David walked the two or three miles to the nearest petrol station, where the CCTV cameras would later show a man buying a green plastic petrol container, and then a few minutes later, filling the five-litre container at a petrol pump in the forecourt. He didn't attempt to cover his tracks by paying for the container or petrol with cash. The bank card receipt would also later confirm the purchases and his presence at the petrol station.

He then walked to his own home, sitting in the front room until around 7 p.m., with the petrol container at his feet. At just after 7 p.m., he left his house and walked around to the Armstrong property, confident that all or most of them would be at home, probably laughing and joking over a drink, bragging about the crimes they had committed that day, which as far as David was concerned, included the murders of his three daughters, for which he had no evidence, but didn't need any.

He splashed and poured petrol around all of the ground floor windows and the front and back doors of the Armstrong home, and then retraced his steps, using his lighter to set the petrol on fire at each of the locations that he had laid it. Tightly gripping the petrol container, he stood in front of the house, watching as the flames began to lick and grow, as the wooden doors and window frames welcomed the fire into their combustible lives. The fingers of his right hand stung from where the petrol had burst into life as he lit it.

A few minutes after starting the fires, Kelvin Armstrong burst out of the front door screaming, "Help, help, my house is on fire!"

He stopped in the doorway, the flames licking around the doorframe just inches from his body, as he saw his pathetic neighbour standing in front of him, his face emotionless. Only his eyes gave away the pure hatred he was feeling.

"What do you want, you fucking prick?" screamed Kelvin

Armstrong, just about finishing the sentence, before receiving a huge splash of petrol in his face.

The fire looked in his direction and leapt at the new source of energy. As his face caught fire, Kelvin Armstrong covered it with his hands, screaming in agony, as the flames tried to melt the flesh from his face. He fell to his knees and David poured more petrol over him. As he watched Armstrong burn, David unzipped his jeans and pulled out his penis.

As he urinated all over his screaming victim he calmly stated, "I always told my wife that I wouldn't piss on you if you were on fire. Looks like I lied."

The fire engines arrived and put out the fire. The paramedics treated and quickly got Kelvin Armstrong into the back of their ambulance, and with sirens wailing and blue lights flashing, sped toward the hospital, neither of them expecting the burned man to survive the journey. The police arrested David and sat him in the back of a police car. David did not say anything.

It was an hour later, before the dead bodies of the three young girls were found.

A young police constable, who had been given the task of looking around David's home, staggered out of the front door and puked just after shouting, "Oh my God."

David was not allowed to attend the funerals of his three girls. The authorities decided that he was not in a fit mental state to leave the prison. From the moment David had found the dead bodies of his daughters, throughout the time he was interviewed by the police, his entire time on remand in prison, the trial and sentencing and the time spent to date in the Greenhill Secure Mental Institution, he never spoke one word. The evidence against him had been overwhelming and a finding of guilt was inevitable, and yet the only time that any reaction from David was observed, followed the words of the judge, who at the end of the court case made this announcement:

"The court fully appreciates the impact the deaths of your wife and daughters have had upon you, and any decent person could only empathise with you, however, your actions cannot and will not ever be condoned. Taking the law into your own hands, can only ever lead to anarchy and unforgivable actions. No evidence has been found to connect your victim, or his family, to the crimes that preceded your blatant and purposeful attempt to kill him, and while the court acknowledges the way you and your family were treated by Mr. Armstrong and his family, no such revenge can be allowed to happen in a civilised world. The impact of your violent attack on Mr. Armstrong's life will be both dramatic and traumatising to him until his dying day. Your refusal to communicate, and the subsequent evidence from mental health experts, has unfortunately left me with no other choice, but to detain you under the Mental Health Act 2007 and the Mental Capacity Act of 2005, section 40. You will be detained in a secure mental institution until you are deemed fit to be returned to the prison system, where you will serve a life sentence of no less than thirty-five years, and should your mental fitness never be achieved, you will remain in the care of the mental health authorities for the rest of your life. Mr. Warriner, do you understand what I have just said to you?"

David just smiled.

Picking up the Fallen Pieces

Eighteen months on from his conflict with the Messenger, from the deceit and horrors of the Bloom Foundation, Grant sat on the bench beneath a large tree, looking over the open land between him and the outdoor ménage. He often sat in this very spot for hours, watching his wife riding her favourite horse.

The money he had been given by the organisation that had controlled and influenced his life for longer than he wanted to remember, along with the money from the sale of his house, a building that neither he or his wife would ever have been able to live in again, had allowed him and Julia to buy an old farmhouse off the beaten track. As well as the main property, it also included a stable block that contained four stables, the outdoor ménage, upon which his stare was still glued, and twelve acres of land.

When they had purchased it, the boundaries of the property's land had been contained within a stone wall that had been about four feet high. The only change he had really made since moving in, had been to increase the height of that wall to ten feet, install a large wrought iron gate and twenty-four CCTV cameras at strategic locations around the boundary wall and gates, as well as four others that provided video coverage around the house.

For the past year and a half, he had watched Julia make slow progress, with the aid of weekly counseling sessions and medical intervention, to reduce and eventually eradicate, the effects of the drugs that had kept her memories suppressed inside a locked down mind. The first three months had been the toughest, as her brain began to unlock itself further than the therapy she had received could ever have done, and slowly release the memories that had been locked away for so long. These memories had sent his wife into a deep depression. Psychiatrists, doctors and neurological specialists had regular telephone conferences and meetings to agree on plans that would have resulted in her being sectioned under the Mental Health Act. Grant's only response to this, when he had eventually been included in the discussions, was to say, "Try to do it and one of you dies, I just haven't decided which one yet."

Strangely, sectioning had not been discussed again after that, well, not at least within earshot of him.

Grant continued to gaze at the riding school area. Watching his wife effortlessly ride one of her horses always thrilled him. It also pleased him, as this was the one and only time that Julia seemed to be at absolute peace, free and unstrained from the memories of the abhorrent things that she had managed to survive. To this day, though, any discussion about the death of their daughter, Sharlee, had been a taboo subject.

The counselor had been the first to try and talk about it. Julia had remained seated, and seconds later, the tears had started to flow, and so did the urine. She completed a full and uncontrolled piss, and as she remained sat on the soaked chair she had said, "Do that again and I will burn your house down."

It was said without any sign of emotion—a cold but believable statement.

She had decorated her house and seemed to enjoy doing so, making sure that photographs of Sharlee were included in the décor. Despite a few backward steps, she did make good progress, and her horses were certainly a large part of the happy periods of her life. She'd had horses in her life since she was about five years old, progressing to a good riding standard, taking on the challenges of show jumping and hunting. She had no interest in the hunting of a fox. She had just wanted to feel the thrill of leaping over wide and wild bushes and hedges, and ride the unpredictable and undulating land.

Grant spoke to her, despite knowing that she was too far away from him to hear his words.

"I'm sorry for not being there to protect you and Sharlee, my darling. I am sorry for the reason that I was not there with you, the family that I did truly love."

He followed her around the ménage as she walked, trotted and cantered, exercising the horse physically and mentally. Small and large circles were completed, interspersed with figures of eight, and making sure that each of the schooling exercises were completed on both reins.

"You ride so well, babe," Grant called out.

He dropped his head so that he now looked at the grass between his feet and quietly said, "I cannot begin to imagine what you went through, locked away in that place, not recognising me, not remembering anything, and being used as some kind of experiment by that deluded monster. I just hope that you know that I have always loved you, and always will, my darling."

He looked up again and the image of his wife riding her horse faded away, only to be replaced by the horrific memories of coming home to find the house empty, or at least he thought so.

Taking the opportunity to have a few minutes for himself, he decided to take a shower. By the time he had arrived at the door to the bathroom, his shirt had been removed and dropped halfway up the stairs, and he had begun to undo his belt, when everything, absolutely everything in his life, came to a crashing stop.

Julia lay in the bath. Both wrists had been cut upwards from the wrists to just below the elbow joint. If he had been able to ignore the blood-stained water dripping over the lip of the white tub, located in the centre of the large bathroom, and forming rivulets of pale red rivers across the tiled floor, he could have easily believed she was just asleep. She looked so peaceful, and that was because she had at last found the peace she longed for.

The post-mortem had discovered that she had taken in excess of a hundred tablets of different kinds—antidepressants, sleepers, anti-anxiety pills and varied pain killers. This amount of medication would have killed her, without having to cut open her own wrists, but Grant just viewed this as a message from his dead wife that this had been something that she wasn't willing to allow to fail.

That had happened just two days short of three months ago, and the tears now pouring from his eyes were the first he had cried since Julia's death.

He looked at the white headstone that sat at the head of the still fresh looking grave, flowers still adorning the carefully heaped soil that covered her body. The engraving on the headstone read:

Here lies a mother who lost a daughter and is now reunited with her, and a wife who hopes one day to be once again holding her husband close. Until then, she watches over him and prays.
Julia Anderson
29.02.1964 ~03.01.2017

Grant stood up and made his way to the side of the beautifully simple headstone, and laid a hand on the top of it, caressing it slightly.

"Save your prayers, babe. I'm not worthy of them."

He dropped to his knees and wrapped both of his arms around the stone memorial and sobbed large tears. When they eventually came to a stuttering stop, he whispered, "I miss you, Julia. I am nothing without you. Many will be saying that I have got what I deserve, an empty and pointless life. The only purposeful thing to do is to wait for death to come along and take me."

If he had been waiting for some kind of spiritual sign from beyond the grave, he was disappointed. The only noise he heard was the neighing of one of the horses from a field behind him. A tall chestnut coloured mare named Willow looked at him.

"I'll get you in, give me a few minutes," he shouted to the horse, knowing that it and the others would be spending another night out in the fields, for he had not been able to bring himself to return them to their stables for about a week now. It may even have been longer, ten days, maybe. He did the basics: performed a visual check on them once a day, made sure their water feeders were working, and threw a bit of hay into the fields occasionally. The horses had been Julia's life and he just wasn't ready to make that connection yet.

He remained kneeling at the graveside for a while longer, always making sure that he was in contact with it in some way, as he spoke to his dead wife. He ended this daily ritual with the same words: "Please let this be the day that I die, so that I can be with you again."

He was convinced that every day that he said these words, he felt the marble headstone turn slightly colder, just for a second or two, and he always responded with, "Not today then, eh? See you again tomorrow, my love."

Grant walked back toward the house, ignoring the now more insistent complaints being made by Willow. He made it to the front of the farmhouse, only looking back at his wife's grave twice, and only once having to stop himself from returning to it and spending the rest of the day there. He pulled his pack of small cigars from his back pocket and lit one of them, rolling the smoke around the inside of his mouth, before taking it down into his throat and exhaling, before it went all the way down. He watched the grey smoke rise into the air, and through it, saw a moving dust cloud making its way up the dirt track that led from the property gates up to the house.

He hadn't closed the gates since the hearse had bought his wife's body, which lay inside the wicker coffin that she had requested, up to the property to be buried where she had lain ever since. The unusual dry spell since before Christmas meant that the dirt path was parched, hence the cloud of dust that Grant could now see was being thrown up by a black vehicle.

He went inside the house and returned outside after a few seconds with a fully loaded shotgun in his hands, and sat down on the rocking chair that sat a few feet left of the front door. The rocking chair had been a romantic dream of his when he bought it. He had imagined himself sitting in it on an evening, smoking his cigar and drinking a large brandy or good glass of white Riocha. This dream never quite met up to the reality. Grant had quickly learned that he hadn't grown up one bit, and had found himself rocking the chair backward and forward so rigorously that it would end up toppling backward, hurtling him unceremoniously to the ground. The chair now rocked no more, temporarily held in an upright seating position by the placement of two wooden wedges hammered into place underneath the back of the two rocking plates.

Grant sat in the chair and crossing one leg over the other. He placed the butt of the shotgun into his hip region and rested it on his higher positioned thigh and knee. It was a relaxed, but somehow intimidating stance.

The sun was low in the sky. Grant reached to retrieve his glasses that were hooked over the neck of his T-shirt, a pair of round blue lens sunglasses that he treasured, because he thought they made him look cool. He had owned them for years, and Sharlee had often told him that they made him look like an aging hippy. He preferred to think aging rocker.

The car approached quite rapidly, throwing up more brown dust behind it, at times almost disappearing within it. It came to a stop directly in front of Grant—a black Mercedes with fully blacked out windows all round and a grey tinted front windscreen. He waited for the occupant or occupants to get out of a style of vehicle he recognised, one used by the agents of C.O.R.T., or The Bloom Foundation, whichever you choose to believe.

The driver was the first to get out, a man who Grant did not recognise. From the rear of the vehicle appeared a man who he did recognise, but whose presence surprised him.

The driver, carrying a small soft briefcase, walked toward Grant, who in turn lowered the shotgun slightly, so that both barrels were pointing directly at the chest of the man.

"Mr. Anderson, nice to meet you, sir. My name is Pheasant," the driver said.

"Un-fucking-believable," Grant replied. "What are you people, an organisation of killers, or a fucking petting zoo?"

Agent Pheasant clearly didn't get the joke, not putting together the Fox-Pheasant-agent-animal-names-connection.

"And for the one and only time, it's Grant. Didn't Fox inform you?" Grant added.

"My apologies," Pheasant said. "It was our understanding that your wife had convinced you to change your name back to John Anderson." Realising at that point that he was referring to a woman who had quite recently passed away, he said, "Please accept our heartfelt condolences for your loss, sir."

The passenger, who had remained standing by the rear door of the vehicle, had not said a word, and was still standing by the car, studying Grant. The shotgun moved slightly so it was pointed toward him and Grant addressed him.

"And what do you have to say for yourself, Mr. Lambden?" he enquired of the well-dressed man.

Godfrey Lambden took a few paces away from the car. His eyes never left Grant, and more importantly, the shotgun, for he was not sure whether or not the man intended to pull the trigger. Secretly, he wouldn't have blamed him for doing so, after the way he had been treated by the organisation he now effectively headed up, even though it had been swallowed up by the larger Secret Services Intelligence Agency.

"Well, are you going to keep me waiting and run the risk of my trigger finger getting weary?" Grant said.

"I am not here to cause you any trouble, Grant," Lambden replied.

"Surely you are not here to try and persuade me to come and work for you again? We had that conversation the last time we met. I am sure that you were not confused by my reply then, and I can assure you that the answer has not changed one bit," Grant said.

"Absolutely not," Lambden replied. "While the establishment fully acknowledges that your involvement in the Messenger case certainly brought about an earlier than expected demise for the killer, even if your actions were characteristically unorthodox and direct, the organisation that I am in charge of has changed. Let us say that your methods are no longer desirable."

"Then your pointless visit is over," Grant replied, moving the end of the shotgun between the two men several times. "Thanks for coming to see me. It has really moved me. Now fuck off and close the gates behind you on the way out."

Neither Agent Pheasant or Godfrey Lambden moved.

Lambden coughed, and said, "Grant, I learned one thing about you, and that was that friendship and trust, or as you would describe it, brotherhood and respect, are important, no, crucial to you."

Grant listened without showing any sign that he was listening. Lambden continued.

"Many years ago, you left your childhood home to join the military, and left behind a person who had been your best friend since you had both been very young boys. I am aware that you parted on bad terms, but that since then, you have tried to find him again, without any success."

"You came all this way to read me a historical story, a vague memory from my past," Grant replied sarcastically. "Have the threats to our country fallen so low that you have this much pointless spare time on your hands?"

"And yet right now, you are thinking of that friend," Lambden responded coolly. "You recall his name with ease, you are remembering the rock concerts you attended together, the times you spent at each other's homes listening to records, the dreams you shared of forming the greatest heavy metal band in the world."

Once again, Grant did not react, although everything that Lambden spoke about was exactly what was going through his head.

"I bet you even remember dating his sister," Lambden added.

The emotional weariness caused by his daily visits and chats to Julia's graveside was being increased by the trip down a troubled memory lane, courtesy of his visitor. Grant was too tired—emotionally and physically—and too weary to be involved any further in a game of tit for tat verbal competitiveness.

"Two fucks could not be given, now please leave, before I shoot you both and then myself," Grant said.

"Well, at least there is some effort left inside you," Lambden replied.

Grant looked up quizzically, not quite understanding what he meant. Lambden picked up on Grant's confusion and helped him, by saying, "You would have to reload to shoot yourself."

Pheasant reached inside the briefcase he had been carrying, and Grant reacted immediately, bringing the butt of the shotgun to his hip and pointing it directly at the chest of the agent.

"Easy cowboy," Pheasant said, his hand still inside the briefcase, but momentarily frozen in place. "Just getting a bit of reading for you," he said, pulling an A4 envelope out of his bag.

He stepped forward just enough to be able to place the envelope on the wooden floor of the outdoor porch.

"I don't need any more of your money," Grant said without casting an eye at the envelope.

"Good," Lambden replied. "Because you will never get another penny, but, and please pardon the pun, don't bite the hand of this messenger. We cannot offer money, but we may still be able to offer assistance, should you be able to lower your stubborn pride long enough to request it."

Grant leaned forward in his chair and stared at Lambden.

"Well, there is one thing," he said, his voice bordering on sounding needy.

A surprised Lambden responded immediately. "Just ask."

"Close the fucking gates on the way out," Grant said, delivering his final piece of sarcasm.

Lambden called Pheasant back to the car.

"Let's go, Mr. Pheasant, and leave this broken man to his empty pitiful life," Lambden said. "I wish you well, Mr. Anderson."

Both men began to get into the vehicle when Grant called out, "It's Grant, for fuck's sake."

Lambden stopped, one leg inside the car and looked toward Grant, a look of genuine pity on his face.

"Not any longer, Mr. Anderson. The man I knew as Grant would not have allowed heartache, pain and an unbelievable and undeserved amount of blows to his life to turn him into the person I see before me today," Lambden replied.

"Just close the gates," Grant replied, a level of tiredness in his voice that almost suggested that he could not disagree with what had just been said.

"Certainly, Mr. Anderson," Lambden replied politely. "Say hello to Grant if you ever see him again."

Lambden climbed into the rear seats of the car and Pheasant drove away. Grant followed the car's journey down the dusty road, watched as it came to a stop and someone, almost certainly Pheasant, closed the gates, before eventually the car was gone from sight. Only then did Grant allow himself to look at the envelope sitting a few feet from him. Written on the front was his name. *Or was it?* he thought. In neat capital letters, it read FAO GRANT.

A Trip Down Memory Lane

G rant walked back into his house. Coming to a stop by a large wall mirror, he looked at his reflection. A tired face looked back at him, at least a week's worth of hair growth had taken the shine from his normally closely shaved bald head, and his facial hair was threatening to turn his goatee into a full face beard.

"You pathetic mess," his reflection said to him.

He had no doubt that Lambden would have thoroughly enjoyed seeing him in this state, a broken man who no longer gave a shit about the way he looked, who couldn't even cope with the basics in life, such as washing and shaving. He lifted the neck of his shirt to his nose and sniffed it. He had probably been wearing that for the last week, too, including sleeping in it, and his sense of smell confirmed that fact.

He sat down in a large, old armchair he had picked it up at an auction the year before, and Julia had immediately hated it.

"It's old, smelly, and broken," she had said.

Grant silently laughed inside, thinking how strange it was that he had now basically turned into this chair, but he still loved it, because he and the chair fit each other so well.

He ripped open the envelope and pulled out the contents,

several pages of printed information on the unheaded A4 paper. He immediately recognised the name at the top of the first page, Mr. David Warriner, his old schoolmate.

He placed the pages on the wide arm of the chair and wandered over to the wooden unit that stood beneath the small window, which allowed a view to the side of the property. His wife would stand by this window for hours, watching her horses in the fields adjacent to the property. He lifted the brown coloured translucent lid of the record deck and selected an album from one of the black metal album cases that stood, one next to the other, in front of the sound system. Lifting the needle, he placed it onto the vinyl and cranked the volume knob to ten. He listened to a few seconds of crackling as he walked back to the chair, sitting down as the first track of the album began to play. He had owned the album for years, decades, it was the first album he and David had listened to as young teenagers, discovering their love for rock music, and it still sounded as good now as it did all those years ago.

The opening words of the live album blasted around the room, a deep booming voice of a man announcing: "You wanted the best and you've got the best … the hottest band in the world … KISS."

The throbbing beat of the opening song, "Detroit Rock City," took over Grant's mind, as he began to read through the information written on the pages. His head rocked slightly back and forth to the beat of the music, just like it had with David, the first time they had listened to this album, only back then, the head-banging had been done with the energy and neck strength of youth.

As track five began to play, he placed the papers back onto

the arm of the chair. The voice of Paul Stanley spoke in the background: "Here's a song, the new single, title track off the new album … called 'Love Gun.'"

Grant was suddenly plunged back to 1976, and began to sing along with the track. Playing air guitar, he jumped on and off furniture, just like he and David had done back in that year when they first heard this track. Every time the title of the song was sung, he screamed it out himself, thrusting his groin back and forth in a sexual way. He began to laugh, as his crazy air guitar antics continued around the room, his head shaking in every conceivable direction. The song ended and Grant stopped and dropped to his knees. Letting go of his invisible air guitar, he lifted his arms upwards, fully outstretched with the palms of his hands turned upwards. Screaming like a madman, he turned his face up to the ceiling of the room.

"You wanted the worst, you've got the worst … the most evil bikers on the planet …" He paused and then lowering his head, he whispered, "I'm coming, David."

* * *

Grant sat back down in his favourite old smelly chair and reflected on what he had just read. His breathing was heavy from his music-driven antics, which had reminded him that an aging rocker can still rock, but should do it in shorter bursts.

His initial reaction to the story of his old friend's downfall had been anger and revenge, and the rock music selected had made those emotions increase tenfold. Now, as he sat down in relative calm, he could only think, *what the hell can I do?*

He laid his head back in the chair and closed his eyes, allowing his mind to wander around the imaginary world of possibilities. It was almost an hour later, before he opened his eyes, not absolutely sure if he had been in some kind of deep almost meditative thought process, or if he had in fact, taken a post-rock nap. The one thing he was certain of was that he now needed to talk to two people, but before anything else, he needed a good old fashioned military style shit, shower, and shave.

As he shaved his head and face with a new razor blade, his body still tingled from the heat of the shower, which he had increased, bit by bit, trying to wash away the images he had in his head, formed from the information he had earlier read. As the sharp razor blade swept through the foam-covered stubble, he thought about his childhood and Dave, his best mate since the age of six or seven.

They had skipped school together, listened to music in each other's bedrooms, gone to rock gigs together, fallen out and made up, and never let girlfriends affect their close friendship. Grant had loved Dave's family and especially his sister, Kerry, who he had dated for about eighteen months, and even when they had split up, it had no negative impact on the friendship between the two lads.

As young boys, they were both described by neighbourhood adults as scamps and loveable rogues, if there was a bit of harmless trouble or a prank had been played, then generally it was Dave and John who everyone looked at, for they were normally the source. Times with Dave had been the best and happiest parts of Grant's childhood. He was more like the brother he had always yearned for, and it was this that made it difficult for Grant to forgive himself for dumping his friend without a second thought.

He was a relic of what Grant was trying to run away from, a painful memory of the town he grew up in and so badly had to leave behind. A few years after leaving the Army, while living in London, Grant had made a feeble attempt at finding Dave, but it came to nothing, and except for the occasional recollection, normally when swapping tales of the past with a fellow drinker, he rarely thought about his childhood past or Dave Warriner.

A shot of pain brought Grant back to the present. A lack of attention and a new blade was never a good mix. He wiped his hand over the back of his head, where seconds before the razor blade had been, and found the source of the pain. He looked at his watery blood and foam covered hand and cursed himself.

"Fucking daft twat! That's going to take ages to stop bleeding," he said out loud.

He tore a small piece of paper from the toilet paper roll that was stood on the worktop next to the sink, a habit of his that his wife had hated.

"Put the bloody toilet roll on the toilet roll holder. That's why it's called the toilet roll holder," he could hear Julia saying. The memory made him smile. He placed the strip of paper over the cut on his head and dabbed his closely shaven head and face with the towel. *They don't feel as soft as they did when she was here,* he thought to himself. He looked at his smarter, fresher looking reflection.

"Washing them might fucking help, eh?" he said to nobody but himself.

He dressed and walked back outside, before lighting up

another cigar. Despite being the only inhabitant of the house these days, he still couldn't bring himself to smoke indoors. Julia had hated him smoking in the house. He leaned on the wooden rail that ran around the outside of the veranda and sucked in the smoke, taking it deep down his throat, before breathing it out as a controlled stream of smoke.

Walking away from the house, he stubbed out the butt of the cigar with the tip of his boot into the ground, and made his way back to his wife's grave. Kneeling down on both knees, he placed his hand on the ground in front of him and grabbed a handful of soil, letting it fall through his fingers.

"I need to go away for a while, darling," he said to his wife's grave. He stroked the soil, imagining it was his wife he was caressing. "It won't be for a while. I have a bit of planning and preparation to do first, but after, I may be away for some time. To be honest with you J, I may not come back from this one at all. A friend of mine needs my help, and I know you would say, *'Why does it have to be you?'* and I can only say that it just has to be."

He wiped his eyes. Talking to his dead wife made him cry once again.

"It is time to unleash the old me," he said, as his face hardened with each word. He swallowed back the next wave of tears and continued. "I will make sure the horses are taken care of, I promise. Vicky will step up, she always has."

Vicky had become a good friend to his wife. She had always been there to look after the horses when Julia had not felt up to it. She never complained, never said she was unavailable.

"I'll be around for a few months, and after that, I can't really say, but one way or another, I will see you again, my darling."

He got back to his feet and walked away, before the tears

overwhelmed him and he turned back again. Looking down at the grave, before finally walking away, he said, "I have always loved you, babe, and I will love you for an eternity and a bit longer, but I am so glad you are not around for this one."

Walking away, he took his mobile from his pocket and, after unlocking it, he opened the contacts screen and pressed his finger to the screen on the name of an old friend. The call was answered after just a few seconds.

"What do you want, you old scrote?" the man asked.

"Hello Shuffler," Grant replied. "I thought you might like a ride out and a catch up."

"Pleasure or business?" Stanley "Shuffler" Dawson asked.

"Bad business," Grant replied.

"It's the only type that interests me," Shuffler said.

"I'll text you where and when," Grant replied.

"Thanks for reaching out to me, bro. Don't take this the wrong way, because I really appreciate the help you gave me to get out of that shithole, but life was beginning to get a bit boring," Shuffler said with what sounded like genuine gratitude.

"You may not be thanking me when I tell you about the business," Grant said.

Shuffler didn't acknowledge Grant's statement.

"I was sorry to hear about, well, you know," he said sadly.

"I'll talk to you in a few days, bro," Grant said, ended the call and then searched for the next number he had to call.

"Hello Grant," Godfrey Lambden said. "I hoped I would hear from you."

"I will need a few life histories deleted," he said and immediately ended the call, before Lambden could reply.

In the back of the car, Lambden smiled.

"He is on board as expected," he said, addressing Pheasant who continued to drive, not looking over his shoulder, as he heard his boss speaking.

"Fox will be pleased, sir," he replied to Lambden.

Lambden stared out of the window at the passing scenery, his thoughts elsewhere.

"This isn't for Fox. That amateur vigilante set back my plans when his actions resulted in the closing down of The Bloom Institute. He was always going to pay for that."

* * *

After calling Vicky and explaining that he would probably need her help to look after the horses and take care of the house for an extended period of time, Grant sat in his chair and began to add meat to the bones of the idea that had formulated in his head, almost immediately after reading the story of his old school friend's plight. Vicky had agreed without hesitation, asking only why Grant was going away and accepting his story of needing a long holiday away. He also told her that he was planning on doing a bit of traveling around parts of the world that he and Julia had always wanted to visit.

He sat quietly, allowing his thought process to guide itself around the basis of the plan in his head and slowly it began to grow and develop. He mentally noted each possible problem as his brain identified them, and after about two hours, he reached for his phone again. Grant had never been one to stay in touch with large numbers of people whom he had worked with over the years, but he knew one man who did exactly that.

He found the number he needed and hoped that the person he needed to speak to had not changed the number since he had been given it many years ago at a military reunion he had reluctantly attended, only going because Julia had said that it would be good for him to see some old faces.

She had been wrong. Grant had decided to leave the function after only a couple of hours. Being surrounded by old sad bastards, most of whom had not managed to move on with life since leaving the military, was just too much to bear for him, with the exception of one person. He had served with McGill in Ireland, and the singular reason that this man had always been remembered by Grant, was because of the level of insanity demonstrated in everything that he did.

Corporal McGill had applied, successfully, to join the bomb squad team nicknamed Felix. His reason for wanting to do the dangerous job of making safe unexploded terrorist bombs was simple, and clearly showed the madness of the man.

During a routine patrol in the South Armagh area of Northern Ireland, in the small town of Forkhill, McGill being the "brick" commander, they had been the victims of an explosion. Thankfully, nobody had been seriously hurt, but Grant had been thrown through a shop window by the blast of the explosion. Through the smoke, dust and shattered glass, McGill had looked through the damaged shopfront to find Grant laying on his back in the middle of what had seconds before been a display of cornflake boxes. Grant was dazed, and the ringing in his ears blocked out everything else, but he watched the movement of his patrol commanders' mouth and made out that he was being repeatedly asked if he was okay. He had nodded his head to confirm that he thought he was

21

all right, and watched in amazement, as McGill ran farther into the shop and reappear a minute or so later with a bottle of milk in one hand and a plastic bowl in the other, his rifle hanging over his shoulder.

The ringing in Grant's ears had dissipated just enough for him to hear McGill say, "There is never a fucking spoon when you need one."

McGill had joined the bomb squad, because he loved cornflakes and hated the idea of the IRA ever being allowed to hurt another box of them again.

Grant had worked with Frank McGill for three months, but over that short period, they had become good friends and got into a few scrapes together, as you would expect from a madman and a maverick. They had a saying that only the pair of them understood the meaning of, something one would say to the other, just before going out on patrol—a phrase that meant they anticipated trouble ahead and that they were ready for any trouble that came their way.

The phone rang and rang. Eventually, a recorded voice stated, "This number is not available at this time." Grant tried again and got the same end result.

He typed out a text and pressed the send button. The text message said, "I need to get this fucking monkey out of my brain."

About three minutes later, Grant's mobile phone began to ring. A deep voice with a broad Yorkshire accent said, "Hello, ya fucker, what do thee want?"

"I've got a fucking monkey in my brain and I need to get rid of it," Grant replied, repeating the content of the text message.

"Abaart fucking time," McGill said. "You going t'tret me with some respect this time?"

"There's more chance of me sucking your cock," Grant answered.

"Reet, I'll wash the chap then, speak soon." McGill ended the call.

Grant placed the phone on the arm of the chair and smiled. It never ceased to amaze him how readily some service veterans, military and civilian, would come to the assistance of someone they had respect for.

He sent two more texts, one each to Shuffler and Frank McGill. Both simply gave a date, time and location for a meet. Nothing else could be done now, so once again, he allowed his thoughts to take him wherever they wanted to. Thoughts of school days, military days and prison service days paraded through his head. Some were good memories, while others were terrible, but he allowed them the time they wanted. Some he tried to hold onto and others, the ones that had the potential to take him to places he didn't want to visit, he allowed to leave easily.

Many of the memories brought with them faces from the past, faces of people he had interacted with over the years. Some he had completely forgotten and was surprised that their memory had been locked away somewhere in his head, and others he remembered fondly. These he once again made a mental note of a handful of people who had the potential, and the devil-may-care attitude that could make them suitable to be involved in what had to be done. Each had a connection through their unique characters. Each of them was either brutally cruel or borderline insane. Grant relaxed deeper into the chair, as a collection of misfit and Fortunates gathered in his head and he drifted into a deep sleep.

* * *

"David," exclaimed the high pitched nasal voice of the psychiatrist. "David, earth to David."

David Warriner stared out of the window of the small office, an office he had spent many hours in during his time at Greenhill's. He could see nothing but sky through the window, as it was located high up on the wall. The bars on the inside and outside reminded him of the level of security in place.

"David, if you do not take an active part in these sessions, there is nothing I can do to help you," said the voice that grated through David's brain like the noise a fork made when slid across a dry china plate.

He knew that a member of staff would be stood directly outside the door of the psychiatrist's office, and others would be close enough to respond to any incident. They were always the same individuals who seemed to respond to the alarm bells or shouts for help from colleagues. They arrived quickly, and were always willing and capable of handing out a heavy dose of pain when applying their restraint techniques. He had never been on the receiving end of these Home Office employed thugs, but he had observed them, and got to know each and every one of them.

He could hear the psychiatrist's whiny voice saying something or other, but he had tuned out, a skill he had developed from day one of walking into the secure mental health wing of Greenhill Secure Mental Hospital. It helped him to keep his sanity and it blocked out the agglomeration of insane noises made by the other inhabitants of this island of delusion.

He heard the door open, and assumed that Dr. Ainsworth

had called for the member of staff to escort him back to either his room or the patients' day room.

"Take him back to his room," Dr. Ainsworth instructed the burly mental health orderly. "No interaction with the mainstream population for forty-eight hours," he added.

The orderly nodded to acknowledge that he understood, and placed himself close to where David was sat, towering over him menacingly. David stood and walked toward the door, the orderly only a few feet behind him.

"David," said the psychiatrist. David turned and looked at him blankly. "Until you talk about what you did and start to demonstrate some kind of emotion about what happened, be that an understanding, an admittance of guilt or God forbid it, remorse, your life here is only going to become steadily more unpleasant."

David stared at Dr. Ainsworth for a few more seconds and then turned away, and continued to walk through the open doorway into the corridor outside. He turned right and began the familiar walk back to his room, the orderly extending his stride to catch up with him.

"Slow down you fucking freak. You walk at my pace, not yours." the orderly instructed.

David slowed slightly and wondered why the usual abusive thought did not mentally form in his mind, and began to worry that his self-imposed distancing of himself from humanity was, in fact, starting to make him actually insane.

* * *

Kelvin Armstrong sat in the darkness of his bedroom. A small wooden trolley on wheels sat in front of the chair in which he sat. His permanently curled up and twisted right hand held the fork awkwardly and he brought it up to his mouth. The tight scarred skin of his face, mixed with the many scars left behind, following a dozen skin graft procedures, prevented him from opening his mouth very wide, which meant anything more solid than mashed potatoes, a small amount of which now sat on the end of the fork, proved very difficult if not impossible to get into his mouth. He lived his life, consuming nothing more than soup or food blended to the point of turning into baby mush.

The prongs of the fork dug into his lower lip, as he tried his best to guide it into the small slit provided by the limited movement of his mouth. He swore because of the pain caused by the gentle contact between metal and his flesh. He threw the fork in the direction of the plate, which contained a sloppy mixture of gravy and mashed potatoes. It missed its target and bounced off of the top of the wooden trolley onto the carpeted floor.

He was looked after these days by his two daughters, both of whom hated the fact that this duty had been left to them. Their three older brothers were incarcerated at Her Majesty's pleasure and their father's brothers, sisters, cousins and other members of the huge extended family, only made an appearance if free food and booze were on offer.

He slowly pushed the trolley away from him and stood, taking his time to allow the tight burn-scarred skin down the right-hand side of his body to slowly compensate for his movement. The fire had barely touched the other side of his body, but it had left memories of that eventful da—clear down his right torso, arm, leg and foot, as well as across most of his face. He half limped, half shuffled his way to the door of his bedroom, and using his left hand, awkwardly turned the door handle and opened it toward him. It was time to get this family back in order and start to demand a little more respect like it always had been before Warriner had done this to him.

Fuck you Warriner. Fuck you and your wife and your bitch children, he silently thought.

Standing at the top of the stairs, he shouted through the almost immovable mouth. "Courtney, get your fat ass up here and tell your twat of a sister to arrange me a prison visit to my boys."

Downstairs, his daughters, Courtney and Leanne, looked at each other with dread. The day they had feared had arrived. Their father was in charge again.

* * *

Grant stood in the open doorway of his triple-sized garage and surveyed his collection of motorbikes. His trusty and much adored black Yamaha Midnight Star took centre position between the other two. She was starting to look a bit jaded these days, despite his valiant efforts to keep her in pristine condition.

Crashing it after being pursued by the Crippens hadn't helped, but then neither had neglecting her slightly because of the need to look after his wife and try to put their lives back on a normal keel. The bike to the left of the trio had been an indulgent purchase. The gold and chrome Harley Davidson

Fatboy had only been ridden twice and he had quickly learned that this girl had been built for the Californian climate. She did not like the cold, and living in England, that was never going to be a good thing. Grant had decided to keep her as his summer ride. The third bike in his collection, however, certainly did not mind the British weather. The silver Norton Dominator was built to maintain the classic appearance and style of Norton bikes with a modern twist mixed in—961cc air and oil cooled with a crank fired fuel injection system. She was not the type of bike that Grant would normally ride, but she was tough, fast and loved being thrown around the twists and turns of the British countryside's tight and winding narrow roads and lanes.

As it was a warm and sunny day, he decided that the Harley would be his choice for the day. Choosing a classic, open-face helmet from his selection of six different helmets—something his wife had never understood—he sat astride the Fatboy and gunned her into life.

Love them or hate them, you can't help loving the sound of those Harley pipes, he thought as he ripped the throttle back and forth. He rode out of the garage, stopping briefly to press the security fob attached to the keys that electronically closed and locked the garage door behind him, and rode down the long dusty driveway and onto the open road, leaving the large gates once again in the open position. His destination was about a two and a half hour ride away, chosen because it was fairly central for all three men to meet up, and Grant intended to enjoy his first long ride out for several months.

Opening up the Harley and easing her around the smooth, long curves of the country lane that led away from his house was a thoroughly enjoyable experience. When he arrived at the first small town with its narrow roads and fairly busy traffic that slowed his progress, the admiring looks that the bike attracted was an equally satisfying experience. He nodded at each and every person he saw admiring the bike as he went by, or those who waved at him, eagerly awaiting and hoping for a wave back from him.

This was one of the many things that made being a biker so special—complete strangers wanting to engage and interact with you, just because of the lifestyle choice you had made. He was also sure that his attire made it easier for the people to be so polite and welcoming—no leathers, except for a sensible jacket, and no cut or colours emblazoned across the back of them. He especially knew how different the reaction was when someone with that look rode into a town. He also knew that with a few exceptions, those riders were also just bikers, fans of the open road, or people who didn't want to travel trapped inside a metal cage. They just had a different way of advertising that fact.

He continued his journey, stopping once for a smoke and a cup of coffee at a small roadside café called Roll In, Roll Out. The sign outside the building proudly announced that rolls with all fillings were available: Breakfast Rolls, Rolls for Lunch & Dinner, and even a few with a dessert in them. Grant was more pleased to read the smaller sign beneath that heralded Bikers are Welcome.

After this brief interlude from the road, he continued on an enjoyable and uninterrupted ride, eventually arriving at the agreed destination. He was instantly pleased when he saw an Indian Storm parked outside. Shuffler had arrived, and unsurprisingly, was the first to do so. The ride for Shuffler had, in fact, only been about thirty minutes, but Grant had not told Frank Magill that fact when informing him of the location of their meeting. Magill would not have cared that long rides caused Shuffler agonising pain, because of the many injuries he had sustained over the years. He would have merely focussed on the fact that one of the three of them was, in his opinion, of which he had many, was not pulling his own weight. Grant could only imagine Shuffler's reaction to that, so he had not bothered to mention it.

He pulled his bike up alongside the Indian and secured her with the central lock, and even remembered to switch on the theft alarm, something he had never had on a bike before, and more often than not, forgot to engage.

Taking off his helmet, he turned to see Shuffler walking out of the front entrance of the small country public house and approaching him as quickly as his broken body would allow him. They greeted and embraced each other as only biking brothers can—a standard handshake that turned into a thumb grip style handshake, followed by a one-armed hug and a couple of slaps on each other's backs.

"How you doing brother?" asked a smiling Shuffler, his smile so wide, it looked like it was capable of splitting his face into two pieces.

"Yeah, I'm doing all right considering," Grant replied, smiling back at his old friend.

Shuffler stopped smiling, his face adopting a sombre look.

"Yeah bro, really sorry to hear about everything that has happened, sad loss bro, sad loss," he said to Grant.

"Thanks Shuffler, appreciated mate, but shit happens don't it?" Grant asked his caring friend.

"Yeah, but to get her back and then, well ya know, lose her again. That's fucked up bro."

Grant patted him on the back and smiling, jokingly replied, "Oh sorry, bro. I thought you were referring to me buying a Harley."

"You fucking wanker," Shuffler yelled out, and the two men slung an arm across the shoulder of the other and they walked into the pub together laughing.

The two friends had been in the pub, sat in a quiet corner, for around twenty minutes, enjoying a pint of good ale and reminiscing over old times, when the doors of the pub burst open and a large frame stood between them. The man was easily over six-foot-tall and must have weighed more than seventeen stone, his long, black greasy hair and scraggly beard finished off the look of a man who didn't care about his appearance and cared even less what anyone else thought.

"I'm looking for two old fuckers who ride pissy old man cruisers. Anyone seen them?" he shouted out loudly.

Shuffler whispered over to Grant, "I'm guessing this is your mate?"

Whispering back, Grant answered, "I wouldn't go as far as calling him a mate," and then standing, he addressed the loud man still stood in the doorway. "Frank Magill, as I live and breath, you've changed a bit."

"Yep, I decided the dirty grunge look needed bringing back," Magill said walking over to Grant and shaking his hand firmly.

"I see you went for the bald head and goatee beard. The 'I want to be a real biker even though I'm not,' look," he said as he released his hand-crushing grip, much to the relief of Grant.

Magill glanced over in Shuffler's and direction and exclaimed, "And fuck me, if you haven't gone and got an interest in animal protection and brought along your adopted chimp."

Grant heard the scraping of the table legs on the pub's wooden floor, and didn't need to look back, to know that Shuffler had just stood up and pushed the table away to give himself some fighting room.

"Magill, may I introduce Shuffler, a chimpanzee who is more than capable of ripping off your bollocks and juggling them," Grant said.

Shuffler walked past the stationary Grant and squared up to Frank Magill, the top of his head reaching no higher than the top of Magill's chest. He arched his neck back and looked up at Magill, trying his best to stare directly into his eyes.

"One more chimp remark out of you, and not only will I rip your balls off, but I will also feed them to your mother … the minute she has stopped rolling mine around inside her fucking mouth of course," he said angrily.

Magill let out a raucous guffaw type laugh and slapped Shuffler on his shoulder, having initially thought about slapping his bald head, but quickly changing his mind, after deciding that he liked his testicles where they were and didn't want to carry on with a conversation that involved his mother sucking the balls of a small monkey.

"Nice one, Shuffler. I like you. Anyway, my mother is dead and buried," he lied.

"Wouldn't stop me, I have a fucking shovel," Shuffler replied, returning to where he had been sat.

Could have gone worse, Grant thought, as he and Magill joined Shuffler in the corner.

"A pint of your best mead, my good innkeeper, and make it snappy," Magill called out, clicking his fingers in the direction of the middle-aged man stood behind the bar. The three men sat at the table in silence until the barman placed a pint in front of Magill.

"That'll be three pounds and eighty pence of your good money, squire," he said sarcastically.

Magill cocked a thumb toward Grant.

"He's paying," he said and glugged down half of the pint in one go.

Grant paid the man, thinking to himself, *may still get worse though.*

Planning for the future

The three men talked and drank for just over three hours, the drinking mainly being done by Magill. Twice, during visits to the toilet by Magill, Shuffler had asked Grant if he was sure about this guy, and on both occasions, Grant had assured his friend that Magill was the man he needed, because of his contacts.

"He knows the people I need," Grant told Shuffler despite his protests.

After Magill's first piss break, and feeling that enough banter and swapping of old war stories had taken place, Grant had got down to business.

"Listen up, fellas, I have a situation that requires my attention, but I cannot do this one alone. I need help, and lots of it," Grant said quietly, aware that this was one conversation he didn't want anybody overhearing.

"Magill, I need you to use your contacts, and more importantly, your knowledge of those people to come up with a short list of ex-forces who can bring certain skills to the table. When I say skills, what I mean is a willingness to get dirty, not be too bothered about bending a few rules, and if they have no family that would be a bonus. I will pass on the names of a few who I would like you to find, but the others I am happy for you to recommend."

"Why no family?" Shuffler asked.

"Less people to get hurt, simple as at that, bro," Grant responded.

"This thing going to get that dirty, is it?" Magill asked.

"Yeah probably," Grant answered.

"Fucking ace," Magill said, causing Grant to ask him to keep voice down.

"Oh, whoever you come up with must be able to ride and have their own bike, too," Grant said to Magill.

"So you want a list of fucked up, mental case veterans who love bikes," Magill said, almost sounding excited by the task he had been given. "Should easily be able to come with a couple dozen of those fuckers."

"I only need a group of twelve, so come up with a list of twelve, and we can select ten of them and have the remainder as a reserve," Grant said.

"I also need you to find me a building, within its' own secure compound," Grant said and slid a folded piece of paper over to Magill. "That gives you the specifications that the building has to give us, and the area it needs to be in."

Magill unfolded the piece of paper and scanned his eyes down the list.

"Not asking for much, are you?" he asked after a few seconds. "Would be easier to build one to your requirements."

"Do your best, and if it isn't good enough, I will get someone else to find somewhere," Grant said, his tone suggesting that failure was not an outcome he was willing to accept.

"And what about me?" Shuffler asked.

Before Grant could answer, the quick wit of Magill struck again.

"I know of an organ grinder with an organ, but no monk...."
He didn't get to finish his sarcastic sentence, as Shuffler raised
his middle finger at Magill.

"Just get the image in your mind of my hairy balls being
forced into the mouth of your rotting mother, you piece of
shit," Shuffler cut in.

"Let's play nice, boys," Grant said sternly, wondering if
Shuffler was right about Magill's involvement. He slid another
folded piece of paper over the top of the table, this time toward
Shuffler.

"You, my friend, need to get this list of resources. You will
see that some do require Magill to pass on certain information
to you, before you will be able to get some of those items,"
Grant told Shuffler. "And you, Magill, that information is on
your list, so make sure you get it to Shuffler pronto."

Magill threw a quick salute, and then turned it into a
childish wave of his hand.

"Yes sir," he said.

Grant ignored him and looked over at Shuffler. His
expression was now deadly serious.

"There is one thing I need you to do that isn't on that list
mate," he said.

"Fire away, bro, anything to help," Shuffler replied, pleased
that it sounded like he was about to be asked to do something
that was more important than Magill could be trusted with.

"You may not be saying that after I tell you what it is," Grant
said.

Shuffler waited silently, so Grant just said it.

"I need you to go to prison."

To Grant's surprise, Shuffler's first response was, "Okay."
And then he asked, "Who do you need me to visit?"

Grant shook his head.

"No mate, I mean I need you to … go to prison. Ya know, get yourself nicked," he said.

As if not hearing what Shuffler had been asked to do Magill asked, "Who is paying for all of this shit?"

Keeping his eyes on the face of Shuffler, who held his gaze looking back at him, his mouth hanging open and a look of disbelief on his ravaged face, Grant finally replied to Magill.

"Over the past two weeks, since I contacted you both, I have busied myself putting into place an overseas company that will be responsible for all of the payments. The information is on your piece of paper."

This he had managed to do with the help of several departments that were under the command of Godfrey Lambden, a favour that had meant him eating a huge spoonful of humble pie and experiencing a level of humiliation that Grant was not familiar with.

"May I now suggest you take ten minutes, shut the fuck up, and read that information thoroughly," he added, angry that Magill was already proving to be extremely high maintenance. He turned his full attention back to Shuffler, whose mouth had now closed. It looked like the full magnitude of what he was being asked to do was sinking in.

Shuffler looked down at the list of information on the piece of paper being held in his hands and said to Grant, "So you want me to go shopping to get this stuff?" He scanned his eyes down the list again. A whole array of weaponry, an eclectic mix of clothing and several different chemicals were on his shopping list. Continuing, he said, "Well, as it is highly unlikely that I can shoplift most of this stuff, I take it you want me to do something else that will result in me going to jail?"

37

"To be fair, bro, with your record, it shouldn't take much," Grant replied, trying his best to lighten the mood, and failing.

"Thanks for pointing that out to me, Grant," Shuffler replied. "It's really nice to know that you realise that if I ran a red light, I would probably be sent down for a three to five stretch."

"I was thinking more along the lines of something that would get you an appearance in a magistrate's court, and then piss off the judge and get a few weeks for contempt," Grant said.

"And what am I expected to do when I get there?" Shuffler asked.

"We will chat about that when we are alone, mate," Grant replied, casting his eyes quickly in the direction of Magill.

"Do you really need all these fucking rooms?" Magill asked.

"Oh for fuck's sake, Frank, shut the fuck up," Shuffler and Grant said in unison.

* * *

Kelvin Armstrong had arrived at HMP Swandale, courtesy of his eldest daughter, Leanne, the only member of the Armstrong clan to own a car. They sat in the car for a while, looking at the front of the imposing newly built modern prison.

"Nothing like the real jails that used to house me. This place looks more like a large Tesco," Kelvin said scornfully.

"I think the large bloody wall suggests it's a prison though, Dad," his daughter replied.

"Shut your mouth, bitch," her father hissed.

He got out of the back of the vehicle and walked toward the visitors' centre where, after identifying himself, he was asked to take a seat until visiting time started. The room was like a large doctor's waiting room—hard plastic chairs that hurt him when he sat on one, so after just a few minutes, he decided to stand. Posters and signs on the walls that warned of the consequences of bringing any unauthorised articles into the prison were right next to self-help advice and a couple of paintings that were supposed to help you forget that you were in a prison building. A few young children were playing in the play area at the far end of the room. A few books, toys and activities were scattered around in a token effort to keep the children entertained, while they waited to visit their fathers, grandfathers or brothers.

The middle-aged woman, probably a volunteer, behind the counter where visitors had to book in, announced that visiting time was about to start and could the visitors please make their way to the main prison building.

"Please head for the door that has the sign above it saying 'domestic visitors' entrance,'" she said politely.

Kelvin Armstrong and the dozen or so other visitors, not including the children, of which there were about eight, made their way as directed. Kelvin made slower progress than the others, due to the injuries to his right leg and both feet, and also because this was the part of the visiting process that he hated the most—the part where the screws searched the visitors. He wasn't overly bothered about being searched, that he had gone through on countless occasions either by screws or the police. It was the pain that it caused him ever since being burned, and he was convinced that the screws performed their rub down search procedures more rigorously on him if they knew about his injuries. And most of them did, because most of them knew the Armstrong family very well.

Entering the prison, he placed his few meagre belongings into one of the lockers provided for visitors. Nothing except a small amount of cash was allowed into the visiting hall, and he had no intention of buying anything from the small canteen for his eldest son to gorge on. He placed his wallet, watch and mobile phone into the locker and placed the small key into his pocket after securing the locker door.

He approached the visitors' search area and scanned the staff working there. Luck was not on his side, as he recognised every single screw on duty, and by the smiles on two of their faces as they watched him limp in, they recognised him, too. One of them beckoned him over—an officer he remembered from his last sentence a few years before. He walked over, placing the locker key into the tray that would go through the X-ray scanning machine, and then stepped onto the low raised platform in front of the prison officer. He winced, as the skin around his knee resisted the unwanted bending movement he had to make to step up onto the platform—a reaction that didn't go unnoticed by the member of staff.

"Raise your arms up, Armstrong. You know the drill," the officer said.

"Shouldn't that be Mr. Armstrong?" Kelvin replied.

"The title of mister is one I reserve for those I have respect for, so just do as you're told … please," the officer responded, his eyes squinting slightly, as he put on his best fake smile.

"Trying to make it look civil for the cameras, are you, Norbit?" Armstrong asked, raising his arms slowly.

Officer Norbit didn't respond. He started his body search of Armstrong, starting with the left arm first and then the right, increasing the pressure on what he knew bore the worst of the burn injuries the man had sustained. He ran his hands, lightly locked together by the two thumbs and hands fanned out like the shape of butterfly wings, down the front of Armstrong's chest once again, applying more pressure than was needed. Throughout it all, Armstrong gritted his teeth in pain, but refused to ask Officer Norbit to take more care.

Thirty seconds later, the agonising search procedure was completed. The officer looked at him and once again smiling that annoying cheesy smile, he said, "You should have reminded about your horrific injuries, Mr. Armstrong, then I would have used the handheld metal detector instead. Never mind, next time, eh?"

Armstrong stepped off the low platform and collected his locker key from the waiting tray that had completed its journey through the X-ray machine, a pointless exercise in his opinion, but one that had to be done, because screws needed their procedures. He joined the other visitors and they made their way through the series of electronic doors to the visitors' hall. Their progress was slowed by the opening and closing of the doors, which pleased Armstrong who, because of the over-exuberant search he had been subjected to, was suffering a bit.

Once in the hall, he took his seat at the table indicated by a member of the visitors' team, and awaited the arrival of his eldest son. A door in the far corner of the room opened. A steady trickle of prisoners filed through it and a throng of red bib wearing prisoners began to fill the hall. Prisoners and visitors greeted each other with hugs and kisses.

Armstrong remained seated watching a young prisoner grope the arse of his girlfriend through a tight fitting short skirt, which left nothing much to the imagination. It was clearly obvious she had forgotten to put any underwear on that day. He smiled, as he remembered doing exactly the same to his girlfriend in his younger days. The only difference being that in his day, he was told to keep his hands to himself by one of the rule-abiding observant screws, and would then receive the punishment of closed visits for a period that was usually for his next three to five visits, depending on how good or bad a mood the wing governor had been in. On this occasion, as Armstrong watched the lad's grip get tighter, not one of the inadequate number of staff members said a thing.

An unshaven lad sat himself down in the chair on the opposite side of the table he was sat at. He looked over at his son and nodded his head. There was no attempt to greet each other with a handshake or hug.

"Wasn't expecting a visit from you," Michael Armstrong said to his father.

"How are the other two scrotes?" Kelvin asked.

"They're fine. We are all on the same wing now," Michael replied.

"Any progress yet?" his father asked, his voice was emotionless.

"It isn't that easy, Dad. None of us has even been accepted onto the therapeutic wing yet. Convincing these cunts that one of us is a nutter, is more difficult than we thought it would be," Michael said. His voice had a tone of fear, as he tried to explain the situation to his father.

Kelvin stood up, and before walking away and heading toward the door, he had entered only a few minutes before, he looked at his son, and said, "If at least one of you doesn't get into Greenhill's soon, all three of you will be needing the services of an undertaker."

Kelvin Armstrong walked away from the visitors' table and out of the hall. The visit was over.

* * *

Grant and Shuffler had carried on their conversation, as Magill laid himself down on the bench-style seats against the wall of the pub, and fell into an alcohol induced sleep.

"Are you absolutely certain there is nobody else who has the friends this guy has?" Shuffler asked, nodding his head in the direction of the sleeping biker.

Grant shook his head.

"Magill has contacts, not friends. He likes to think they are friends, but most are not," he said. "After leaving the Army, he found himself alone and unable to integrate into the civilian population. Let's face it, who else but military people, would understand and tolerate his behaviour?"

"Okay bro, it's your game and your rules," Shuffler replied, clearly still not comfortable with the involvement of Magill.

"Anyway, what do you want me to do when I get myself put away?" Shuffler asked.

Grant smiled, grateful to his old friend for not putting up resistance or asking any awkward questions about his request.

"Just observe a few people and report back," Grant replied.

"Sounds simple enough," Shuffler said.

"Not really," Grant replied. "They are brothers, very close-knit, and from a very controlled and equally dangerous family."

"I have to ask," Shuffler said, "what is this all about bro?"

Grant dropped his head and stared down at the table. He answered the question without making eye contact with Shuffler.

"Many years ago, I left a man behind, a true friend, and I have felt guilty about that ever since, bro. I left him, knowing that his life would be difficult, surrounded and influenced by the wrong people, and left even more alone if he walked away from them." Grant paused for a moment, as he thought about the situation his friend was now in. "He chose the latter, and now he has lost everything, and unlike when I found myself in that position, there is nothing he can do about it. But I can, with the help of people like you." Grant now looked up and made eye contact once again with Shuffler.

"Say no more, brother," Shuffler said, and reached his hand out over the table and placed it on top of Grant's hand. "We are brothers from different mothers, and any friend of yours, is a friend of mine."

A huge grunting snore broke the emotional moment between the two men, and Grant laughed.

"Please tell me that once he has done the job you have given him, his involvement is over," Shuffler said. He was reluctantly smiling, too

"Guaranteed. This job doesn't need a cannon as loose as Magill having a part in it."

The two men shook hands, and Shuffler slapped Magill on the top of this head.

"Hey Babe the Pig, it's time to return to your pigsty, you noisy fucker."

The reaction from the apparently deep sleeping man caught out Shuffler, who suddenly found his wrist encapsulated by a grip so tight, that he instantly thought he could feel his blood stop flowing <u>into</u> his hand.

With his eyes still closed, Magill said, "You touch me again, you fucking hairy little chimp, and I will bite off your fingertips, one by one."

Shuffler tried his best to free himself from Magill's grip, but only managed to do so once the grip was released. Magill sprang up from a laying down position to a sitting position, with surprising speed and agility.

"I need to freshen up and have a piss," he said as he stood up, and then winking at Shuffler, he added, "I might even think about your hairy little ass and throw out a quick five knuckle shuffle while I'm in there."

Shuffler raised two fingers in the direction of Magill—the universal sign for fuck off—and added clarity to his hand gesture, by responding, "Fuck off, you freak."

Magill walked toward the public toilets, rubbing his crotch, and without looking back, he shouted, "Ooh ooh, I'm feeling some movement downstairs."

Grant looked at Shuffler and shrugged his shoulders.

"You are as bad as each other, mate," he said. "Just ignore him and let him do his job, and then you won't have to see him again."

"Do you know how difficult it is to ignore someone you want to kill?" Shuffler replied.

"More than you know, brother," Grant answered. Neither of them needed further explanations about that response.

* * *

45

DS Richard Bradley ran his fingers over the crime case folder that sat on his desk. Large red letters had been printed on the front cover of the file, which declared that the case had been solved. Bradley couldn't get rid of the nagging doubt that lingered in his mind.

He had been one of two detective sergeants in charge of the team who had investigated the attempted murder of Kelvin Armstrong by David Warriner. It had been the easiest case to solve that he had ever worked on, and yet, the most difficult at the same time. The entire investigation, from beginning to conviction, had left him feeling very uneasy.

He opened the file and flicked through the pages, stopping at the occasional page and reading the words printed on them. Reading one of the transcripts, from one of the many interviews of Warriner, reminded him of the frustration they had left him with. Warriner's immovable stance toward total silence had made no sense. What the Armstrongs had done to his family would have been a very strong argument for mitigation, and the fact that his victim had not died, would, in his opinion, have resulted in a shorter sentence for grievous bodily harm.

The local populous had been fully behind Warriner. Many were quite vocally outside both the police station and the courthouse, and even that did not have an effect on Warriner. His silence had contributed toward his harsh sentence, and it was this that had DS Bradley confused and uneasy. Most of the accused people who he had been involved with denied their guilt vehemently. A small handful accepted guilt willingly, but Warriner did neither, and said nothing.

He closed the file and placed it into the tray that was labeled "files for archiving," and then removed it and placed it in his drawer. For some reason, he knew he would need to look at that file again sometime in the near future.

After just a few minutes of mulling things over in his head, Bradley reached for the drawer again, opened it and retrieved the Warriner file. He spent the next hour reading through pages of interview transcripts, all of them being the interviews with Warriner. Question after question fired at David Warriner, from himself and his colleagues, and not one word spoken by the accused. He got bored with reading the words, "for the purpose of the tape, Mr. Warriner has declined to answer, and given no other indication of offering any response." Bradley looked down at the box on the floor next to his seat, a simple brown evidence box rammed full of interview tapes, all of which, were now allowed to be unsealed and listened to. He closed the file again, but before he could return it to the drawer, a head popped around his office door.

"Fancy a coffee, boss?" a young DC named Pete Wood, aka Woody, asked.

"Do you ever knock?" Bradley asked.

"No," Woody replied. He had ironically been given the nickname, because unlike the woodpecker, Woody never knocked.

"I find it a waste of time, boss. I used to knock, but it always resulted in being told to come in. I was never told to go away", Woody explained. "So I am saving time and missing out the middle man."

"Go away and knock next time," DS Bradley said, a hint of humour in his voice.

Woody mentally waved away the response and looked at the file on his DC's desk.

"The Warriner file. Do you want me to take that over to

archiving?" he asked.

"No, I'll keep it for a while and get it down there myself, thanks," Bradley replied. "Tell me though, you worked on this case. What are your thoughts on Warriner?"

"Quiet," Woody replied with a smile.

"Everyone in this department is a fucking comedian," Bradley said sarcastically. "No, come on, tell me what you really think?"

"He tried to kill the bloke who he thought had killed his kids. He got it wrong, but he has got what he deserved," Wood said in a matter-of-fact way. "In fact, if you want the truth, boss, he should have gone to prison, but instead, he played the mental game very well, and now has a cushy life in Greenhill's, probably masturbating himself silly, fantasizing over some of those hot nurses who work there."

"Thanks, Woody, for that very insightful summary. Now go away," Bradley replied, sorry that he had asked the young DC the question.

"Okay, boss, I'll get you that coffee," Pete Wood replied, and his head disappeared from around the door, which he pulled closed as he left.

Despite not wanting a coffee, Bradley didn't bother arguing. He would allow it to go cold and let the cleaners get rid of it, like every other cup of coffee that Woody had brought him had been dealt with.

He lifted the lid from the box and pulled out a handful of tapes, all of which were labeled with the time and date that they had been used. He placed the first tape into the tape recorder on his desk, pressed the play button, and leaned back in his chair, making himself as comfortable as he could, in preparation for the hours of listening that lay ahead of him.

* * *

The three bikers walked out of the public house and toward their bikes. Shaking hands with each other, they said their goodbyes.

"I want those jobs completed within three months, fellas," Grant said to the other two.

"Does that include getting myself put away?" Shuffler asked.

"No mate, I will contact you when I want that to happen." Grant replied. "Until then, you do not contact me unless there is a major problem. I will contact you if I need to speak or give further instructions."

Shuffler and Magill nodded, and all three men split away and walked to their respective rides. The three bikes were fired up within a few seconds of each other, and the combined noise of all them was deafening.

As they prepared to leave, none of them noticed a shadowy figure sat in a parked car in the far corner of the car park. A young man, in his late twenties or early thirties, sat in a black BMW rental car, watching the three bikers closely.

Magill was the first to ride off, and turned right out of the pub car park, throttling his bike hard and disappearing up the road in seconds. Grant and Shuffler headed left at a more easy-going pace, and rode together for a few miles, before Shuffler took a right turn, holding up his left hand as a goodbye to his fellow rider. Grant responded in the same fashion, as he continued his journey home on his own.

The initial foundations of his plan having now been laid, he gave more thought to the details. The lonely journey allowing his mind to focus on nothing else, slowly each detail was mentally ticked off. Even if he had been fully focussed on everything around him, he would not have noticed the black BMW following him, because the driver was doing an excellent job of not being noticed, following Grant at a safe distance, like it was a natural thing for him to do. By the time Grant got home, he knew what lay ahead, and what would be required of each and every member of the team he was going to put together.

The BMW had continued its journey along the road, as Grant had turned into the driveway that led to his house, and disappeared into the distance.

Returning his bike to the garage, he then walked around to the house, stopping before he got there to look over the open ground, to where his beloved wife peacefully lay.

"I'm glad you are not around to witness what I am about to do, darling, but wherever you are, I hope you can understand and forgive me," he said quietly. He could hear his wife's reply—a reply she had given him before.

"I do understand, and eventually I will forgive, but I will never be able to forget and that my love has always been the problem," *she had said.*

Clubhouse, Acquisitions and Prison

Over the months that followed the meeting between himself, Shuffler and Magill, Grant had only had contact with the other two on a handful of occasions. The first time, Magill had contacted him, despite Grant having made it clear that all contact between them would be instigated by him.

"Some of the guys want to know details," he had said to Grant.

"Tell them that they are either in or they aren't, and that there are no guarantees that they will be going home when it's done. Now, do not call me again," Grant had abruptly ended that call, in the hope that combined with the sharp-toned reply, Magill would get the message. It had worked, because Magill did not call him again.

He had called Shuffler twice. The first time was to enquire about how things were progressing and to see if he was having any difficulties obtaining any of the items on his shopping list. Shuffler had only said that some of the items were coming in more expensively than anticipated, and Grant had assured him not to worry himself about the cost. The second contact was purely a catch-up, because Grant had been feeling very lonely and extremely low—the old dark enemies had filled his head again after being away for a long time. His friend did what was necessary—he listened, and then at the end, advised alcohol as a solution, only for medicinal purposes, apparently. Then it had been Shuffler's turn, as he expressed his apprehensions about returning to jail.

"Can you offer any protection, bro?" he had asked.

"I still have a few contacts in the job, mate. I will reach out to them and see what I can do," Grant had said.

"I would appreciate that," Shuffler had responded.

The final three contacts had been with Magill, all instigated by Grant. The first to request an update, which Grant had been pleased with. The second was for a further update, during which he was told that the list of names was complete. Grant issued Magill with instructions about a drop location and a date and time when the drop should be made. The final call was to change the date and time.

"Eleven-thirty p.m. on Tuesday night, mate, and make sure nobody sees you. And don't hang about once you have placed the list in the rubbish bin."

Three nights later, Grant had taken the Midnight Star for a night ride. He rode into the small quiet town and parked his bike on the side of the road, about fifty metres beyond a small convenience store. He looked at his watch, which told him it was 23:48. He walked back toward the store, and before disappearing into the dark alleyway next to it, he looked around to make sure nobody else was around. Assured it was all clear, he made his way to the end of the alleyway, where a large industrial rubbish bin stood. Lifting the lid, he looked inside and immediately saw a large brown envelope, which he took out of the bin and quietly lowered the lid.

He pulled out his phone, and briefly switched on its torch

facility to check the contents of the envelope. Six sheets of paper were inside. The top one had a list of names typed onto it. The other five had a few details about the people who were on that list. He switched off his phone torch and returned the phone to his jacket pocket. He tucked the envelope inside his jacket and zipped it all the way up to secure the envelope tight against his chest.

Returning to the dark town street, badly lit because only one out of every three street lights were in use, he glanced left and right down the street. Once again happy that the coast was clear, he made his way back to his bike. The poor lighting had made it impossible for Grant to see into the back of the parked black Mercedes, an old model that had been bought two months previously by its new owner, who now sat quietly in the darkness of the back seats of the car. The man watched Grant go about his midnight business, and also witnessed the next event.

The next contact with Magill occurred that very evening at exactly 23:54 hours. On this occasion, it was a face-to-face type contact.

Magill appeared around the corner of a sidestreet, catching Grant off guard, as the large man walked briskly toward him, stopping about three feet from him. Despite the badly lit street, Grant could see that the man was on edge. His right hand was inside his jeans back pocket, and he was moving his body weight from one foot to the other, his eyes rapidly moved left to right.

"What are you doing here, Frank?" Grant asked him. "I told you to drop and go."

"People have told me what to do all my life, and you know that I've done as I've been told. I've wanted nothing but friendship, but all I got was turned away," Frank replied nervously.

"Yeah, I know that, Frank," Grant replied, immediately recognising that this was a situation that could quite easily get out of control. He moved his body slightly, so his left arm became his leading limb. "Right now, though, I just need you to go home and I will be in touch."

"No," Frank replied, his voice now louder and more frantic. "I want to know what happens next, bro. My name's on that list, I have a right to know."

"Frank, I didn't ask you to put your name on this list," Grant replied calmly. He was aware from the small shoulder movements that Frank was moving his hand around in his back pocket.

"I gave clear instructions about what I needed from you. Your contacts were invaluable to me," he said, keeping his eyes solidly on the man he now considered to be a potential threat.

"See, there you go again. Instructions all the time, and what do you mean my contacts *were* invaluable to you? What about me? Am I still valuable?" Frank Magill was now highly agitated.

Grant chose his words carefully as he spoke to Frank.

"Magill, I would like you to go home now. I can see that you are not in the right frame of mind to continue this conversation, and I also think that there is something in your pocket that you are considering using. I just need to let you know that I think that would be a really bad idea." As he spoke, he turned his body slightly more side-on, slowly bringing his left foot forward and shifting his body weight over his lead leg.

"Fuck you, Anderson, or Grant, or whatever your name is,"

Magill said, as he pulled the flick knife from his pocket and held it at arm's length between himself and Grant. He moved his thumb over the silver switch that would release the blade, but Grant, anticipating what was about to happen, moved in toward Frank's extended arm, before the blade appeared from the front of the handle.

Grant's lead forearm struck his attacker's weapon arm, moving it upwards and inwards. At the same time, his trailing arm followed in, and struck down on Frank's upper arm, just above the crook of his elbow. Bending Frank's arm inwards, Grant allowed his loose arm and hand to slide around Magill's arm and lock his inside hand around his outside forearm, as his left hand cocked the wrist of the hand holding the knife.

A man with a weaker grip than Frank Magill's would have, by now, dropped the knife, but Magill held onto it, which did him no favours. By the time he knew what had happened, he found his arm locked into a figure of four arm lock, and the tip of the blade of the knife he refused to let go of had, during the technique performed by Grant, flicked out of its housing, and was now just millimetres from Magill's clavicle area, between his shoulder and upper chest.

Grant applied more pressure through the back of the weapon hand, and whispered an assertive order to Magill.

"Drop the knife, Frank, and walk away."

Through gritted teeth, Frank turned his head slightly and eyeballed Grant angrily.

"Fuck you, you using bastard. All I wanted was to be part of your plan," he said.

"This is why you cannot be part of it, Frank. You don't have the loyalty required. You think you do, but look at what is happening here. Now, drop the knife. I won't be asking you again," Grant replied, his voice calm and totally lacking in emotion.

"I know everything. I will go to the police. I will go to the papers," Frank screamed.

Grant applied more pressure, and the tip of the knife entered the flesh of Frank Magill's chest.

"Don't scream, Frank. Be that soldier you once were, and suck it fucking up," Grant said, his voice now contained emotion—pure anger. He could see the pain etched all over Magill's face, but to Grant's admiration, he did not make a sound.

"Now, I want to trust you to stay quiet, Frank," Grant, said his voice once again returning to the calm, almost robotic tone. "I want to be able to stop this, shake your hand and thank you for the work you have done, and then say our goodbyes. Can I do that, Frank?"

Still staring straight into Grant's eyes, and now with beads of sweat dripping down his brow, because of the pain he was suffering, Frank replied through his still tightly gritted teeth.

"I am going to fucking destroy you."

Grant moved his body weight forward, bending Frank's arm farther toward his chest, and the blade of the knife slowly and agonisingly embedded itself farther into Magill's chest. The injured man dropped to both knees. This also happened slowly, as Grant controlled the fall and lowered himself down to one knee.

He whispered into Magill's ear, as he watched the wretched man's head starting to drop forward. Grant assumed that the pain was forcing Magill to fall into unconsciousness, and still, he did not scream out.

"I don't want to kill you, Frank, but if I even think you

are going to say one word to anyone, I will send a horde of maniacs your way. And I think you already know what the end result will be."

He quickly released his hold on Frank's arm, and with as much force as he could muster, he swung his left elbow around, striking Magill in the side of the head, his forearm hitting the man's cheekbone and jawline like a hammer. Frank was unconscious, before the side of his head hit the pavement.

Slowly, Grant walked toward his bike and pulled a rag out of one of the side panniers—a rag he used to clean his visor. For a man who had just slowly pushed a blade into the chest of a man he had considered an ally, and then viciously knocked him unconscious, Grant remained unbelievably calm. He returned to where Frank's limp body lay, and wiped the rag over the handle of the knife.

"If you wake up before someone finds you, get yourself to the hospital, Frank," he said to the unconscious man. Leaving the knife in place, so it helped to stem the flow of blood, he left Frank Magill in the middle of the dark street.

As he rode past the still unconscious body, he stopped for a second.

"Forget about me, Frank, or forget about living," he said, and easing the throttle back, he rode away as quietly as the Midnight Star's exhaust pipes would allow him.

The man in the back of the Mercedes watched with interest, as he saw Grant's tail light disappear into the distance. Once it had disappeared out of sight, he got out of the back of the vehicle. The back door squeaked a little as he opened it. He stood looking at the unconscious body of Frank Magill in the distance, and all he could think was that he had just found himself an ally.

* * *

Grant sat in his favourite chair and began to read through the biographies of the people who had been listed as potential candidates. Some he knew personally, but the majority were unknown to him. By the time he had read the third biography, he knew he had selected the right person to come up with a choice of people. They were a complete mix of rejects and reprobates, but all had certain skills in the areas that would be required. The fourth biography, however, was a complete surprise to him, because the subject was female!

Dee Palmer, nickname Double D, was an ex-Army medic who had been decorated with a Military Cross medal for exemplary gallantry during an incident in Iraq, during which she saved the lives of five soldiers and one young officer. She was in the process of attempting to save the life of an insurgent, when she was told to stop working on the enemy and continue treating the soldiers. By all accounts, she informed the officer that she had triaged all the injured and the injured Iraqi was next to be treated. She had once again been given the order to stop and move on to treating the injured British soldiers.

She responded by shooting the officer in the knee and informing him that she would treat him, once she had finished patching up the Iraqi. The subsequent court martial found her guilty of grievous bodily harm and disobeying a lawful order. They went on to say that they recognised the enormous stress that Cpl. Palmer had been under, and that she had been awarded a prestigious medal for her bravery, however, they still dishonourably discharged her. The lieutenant had his leg amputated, because of the injuries caused to his knee.

Grant stopped tapping his top lip with the pencil and placed a tick next to her name. *We may just need a trained medic,* he thought. *But maybe not give her a pistol.* Grant saw from the short biography that she was a keen bike rider, but currently without a ride. He annotated a note next to the tick. *Bike needed.*

Next on the list appeared to be an interesting character, but not one that would normally be considered during a selection process for any job. Booted out of the RAF after serving twenty-eight days in military imprisonment for endangering the safety and lives of a large number of service personnel, just over three-hundred to be exact, he had been an RAF chef who, having tried on several occasions to leave the RAF early and having repeatedly had his requests refused, had decided to take a more direct and drastic approach. Over a period of three weeks, he laced the food he prepared for the RAF station military personnel with small, but frequent, levels of rat poison. Nine weeks after starting his campaign of mass poisoning, he got his wish, and became a civilian. Grant penciled a question mark next to the man's name. He knew that a good chef would be a potential morale booster, because if there was anything hard working military people appreciated, it was being fed. How much they would appreciate that food being prepared by a known poisoner, Grant had no idea. He placed a heavy-handed cross over the question mark, and then after a few seconds of sucking on the end of the pencil, he wrote another question mark. Grant liked a man who made a decision and stuck by it, no matter what the consequences! Mark "Hammer" Hammel was a possible.

He continued to read through the notes when, halfway

through the last biography, his mobile phone began to ring. Grant looked at the name of the caller on the screen.

"I wasn't expecting a call from you," he said out loud to himself, before answering it with an abrupt, "What?"

"I'm sorry, Grant," the voice on the other line said. "I was angry. Surely you can understand why, after all the hard work I did for you."

"I can't trust you," Grant replied. "I told you that as I was sliding your blade into your shoulder."

"Please, mate," the man pleaded. "I have nothing else. I am a complete mess, I realise that, but this will really help me. I am happy with a REMF role. Anything, bro. Please?"

"Let me give it some thought and call you back," Grant replied and ended the call without another word.

* * *

The caller looked over his shoulder, smiling at the man stood behind him.

"He's gonna think about it and call me back," he said.

"If he says no, I will finish off the job he couldn't," the stranger replied.

* * *

Grant returned to the job of reading the personnel briefs, but the call he had just received continued to prey on his mind.

He put down the sheets of paper and went outside for a breath of fresh air and a smoke.

Part of him felt sorry for Frank Magill, but the job had to come first, and that required a collection of loyal and trustworthy people whose moral code and principles would help them make decisions that the law would persuade others not to make. Magill had not proved his trustworthiness or loyalty, but he did have the connections and the ability to compile data and intelligence that could prove useful to the job in hand. Grant also knew that he could probably get his hands on a van that was equipped to pick up and transport motorbikes. He didn't want to waste a good person on the ground by appointing them as the backup driver. He finished his cigar and crushed it flat on the wooden flooring of the veranda with the heel of his boot. As he began to walk back into the house, he spied the offending cigar butt and bent down to pick it up, placing it into the ashtray that was filled with similar looking cigar butts. The rules applied by his wife continued to apply, even after her death.

He returned to his chair, collecting the pile of papers, and was just about to sit down to start the selection process again, when once again, his phone rang. He picked it up angrily and answered it without even looking at who was calling him.

"I said I would you call you back when I had given it some fucking thought," he shouted down the phone.

"And I said I would call you when I thought I had something worth seeing and warranting a fucking visit," came the response from an equally angry voice.

"Shit, sorry, Stacker. I thought you were someone else," Grant responded apologetically.

"That's okay then," Stacker replied calming down immediately. "As long as it's not me who has pissed you off. I've heard what you do to people who piss you off."

"No not all, bro. I take it you are calling to give me a situation update, so shoot," Grant said.

"Oh brother," Stacker replied, sounding rather similar to a southern state preacher. "You are going to shoot your load when you see what I have done to the place."

Grant smiled as he listened to Stacker explaining all the work he had completed at the clubhouse that Magill had found, thanks to Grant's money, nearly two months earlier. Allowing himself to zone out for a moment or two, confident that if he missed anything that Stacker said, he would be able to catch up by riding up to the clubhouse to see things for himself, he thought about how he had first met Phil "Stacker" Filby.

* * *

Grant had been posted to Germany with an Army Regiment that had its base within the boundaries of an RAF airfield. Phil Filby had been the RAF Squadron's store man, and according to everyone, he was the best store man around. Phil had a reputation of being able to get you anything—literally anything—as long as it had some connection to the military. The nickname Stacker came from some of the Army lads on the base who always referred to store men as blanket stackers. Phil did not mind one bit, being considered nothing more than a shelf stacker allowed him to get on with his other, less authorised, existence as the person to go to when you wanted something quickly and off the books.

Over five years, he built up an impressive number of connections, some within the military and others who worked for shadier organisations. Within that same period of time, he had provided RAF colleagues with items of uniform that were never intended for RAF military personnel, arranged for a two-year-old Mercedes Benz that had been the Squadron Commander's military vehicle to suddenly become the personal property of that same Commander, just before his retirement from military service, as well as many other illicit deals.

There were no lows that Phil would stoop to, so as to ensure his reputation as the go-to man remained intact, he had done it all—basic theft, fraud, forging of signatures on requisition orders, blackmail, and the offer of goods or services to persuade people to look the other way. He also earned himself a healthy pension pot in the process ... until he was caught, just two weeks before his last day as a military store man.

Grant had met Phil when returning from military exercise, having spent six weeks in a German forest pretending that a war against the Russians was actually taking place. The land rover he was driving had been damaged in a nighttime collision with a tree, which was nothing unusual, however, the problem on this occasion, was that Grant was not supposed to be driving the vehicle. He was drunk at the time, and the owner of the forest had caused a right uproar the following morning, when he came across his damaged property. Having managed to keep the damaged vehicle out of sight from senior staff, thanks to the clever use of camouflage nets and blankets, he found himself in the store's area in front of Phil Filby, asking if there was any chance of getting hold of some filler and paint.

"I can do better than that, lad," a smiling and confident Phil replied. "I can get you a replacement land rover and just transfer

the plates, then write off the damaged one and nobody will know a thing."

Grant had enquired how that was possible, and Phil had just winked, and said something about anything being possible in the world of military procurement, but that it was going to cost. When Grant had asked what the cost would be, Phil simply asked for a date with a female officer who worked in the same Squadron as Grant.

"You want to shag an Army officer?" Grant had asked.

"I want to take her to dinner and then shag her," Stacker had replied. "She is a captain; I've never done a captain."

Thankfully, for Grant, the female officer in question was not too choosy who she slept with, and the opportunity of a free meal was too much to resist. Two days later, a brand new land rover with the correct number plates was delivered to the hangar where Grant's squadron was located.

Grant had used the procurement skills of Stacker on a few occasions since then, and had never really lost contact with him.

* * *

"So, when are you coming up?" Stacker asked, breaking Grant away from his thoughts.

"Give me a couple of days, mate. I have a few things to do. I will need you to get a few other items for me and I will be paying for these," Grant replied.

"Okay, a bit of a boring old-fashioned way of getting things, but it's your choice and more importantly, your money." Stacker said. "And talking about money, dare I ask how you managed to access these funds?"

"I sold my body," Grant replied, trying to sound serious, but unable to hide the humour in the response.

"Well, that accounts for two pounds fifty. Speak soon, bro," Stacker said and ended the call.

Grant returned to his selection of people. So far, including himself, he had three members of his yet to be formed bike gang, Stacker and Shuffler being the other two. He once again gave some thought to Magill's request, and having mentally made his decision, he continued reading through the personnel biographies, looking for another ten people who bought the right skills and attitude to the table. He knew that, in total, it would make his selection of thirteen people, but also knew that Shuffler would not be around for a while. He needed twelve riders, which had nothing to do with bike gang protocol, and more to do with skillset and superstition.

Three hours later, and with his eyes stinging from all the reading, Grant sat back and looked down at the list he had compiled. He felt confident by his choices, and now only had to hope that the people selected would not back out when he contacted them. The list contained the names and newly applied road names of his crew, as well as the skills they brought to the team, and their position within it.

- Stanley Dawson – Shuffler – Vice President
- Phil Filby – Stacker – Sergeant at Arms
- Mark Hammel – Hammer- Catering
- Dee Palmer – Double D – Medic
- Andy Southall- Shovel – Disposal
- Tony Carr – Chaos – Instigator
- Alec White – Chalky – Full Member
- Terry Filston – Thunderbox – Full Member

- Pete Johnston – Syco – Intelligence Officer
- Dave Silcoe – Ordnance – Demolition
- Micky Maloney – MadDog – Full Member
- Paul England – Reckon – Reconnaissance
- Shane Greenway – Fixit – Mechanic (not a rider)
- Frank Magill – Pickup – recovery (not a rider)

Including himself, the club comprised of fifteen members, two of which, would not be riders. He also included one more than needed, just in case Shuffler was away for longer than expected. After thinking long and hard, he also included Magill, but only as the pickup man. He had no intention of including him in any part of the planning or execution of the mission.

He picked up his phone and called Shuffler.

"Hello bro, what are you going to tell me?" Dawson asked.

"It's time, bro," Grant replied.

"Time for prison?" Dawson asked.

"Not yet, mate. That will come soon. I am visiting the clubhouse and would like you to accompany me. Your thoughts would be welcomed."

"I appreciate that, bro. When and where?" Dawson asked.

"I will text you the date, time and location," Grant replied. "See you soon, bro."

The call was ended by Shuffler, without another word being said, and Grant knew that it was because his friend was not looking forward to going back to prison.

Grant made his way slowly outside to the chair beside his wife's graveside and sat down. He looked at the grave and did not say a word for several minutes. Eventually, he spoke to his dead wife.

"Julia, I have to go, babe, and I have already said that I may not be coming back. Either way, I will see you again, eventually. I know that you wouldn't agree with what I am about to do, but this is a debt that I have owed for too many years." He paused for a few seconds, as if expecting a response from the grave. "Show me a sign that you really do not want me to leave, and I will forget about it, stay here and look after your beloved horses, and await the day that I will be by your side again."

Grant waited, occasionally looking around, as if he was expecting to see some sign from beyond the grave that would convince him to bring an end to the job in hand, before it had even started. There was nothing—not an unexpected breeze, a falling leaf, a butterfly landing on the gravestone, or a floating feather.

"I knew Gump was a load of bollocks," he whispered.

He sent a text to Shuffler, a simple message that read:

Tomorrow, noon, junction of Duke St/King St/Park Lane. Old snooker hall.

"You have a few hours before I leave, darling. If you say no, I promise I will stop it," he said once again to the silent grave.

He stood, and kissing his hand, he placed it on the top of the gravestone.

"I hate it when you give me the silent treatment," he whispered sadly.

* * *

Frank Magill received the text from Grant late that night,

telling him that he was in. His eyes flitted from the screen of his mobile phone to the man sat opposite to him—the man who had repaired his shoulder with some deftly applied stitches, and the man who now was clearly in charge of his life.

"I'm in," Frank told the man who was still a stranger to him.

The man held out his hand, indicating that he wanted Frank to hand over his phone, and when that had been done, he read the short text.

"You are their pick up bitch. Your job will be to run errands and pick up broken down pieces of junk," the man said after reading the words from Grant.

"Yeah, but I am still going to be around them and their clubhouse. I can still do what you want me to do," Frank Magill responded like a young boy trying to impress his father or older brother.

"You had better hope so, otherwise a minor flesh wound will be the least of your worries," the stranger said, his voice cold and filled with hatred.

He handed the phone back to Frank and stood to leave the room.

"How will I get in touch?" Frank asked him.

"You don't," the stranger replied, opening the door. "When I need to talk to you, I will make contact," he said and slammed the door shut as he left.

Frank Magill did not like being treated like a piece of shit on someone's shoe, but he would put up with it for as long as it took him to bring about failure to Grant's plan. Then he would deal with this little overconfident cocksure wanker who thought he could treat him like he was some kind of pussy.

* * *

Grant did not get to sleep until the early hours, after spending almost six hours calling eleven people, and sending a text to one. Of the eleven he had called, only one had responded with anything other than words to the effect that they were in. The one exception was Double D, who had asked if she was the only female member of the team, and had laughed when Grant had confirmed that that was the case.

"Are you okay with that?" Grant had asked.

"One woman and so many sets of bollocks to kick ... I'm in," Double D had replied.

The fact that not one of them had asked what the job was, not one had, in fact, asked for any details, convinced Grant that his selection had been spot on. He had his team, a group of individuals who were loyal, unquestionably loyal to a friend, or a friend of a trusted friend, who needed help.

He sat on the edge of his bed—a bed he rarely slept in since the death of his wife, choosing instead to sleep in his chair or one of the guest rooms. He briefly considered rooting through the bedside cabinet to try and find some of his medication—the Zopiclone that he had not had to use for some considerable time. He decided better of it, knowing that when he did eventually wake up, his head would be clouded with the need for more sleep. He layed down and pulled the top pillow from his wife's side of the bed, and wrapped his arms around it. This was something he would not have been allowed to do during her living years. Julia Richardson let nobody touch her pillows, not even her beloved husband.

He hugged the pillow tightly to his body and buried his face into the top end of it, convinced that her scent would still be on it. He sniffed in deeply. He wasn't sure if it was real or just a figment of his imagination, but he could smell his wife's perfume.

"That's not a sign, darling. That's just a memory," he whispered.

He fell into a deep sleep.

* * *

The Priest sneered at him.

"Entering the dark murky world of bike gangs again, are you?" he hissed. "Did your last experience not tell you that you don't belong?"

A decomposed hand reached out of the soil, opening and closing, as if grasping for something. Higher up the pile, the soil began to form into a small hill, crumbles of soil rolling down its side, before a dirty rotting face with a scar down the side of it rose out of the ground. She smiled, her teeth encrusted in dry dirt. As she opened her mouth to speak, a worm slithered out of it.

"You want to be next to me, do you? You want to lay with me looking like this?" the dead corpse of Julia Richardson said.

His daughter looked at him, and then turning away, she spoke the words, "Why do you continue to kill and say it is in our name? If you cared about us, you would have been there and we would still be alive."

His daughter's body collapsed into a pile of ashes and dust on the floor.

"You are nothing without the agency. You are not capable of

killing without our help," Fox said, laughing uncontrollably as his face disappeared into thin air, to be replaced by the face of Emma.

"Is this what you are to become—one of them, a dog, a filthy murdering biker like those you rescued me from? Is this to be your legacy"? she asked.

Shuffler stood in front of him, his eye sockets empty of the orbs that should have been there.

"Were you blinded by your need to avenge? Did you send me to prison to die?" his friend asked, before opening his clenched fists and dropping two eyeballs onto the floor.

* * *

He opened his eyes and stared into the dark surroundings of the bedroom. He was covered in a fine coating of cold sweat. He hugged the pillow tighter and whispered to it, "That wasn't a sign either, darling. That was just another nightmare."

* * *

He gave Vicky a hug and a kiss on the cheek, and then thanked her for agreeing to look after the place and the horses while he was away. He briefly looked over toward Julia's grave.

"Don't worry, I will look after her, too," Vicky said momentarily squeezing his arm. "Everything will be okay. Go and do whatever it is that you feel you have to do, and then come home. We will be waiting for you—all of us." She smiled at the face of a man who was clearly troubled by something, and could only assume that he was still suffering from grief.

Grant swallowed the lump that threatened to form in his throat, and got aboard the Midnight Star.

"Why don't you go on one of your newer ones?" Vicky asked.

"The one thing I have learned recently, is that you learn to trust those things that have proved they can be trusted," he said, before pulling on the bike helmet and slipping his hands into the soft leather gloves. Nodding his head toward Vicky, he steered the bike steadily toward the driveway and began his northbound journey. As his wife had once asked him, he didn't look back … just in case fate decided that he was never to return.

* * *

Stopping three times, twice for a coffee and smoke break, and once to wait for Shuffler to meet up with him, Grant's journey was initially lonely and uneventful. For the last third, the trip was enjoyable in the company of his biking brother Shuffler, who looked very much at home on the Indian Dark Horse. He had made a few changes to the bike, the most notable being the high ape bars that helped to keep his back in an upright position. While otherwise an uncomfortable riding position, it suited Shuffler, and the only restriction was the number of miles he could cover, before pulling over for a glug of his Oromorph. The journey from Derbyshire to the Staffordshire town did not trouble him too much, and the warm weather also helped. A few minutes more than four hours after Grant had left his home in the capable hands of Vicky, the two bikers arrived at their destination. Shuffler had led the way for the last few miles, as his bike had the built-in sat nav system.

They pulled their bikes over to the kerb at the junction of Duke Street and King Street, looking at the white building that had once been the Plaza snooker hall. Now all signage connected to that previous history had been removed and its walls left bear of any notices or signs that would give away its new purpose in life.

Grant led the way, riding over the narrow width of King Street onto Park Lane, pulling over once again on the left side kerb. A large solid pair of black gates that had to be opened from the inside were solidly shut. As he started to reach into his jacket pocket to retrieve his phone, one gate began to open, and a tall man wearing a broad smile on his face appeared from behind it. Through the gap, Grant and Shuffler could see the ample parking area that backed onto the back of the one-time snooker hall and now bikers' clubhouse.

On the other side of the parking area was a large grey metal and red brick warehouse, entry into which was currently denied by a large green metal shutter door. This was the second building that Grant had leased, and the large yellow and blue *To Let* sign with a board diagonally placed across it announcing *Unavailable,* was a clear indication of the successful transaction that had been secured a few months beforehand.

Grant and Shuffler steered their bikes through the gap provided by Stacker, parking up against the back wall of the clubhouse, ensuring they were facing outwards toward the centre of the car park. A single door in the outer back wall to their right, was the only way into the building that they could see, and it was to this door that they watched Stacker walk to, after he had closed the main gate and bolted and locked it securely shut.

"I am guessing you want to see the results of your money boss?" Stacker asked with a huge, proud smile on his face.

"I'm not your boss, but yeah I do want to see what you have been up to for the past couple of months," Grant replied.

"Come in," Stacker said, sweeping door open. "You are the boss, though. This is your creation, and the people who will be living and working here, are your team."

Grant ignored him and walked through the door. Stacker held it open a while longer, waiting for Shuffler to get off his bike, take a drink from a small brown bottle and hang his helmet on his bike's handlebars.

"Bit early for that, isn't it?" Stacker asked Shuffler as he walked past him and through the door.

"Do I know you?" Shuffler replied.

"No," Stacker answered.

"And do you know me?" Shuffler asked again.

"No, never met you," a slightly confused Stacker replied.

"Well, keep your fucking huge nose out of my fucking business," Shuffler snapped. A mixture of discomfort and the lingering reluctance of going back to prison, had put him in an unsociable mood, especially toward strangers irrelevant of whether or not they knew Grant.

"Wow, what part of the team are you? Recruitment officer?" Stacker asked, answering his own question at the same time.

"Media representative," Shuffler called back from inside the building to a surprised Stacker, who thought he had spoken quietly enough not to be heard.

The two men walked down the short corridor that quickly opened up into a large bar area, where they found Grant looking around it with a set of critical eyes.

"Where's the briefing room?" he asked, happy that the bar and rest area was exactly as he had imagined.

"Do you like the pool table and the jukebox?" Stacker asked, as he walked toward a single door in the far wall.

"I don't play pool and I doubt if you have my taste of music," Grant replied.

This was not going as Stacker has thought it would. He had been expecting whoops and hollers about the work he had completed in a remarkably short time. He walked to the door that led to the briefing room, and opened it up, looking toward Grant as he did so.

"Thank you," Grant said, as he walked past the man and through the door.

The difference in Grant's reaction was just what Stacker needed.

"Now, this I like, well done, Phil," he said.

"Can we stick to nicknames or road names, or whatever you choose to call them?" Stacker asked.

A preoccupied Grant nodded his head, and said, "Yeah, you're right, Stacker. Road names from now on." He looked around at Shuffler. "What do you think, bud?" he asked.

"I won't be spending much time here, if any, will I? So what does it matter what I think?" Shuffler replied sharply.

It was obvious to Grant that the elephant in the room needed to be addressed quickly.

"Shuffler, you are my brother, and I know what I have asked of you is huge, but I have asked you, because I know that I can trust you to do what needs to be done inside. Now, if you don't want to do it, just say the words, and then be on your way," he said.

"So a case of doing it, or fuck off?" Shuffler asked.

"Interpret it how you like, bro," Grant answered, knowing that this was a potential problem to the success of the job.

"I will do it, Grant, but in the future, don't blow smoke up my arse about me being the only man you can trust with this job. Going to prison is easy, anybody can do that. It's the surviving it bit that worries me," Shuffler said. H firmly stood upright as he spoke, a posture that Grant knew would be causing him pain.

"Stand down, soldier. A level of protection has been arranged," Grant replied, and walking over to Shuffler, he gave the man a one-armed hug.

"Now, what do you think about this room?" he asked, as he released the biker's embrace.

"I've shit in worse places," Shuffler said. He and Grant began to laugh, much to the bemusement of Stacker, who was certain that this small stranger had just described his work as a decent lavatory.

Grant sat at the head of the large black wooden table. Twelve other chairs had been placed neatly around it. Other than the deep blackness of it, the table was unremarkable—no elaborate carvings into its top, no gavel or block to bang against it, and no other trappings that are often connected with the many tables in the thousands of bike clubhouses around the world. Hanging from the wall at the other end of the table, were three banners, a skull was emblazoned on each of them. One had its skeletal hands over its eyes, while the other two had similar embraces of their faces—the second covering its ears, and the last had both hands over its mouth. Below each skull head, a word had been printed. The three different words, which as far as Grant was concerned, summed up the rules of this group—honour, truth and loyalty. In the top of the skulls, were engraved three names—Surdux, Sputux and Caecux.

"What's the empty frame for?" Shuffler asked, looking at a simply framed glass-fronted casing on the wall in front of him, and left of where Grant was still sat.

"Well," Stacker proudly replied, "that is my personal addition. I thought you could get me photographs of all the members, and I will place them in there, underneath the name of the club, which you can see I have already put up,"

"No," Grant responded, his tone demonstrating that of a man who had suddenly found his place in life. "I will get you the pictures you want, but they will not be put up in the frame."

"So, what's the point of giving the mugshots?" Stacker asked.

It was Shuffler who responded to the confused architect and builder of the clubhouse, because he knew exactly what Grant wanted.

"What he means, is that the photos will go up ... eventually ... if and when one of our members turns off their engines for the last time."

Grant nodded his head in agreement.

"It will be our in-memoriam board—our way of remembering those who don't return from the war," he said.

He looked once again at the frame, empty except for the rectangular piece of white card that Stacker had pinned behind the glass. Three words printed in blood red finally made Grant realise that everything was almost in place. All he needed now, were the members of the club to turn up.

The Nameless Ones were born.

Reaching Out

Before leaving the briefing room, Grant handed a sheet of paper to Stacker. Written on it, was a list of sizes, mostly large and extra-large. The words small, medium and large had been listed, and one XXXL wrote once among the list, was the only thing that broke from its repetition.

"Contact the address I have written at the end of the list," Grant said to Stacker. "They already have the instructions for what to place on the cuts and where to place them, and I have already paid for their services. They just need the sizes, bro."

"You want me to do this now?" Stacker asked.

"No," Grant replied with a smile, at last replacing the serious look that had been a permanent feature on his face, ever since he had walked into the clubhouse. "Show us around the rest of the place first."

Stacker was pleased to hear this. He had been wanting to show off his work, ever since the two bikers had arrived.

As they entered the bar, Grant turned to Shuffler and asked him to stay put.

"Put on a bit of music and have yourself a beer," he said, and then to Stacker, he asked, "I take it the bar is fully functional and stocked?"

A proud and beaming Stacker nodded his head, a bit too frantically.

"Oh yes, stocked better than a PBX," he replied.

Shuffler was not pleased about being told to stay where he was, and not being allowed to take the full tour.

"Why do I have to stay here? Am I not a member of this club?" he asked, clearly hurt by Grant's instruction.

"Bro, you are as much a member as I am. In fact, you were the first person I thought of when I was planning this out, but I don't need you seeing the layout, or the facilities, from here on in," Grant replied. "If you don't know, you cannot say anything. It's basic plausible deniability."

"You know I don't squeal, bro. Do you need me to remind you of what Fox did to me?" Shuffler asked, still smarting from what he saw as being excluded.

"No mate, you don't need to remind me. That memory will remain emblazoned in my brain, way beyond my eventual arrival in hell." Grant answered. "But Fox is one thing. The people you are going to come across inside are in a totally different league, and you know I am speaking the truth."

Reluctantly, Shuffler had to agree, and immediately re-signed himself to being a temporary outsider. He walked toward the bar sulkily, remarking, "This bar better have some rum."

Before being led out of the bar by Stacker, Grant walked over to Shuffler and slapped him on his back, quietly saying to him, "Have a drink, bro. Put on some tunes, and then go to my bike. There's a gift in my left saddlebag that I hope will convince you that you are a fully-fledged Nameless One."

* * *

The two Armstrong brothers had tied their victim securely to the chair, and were now making threats to cut him up unless they got a transfer out of the jail. The recent transfer of their younger brother to a prison in Northumberland, made their demand appear to be feasible, but it had nothing to do with them taking a hostage.

The negotiator stood outside of the prison cell door, trying his best to build up some sort of relationship with the two perpetrators. He was young, nervous and newly trained as a hostage negotiator. In fact, it was his first live hostage incident.

"Michael, would you put the knife down for me please?" the negotiator asked.

Michael Armstrong held the sharp blade, taken from behind the wing servery, just before they bundled their victim into the cell, and waved it in front of the young prisoner's face.

"Shut up, you fucking twat. You say one more word, and I will cut his face into a thousand pieces," an insane looking Michael Armstrong yelled back.

"Cut him up! Cut him up!" an equally over-excited Harry Armstrong, the younger of the two hostage takers, screamed.

The three incumbents in the cell were all situated very close to the inside of the cell door. This was a deliberate act by the Armstrong brothers who, in order to make a forced entry into the cell both difficult and dangerous, had placed their bound victim right behind the door. Behind the chair, to which their victim was tied, they had placed the cell bunk bed, and then behind that, they had wedged the heavy wooden locker, which

81

fit securely between the bed end and the back external wall of the cell. Any intervention team attempting to force open the door, would potentially cause great injury to the hostage because of this, and the Armstrong brothers knew that this would make the authorities think twice about bringing the situation to a quick conclusion with the use of force.

Out of sight of the Armstrong brothers, a specialist officer had placed himself up close against the outside of the cell door, and was now on his knees, directly in front of the legs of the negotiator. Slowly, he used the allen key to loosen the bolts around the cell door lock, the removal of which would allow the door to be quickly opened outward, allowing a quick entry into the cell without causing harm to the hostage.

His progress was extremely slow to ensure that the loosening of the securing bolts was done with absolute silence. The works department had decided at some stage to paint over the bolts. If the officer could have cursed the idiots who had made that decision, he would have done so with gusto, but he, too, had to maintain absolute silence.

"Will you let me speak to Adam?" the negotiator asked, referring to the hostage.

Michael Armstrong responded by sticking the blade of the knife through the very thin gap between the heavy cell door and its door frame, and sliding it in an up and downward direction. The blade had appeared through the gap, about two inches above the kneeling officer's head, who was now working on the second bolt and hadn't noticed the weapon come so close to causing him a horrendous injury. He only realised that something was amiss when, despite the threat of the protruding blade, the negotiator stepped slightly closer to the door and placed his hand on top his head to prevent himself from accidentally rising up toward the knife. Tilting his head slightly backward and turning his eyes upwards, he stared at the offending article, and silently whispered a *thank you* to the negotiator.

The move toward the door by the negotiator had not gone unnoticed by Michael Armstrong.

"Want me to stick this into you, do you, you fucking stupid bastard?" he screamed.

The negotiator was about to respond, when he felt something splatter against his shirt. Looking down, he saw a red liquid all over his white shirt, and initially thought he may have gone too close to the blade. He placed his hands over the red stain on his shirt, and looked with shock into the cell through the observation window, only to see Harry Armstrong doing a dance inside the cell and laughing maniacally. In his hand, he held a squeezable bottle of tomato sauce.

The negotiator, Officer Ben Hockley, let out a sigh of relief, and noticing that the pressure he was applying to his colleague's head was more than was necessary, moved his hand from the top of his head. The officer on the floor looked up at Officer Hockley and mouthed the word *wankers*, and immediately carried on with the work of loosening the securing bolts.

The negotiator refocused and turned his attention back to the occupants of the cell.

"Listen Michael, Harry, I just want to talk to you both. I want to find out what has made you do this," he said.

Michael Armstrong pressed his face up against the inside of the observation glass and glared at Ben Hockley. He had forced his face so hard up against the glass that his face was distorted and twisted, and as he spoke, his mouth stretched in ways that gave him the look of a ghoulish monster.

"I want ... I want, that's all we hear in this place—what you bastards want all the time. You don't give a shit about us, you don't give a fucking damn about poor little Adam—it's just all about what you want. What about what we want?" The question was screamed out by Michael, who then slammed his forehead against the glass with such force that the reinforced barrier cracked slightly, and blood burst from the wound that instantly appeared.

"I do care," Officer Hockley replied "I really do."

"Do you ... do you really"? Armstrong asked, and then looked at his younger brother and nodded his head.

"Then get us our transfer and this won't happen again," he said menacingly.

At that point, Officer Hockley watched as Harry Armstrong wrapped one arm strongly around the forehead of Adam Batchelor, and with his other hand, used his thumb and first finger to grab a large piece of flesh, stretching it out from his victim's cheek. Michael Armstrong held the sharp blade of the prison kitchen knife against the stretched flesh, and with a startling quick movement of the knife, sliced it cleanly through Adam's cheek. The scream that came out of Adam Batchelor would live with Officer Ben Hockley for the rest of his life, and would prove to be one of the factors that stopped him from returning to work, and having to be medically retired from the prison service. The second factor was what happened next.

As Harry Armstrong held the now dissected piece of flesh that had once belonged to his victim's face and waved it around in the air, Michael Armstrong calmly held out an open hand. Officer Hockley watched in horror, as Harry placed the bloody piece of human flesh into his brother's hand, and then threw up as Michael placed it into his mouth and began to chew. Blood flowed down the chin of Michael Armstrong, who was now laughing between each chew into human flesh, and Adam Batchelor screamed and screamed. Officer Hockley looked down through the now blood-splattered observation glass at Adam, and wondered if the scream was coming out of his mouth, or the newly acquired hole in the side of his face. At that point, he fainted.

Three of the four securing bolts had been fully removed, and the last one was millimetres from being out, when the officer heard the heavy stomping of boots approaching down the landing, instinctively knowing that the order to initiate a forced entry had been given, but not aware of why he moved away from the cell door and managed to slide the prostrate body of Ben Hockley out of the path of the two intervention teams. The first member of staff to arrive pulled on the cell door handle, and the final securing bolt gave up its hold and snapped as the door was wrenched open. Ignoring the screaming and bound victim, the two teams rapidly entered the cell, each team protected slightly by a small shield, and each team member with their extendable batons drawn and in the ready position. The first team slammed their shield into the face of Michael Armstrong, who fell to the floor. The team quickly followed his descent and pinned him to the floor with the shield. Michael Armstrong stared through the Perspex shield, and using his tongue, he forced the partially chewed piece of human cheek out of his mouth, sticking it against the hard plastic.

"Can I have his tongue for dessert?" he screamed.

Despite the pain caused by the arm locks, the subsequent wrist locks and the final application of the rigid handcuffs, the two Armstrong brothers did not respond with cries of pain or discomfort for the entire duration of the removal from the wing to the segregation unit. When finally relocated in separate cells in the segregation unit, Harry Armstrong sat himself up in the middle of the cell cross-legged and rubbed his wrists, while his elder brother slowly and meticulously stood himself upright and walked to the cell door. Through the observation glass, he calmly looked at the duty governor, who was looking back at him.

"Put me back on the wing and I will do it again, only this time I will eat the whole face," he said with such evil in his voice that the governor could only think that he was face-to-face with a monster.

* * *

Stacker led Grant through the door, leaving Shuffler in the bar behind them.

"When do the others arrive?" Stacker asked, as he led Grant down a corridor containing many doors, behind which were simply laid out bedrooms, sixteen in total.

"Should start arriving over the next few days. I am hoping for a full complement by the weekend," Grant replied, briefly stopping to open one of the doors to take a look inside one of the bedrooms, which reminded him of the many single-person barrack rooms he had been billeted in over the years.

"And what about him?" Stacker asked, referring to Shuffler.

"He will be fine. Don't ever make the mistake of underestimating Shuffler. The man is a born survivor," Grant replied.

At the end of the corridor, four rooms had been converted into shower rooms. Three of them were of the communal type, with each of them having an open shower area with four shower heads protruding from the wall. The fourth was a single shower room.

"For the split arse," Stacker said, as Grant perused the shower facilities.

"Female member of the team, the medic, the woman," Grant sharply said. "Let's not start off by splitting the group with terminology."

"Pardon the pun, eh, Stacker said smiling, but Grant completely ignored his attempt at humour.

The final room was a medium-sized kitchen, which looked very well equipped.

"For the slop-jockey … sorry, chef," Stacker said, quickly correcting himself.

The two men stood outside of the kitchen door, as if waiting for the other to say or do something.

"And the other areas I asked for?" Grant asked.

"Well, the large building across the car park has been converted into a bike workshop—full sets of tools, may I add, and I built a storeroom in there for food stock, as there was just no room over here," Stacker replied. "The booze is stored in the same place, too. I put a lock on that door, so the boys couldn't just raid the beer when they are working on their bikes."

"Stacker, stop fucking about … you know what I'm talking about," Grant said impatiently.

Stacker reached his arm back and grabbed a door handle. He turned it and pushed the associated door open. It swung inwards to show a short descent down about eight or nine stone steps.

Grant looked down the steps from the top of them.

"Well?" he asked, confused by being shown a set of stairs that led nowhere.

Stacker smiled and began to make his way down the stairs, reaching the bottom very quickly.

"These steps led to the large basement below the whole building, but I blocked it up," he said.

"So the entrance is somewhere else I'm guessing?" Grant replied. "The garage maybe?"

"Well, yes and no," Stacker replied.

"Bro, I am not in the mood for a quiz or a find the secret door competition," Grant said, his patience beginning to run out, and the need for a beer beginning to consume his mind.

Grant watched as Stacker stepped back up onto the bottom stone step. He dropped to one knee and reached an arm to the far side of the concrete base floor at the foot of the stairs. His fingers dropped into a small indention that Grant had not spotted. Stacker pulled and the floor began to slide back toward him and disappeared beneath the bottom step. The whole concrete based disappeared out of sight to disclose a wooden trapdoor beneath it. Lifting the trapdoor and leaning it back against the stairwell wall, he stood to one side, to allow Grant to take a look.

Grant walked down the stairs and leaned forward to look down into the hole beneath the trapdoor. Another set of stairs could be seen, these made out of wood. Based on the fresh, clean looking wood, these were new.

Stacker reached down and placed his hand under the lip of the trapdoor hole and flicked a switch that had been hidden there, and a light illuminated the area below.

"After you, boss," Stacker said to Grant, who scowled at the use of that word to describe him again.

Grant made his way down the stairs, waiting at the bottom for Stacker to join him. A large open space that was very well lit was located at the bottom of the second set of steps, and Grant could see that several rooms had been constructed within this space.

"The entire space, ceiling and walls, have all been sound-proofed," Stacker explained. "One of the main reasons for the huge dent in the funds you made available.

Grant nodded his head, as if in approval of the additional spending.

"Good thinking," he said. "Now show me the rooms."

Grant and Stacker perused the rooms that had all been built by Stacker, who had decided against involving a building firm on this part of the project, as some of the rooms and their designs may well have attracted the wrong type of attention, or at the very least, too many questions. He was obviously very proud of what he had created, as he explained to Grant the particulars of each room. At the end of the short tour, he looked at Grant and awaited a response. What he got was exactly what he had been hoping for.

"Brilliant job, Stacker. Absolutely fucking outstanding," Grant said, who was clearly pleased with the outcome of his requests. "This is beyond what I expected."

"Wait until you see the additional stuff in the garage then," Stacker said, beaming with pride.

Grant shook the big man's hand.

"That can wait a while. Let's join Shuffler for a drink, before he finds that bottle of Pussers,'" he said.

"Pussers?" Stacker enquired.

"Bloody strong rum—his favourite tipple," Grant explained.

"Oh right, gets a bit punchy on it, does he?" Stacker asked.

"No, much worse," Grant replied, who was now smiling, too. "He starts to dance and fucking sing, and this is one man who is totally tone deaf. His singing has been known to silence hell."

The two men laughed and made their way back up to the bar area, Stacker making sure that everything was slid and shut back into place, so the secret underground area was once again hidden away.

Walking back into the bar, they found Shuffler sat at the bar on one of the wooden stools. A small glass containing a dark fluid sat on the bar in front of him, and upon his back, he proudly wore his new cut. Seeing the two men enter the room, he stood up and did a slow 360-degree turn.

"Fits me well, Grant, and the patches are perfect. I feel like I have come home," he said to both men, but mainly his words were for Grant.

The standard leather cut had six patches sewn onto it. On the front left shoulder area was a small patch showing three numbers. In Shuffler's case, those numbers were 364. On the right shoulder was a patch showing his road name, and beneath this, a smaller patch with his designation in the organisation embroidered upon it—his said *Vice President*. The back of the cut was laid out in a typical bike gang style—a top rocker with the name of the bike gang, which in this case was on a white top rocker with red characters. The words emblazoned across it were *The Nameless Ones*. The bottom rocker, which was also a white background with red characters, was the single word *Loyalty*. Between these two rockers sat the main large patch—three skulls sitting atop of each other with the top skull's mouth covered by a bandana; the middle skull had a banner coverings its ears; and the bottom skull had its eyes covered, once again by a bandana that entwined itself around and across its gaping jawbone.

"We say nothing, we heard nothing, we saw nothing," Shuffler said.

"Except for road name, rank and number, my friend—the way it has always been," Grant responded.

Shuffler reached over to his right and picked up a second similar cut, and threw it over to Grant, who caught it.

"I am guessing this is yours. Let's see it on you, bro."

Grant put the cut on and stood proudly in front of Shuffler, who was smiling back at him.

"You approve?" Grant asked.

The only difference between the two cuts, was that Grant's number patch read 000, and there was no road name or designation patches.

"You have no road name, bro. That's not right," Shuffler remarked.

"Never really had one, mate. I'm just Grant," Grant replied.

From behind him, Stacker spoke.

"Only one name will do," he said dramatically, as if bestowing an award. "I hereby name you … Nameless."

Shuffler started to clap his hands together.

"That will do perfectly," he said.

Grant held his hand up and Shuffler stopped his light applause and the room went silent.

"Shuffler, my friend, it's time to remove the colours. Place your cut on the back of your chair in the briefing room," Grant asked Shuffler with a hint of regret and sadness in his voice.

"It will await your return."

Shuffler did as he had been asked, and the other two men remained silent and solemn, until Shuffler returned to the bar area. Grant broke the uncomfortable silence.

"Shuffler, you know what you have to do now and I wish you luck. Reach out to me when you move into your new home." Turning to Stacker, he said, "Stacker, I need you to wait here and welcome the team. They should start to arrive tomorrow."

Stacker nodded his head to show that he understood.

"Are you not staying then?" Stacker asked.

"I will be back later. Right now, I need to reach out to the local chapter, before the club members start to arrive. I need to shake hands and put peace into place, otherwise, we will end up with more trouble than we can handle," Grant replied. "I will hopefully be back in a few hours."

"Let me come with you," Shuffler said. "My old life and knowledge will be useful. I know the language that these people speak."

"Thanks, bro, but your anonymity is crucial right now. You must have no connections to this club," Grant replied. "Now, get to work, guys. Our mission starts today."

Without any signal, and as if there was some invisible mental connection between the three men, they approached each other and held one hand out toward the space at the centre of the small circle they formed. Stacker placed his hand on top of Shuffler's, and Grant placed his hand on top of Stacker's and in unison, all three men spoke one word.

"Loyalty."

* * *

The young man sat in his plush apartment, looking out of the large glass frontage over the river, and contemplated the future. Having secured an inside man to keep him up to date with the goings-on of Grant's activities, he now gave thought to when he should make his move. *Should he prevent Grant from succeeding, or should he let him feel the satisfaction of success, and then bring him back down to earth and destroy him?*

The destruction of Grant was, as far as this individual was concerned, inevitable, so it was just a question of when to do it. He had grown to hate this man without really ever knowing him, but that didn't matter. He deserved what was coming to him, for what he had done to his life.

The apartment had been rented for three months and it hadn't come cheap, not that this was an issue. He had earned more than enough money over the past five to six years, and more importantly, had picked up skills and knowledge from the people he had worked with who would prove to be invaluable against Grant.

He crossed his arms behind his head and leaned back, content that he had managed to get to this point in his life. The time had come when he could at last payback Grant for all the pain he had caused him—way ahead of the timescale he had set himself. He smiled as he thought about coming face-to-face with the man, trying to imagine how Grant would react.

I hope you piss yourself and die on the spot from a heart attack, the young man thought to himself.

* * *

The first of The Nameless Ones arrived just one hour after Grant and Shuffler had gone their separate ways—one heading out on a bike ride to attempt to make peace with the bike gang whose territory Grant's new clubhouse fell within; and the other heading off to only he knew where, but wherever that place was, it was just a staging point for a short trip to prison.

Stacker had been stood by the entrance door to the clubhouse having a smoke, when he heard the familiar throbbing roar of a bike approaching. From the other side of the large entrance gate, a horn was sounded, followed by three more inpatient honks just a few seconds later.

"Wait your turn, for God's sake," he shouted. "I'm coming."

He pulled the gate open, and without a wave of acknowledgment or an invite to enter the yard, the biker rode straight in and parked her bike back end first at the side of the clubhouse. Stacker closed the gate, and once again secured it shut, and then striding with a purpose, made his way angrily over to the uninvited biker.

"Who the fuck are you?" he shouted.

Dee Palmer removed her helmet and shook out her shoulder-length black hair.

"I've been told that from this point on I am Double D," she responded.

She got off her bike and looked at Stacker standing as tall as her five-feet-four inches would allow her, and pushing out her ample chest.

"And who the fuck are you? The luggage carrier?" she asked.

Stacker's attitude and approach changed immediately upon seeing Double D standing in front of him, or to be more accurate, standing out in front of him. He couldn't stop staring at her large breasts tightly encased inside her leather jacket.

"Hey moron, focus on the face, not on the pleasure bags. They are for comfort, this is for communication," she said pointing at her own face.

Stacker broke out of the trance that the woman's breasts had placed him, and said, "Yeah, yeah sorry, babe. I'm Stacker."

She placed her helmet on the bike seat and placed both of her hands on her hips. What she lacked in height, she more than made up for in solid stockiness.

"Listen, Slacker. I ain't yours or anyone else's, babe," she retorted.

"No, no it's Stacker," Stacker replied emphasising the letter "T."

"That's open for debate," Double D replied. "Now, I take it this is the way in?" she asked, looking at the only door she could see.

Leaving the helmet on the seat of the bike, happy that it and the red Yamaha 900 Virago would be safe, she walked into the building, leaving Stacker to quickly move in an effort to keep up with her. She walked into the bar and sat down on one of the large sofas that had been placed in the bar area—an area that Stacker had named the *R and R area*.

"Thank fuck for that. I am knackered and my arse aches," she said.

"Let me get you a drink, and as we are the only ones here, we can get to know each a bit better," Stacker said, smiling and once again ogling Double D's frontage.

The female biker looked around the bar area, and then

studied the ceiling for a while, before standing up and walking toward Stacker with a smile on her face. She stopped no more than a foot in front of Stacker, who by now was starting to think that his luck might just be in.

"D'you know what this bar could do with?" she asked him.

"What?" Stacker answered.

At that, Double D brought her right knee up and struck Stacker hard in his groin, causing him to fall to his knees and cup his now painful testicles.

"Shiny balls hanging from the ceiling," Double D said with a huge grin on her face. "D'you know where we could find any?"

Stacker remained where he was, still kneeling on the floor and holding his injured parts.

"Why the fuck did you do that?" he asked between moans of pain.

"Oh stop moaning. I am a medic … would you like me to take a look at them?" Double D replied.

"You stay away from my bollocks," Stacker said, unconsciously cupping his balls tighter.

"And that, my little Slacker, is why I did it, so you could learn a lesson," Double D said. "You keep your eyes off my tits, and I will keep my knee away from your balls. Now, my work here is done, so I am off to take my pick of the rooms." And with that, she turned and walked toward the door that she assumed would lead to the bedrooms she was looking for.

"You weren't supposed to arrive until at least tomorrow," Stacker yelled after her.

"Well, I sure am happy I got here early. It gave me a chance to get to know you better," she yelled back without looking in Stacker's direction.

* * *

Shuffler rode off to the local town just a few miles away, and spent about twenty minutes or so, cruising up and down High Street. He had, as requested by Grant, or Nameless if that was what he was going to be called, left his colours hanging over the chair that sat to the right of Grant's chair. Eventually, after completing loop after loop of High Street, he saw what he had been waiting for—a police vehicle. He caught up with it and dropped in close behind it, and then followed it to the side of the street, where it parked up. Instead of parking up in front or behind it, he stopped his bike right next to the driver's door. The copper in the driver's seat looked at him and waved his hand, telling him that he needed to move his bike, but Shuffler stayed exactly where he was.

The copper opened his window and spoke with, or rather to, Shuffler.

"Move your bike, sir."

Shuffler just stared at the copper and said nothing.

"Sir, I will not ask you again," the copper said more sternly on this occasion.

"Does your mother know you are out?" Shuffler asked.

"Very funny, sir. Now, for the final time, move your bike away from the vehicle," the copper said, almost sounding bored as he spoke.

"I don't believe you are a copper. You look like a school kid," Shuffler said.

The copper in the passenger seat got out of the car and walked around the back of it and stood alongside Shuffler.

"Sir, may I ask ... are you feeling okay?" the second copper asked.

Without a second thought, Shuffler raised his gloved hand to the same level of the copper stood aside him, and spreading the first two fingers, firmly poked him in both eyes. The copper staggered back and covered his temporarily injured eyes with his hands.

The driver of the police car opened up the door as far as Shuffler's bike would allow, and slid his lead leg out of the gap provided. Shuffler, waiting for this happen, took the opportunity to raise his foot and solidly kick the door, shutting it on the officer's leg, who yelled out with pain, as his knee and thigh took the full force of the door slamming back toward him.

Shuffler decided he had done enough to begin with, and putting his bike into first gear, sped away, keeping a close eye on where the police car was, as he had no intention of losing them.

The second police officer scrambled back to the car, still rubbing his eyes, which were badly bloodshot, and radioed in the incident, while the driver tried his best to ignore the pain in his upper leg to depress the accelerator and speed down High Street after the bike, lights flashing and sirens wailing. They quickly caught up with Shuffler and positioned their car on the outside of his bike.

"Why isn't he traveling faster? He could outgun us on that thing," the officer asked the driver.

"He is a fucking nutter and he is getting nicked," came the response.

Shuffler suddenly brought his bike to a squealing stop, totally surprising the copper, who stopped his vehicle about three metres farther on. Both coppers got out of their vehicle and looked around for the biker, but could not see him anywhere, which was until Shuffler suddenly appeared between two parked cars and stood in front of the police car.

"Over here boys," he shouted.

The two coppers spun around to see Shuffler climb onto the bonnet of their police car and start to jump up and down like a maniac. As they ran back to their car, they saw Shuffler make his way onto the roof of the police car, and once again, start to leap up and down on it. This time, he also threw in some singing.

"All aboard the crazy train, ha ha ha ha ha, crazy but that's how it goes," he yelled out at the top of his voice.

"Get the fuck down, you crazy bastard," shouted the first copper, no longer worrying about respect for the public.

Shuffler now spread his legs, about shoulders' width apart, and began to play the air guitar on top of the police vehicle roof.

"I've listened to preachers, I've listened to fools." He pointed a finger of each hand at the coppers as he sang the word fools.

This was now all too much for the first copper, who threw himself at the police car, launching himself as far over the roof as he could, and wrapped his arms around Shuffler's feet and ankles. He then allowed his bodyweight to slide himself off of the roof, taking Shuffler with him, who in turn, landed with a dull, metallic thud on his back, causing the metal roof to dent quite badly.

"Cuff this fucker, Brian," the restraining officer screamed at his colleague.

Eventually, Shuffler found himself standing next to, or rather, leaning against the side of the police vehicle, sporting a pair of rigid police handcuffs, and held into place by the hand of the copper, who had restrained his ankles now firmly pushed against his chest.

"What the hell was that all about?" he asked Shuffler.

Shuffler smiled, and then in a high pitched voice screamed, "You're in the jungle, baby."

The two coppers bundled Shuffler unceremoniously into the back seats of the car, and getting back into the vehicle themselves, the driver started the engine and began the journey to the local police station, while the second officer tried his very best to read Shuffler his rights, which was made more difficult by the singing that Shuffler continued to do—something that the copper found quite amusing, much to the annoyance of his colleague.

"Stop fucking laughing and just read the prick his rights," the driving copper shouted.

In the back, Shuffler was giving his own rendition of a well-known Guns 'N' Roses song, and was making up many of the words, because he couldn't remember the real ones.

"If you wanna want to bleed … it's the price to pay, and you a very sexy girl … and very hard to place … you can flash your blue lights, but that don't come for free. Jungle … welcome to the jungle … feel feel feel my turpentine." His singing was just as Grant had warned about earlier that day, absolutely excruciating.

The reasonably short journey felt like a lifetime for the two police officers, as Shuffler refused to shut up in the back of the vehicle, and at one stage, giving them a rendition of a song all about reaching for the stars, much to the amusement of the younger copper in the front passenger seat.

* * *

As Shuffler stood in front of the desk in the cells area of the local police station, once again being read his rights, he responded to everything with the words, "Three, six, four ... Shuffler, Vice President."

None of the coppers stood around him had any ideas about what he was talking about.

* * *

While all of this was going on, Grant was parking his bike alongside about twenty others, outside of a small brick building with a black double door entrance, above which was a sign stating simply Satan's Fortunates. He removed his helmet, but decided to keep his gloves on. If this went south, at least his knuckles would be offered some protection, if he had to lay into a few of the people who were inside, awaiting his arrival. He knocked on the door and waited.

The door was opened by a scrawny young girl who looked like she hadn't slept for days. She looked Grant up and down and opened the door wider, without saying a word. He stepped through and entered the clubhouse.

It was dark inside and the smell was terrible. He looked around a large room, which contained a few tatty old soft chairs and a small corner bar that looked like it had been taken out of a 1970's terrace. A dozen or so bikers were sat in the chairs or on the floor. One biker was kissing a semi-naked girl, although trying to eat her face would have been a better description. She looked at least half the age of the biker, whose hand was feeling around inside the front of her jeans. He cast one eye over in the direction of Grant and winked at him, before continuing with the task in hand.

Although he had been in the room for literally seconds, Grant was already feeling very uncomfortable, when an inner door opened, casting some much-welcomed light into the room. A large man with lank black hair pulled back into a ponytail filled the door space.

"Let's get this done," he said to Grant, and stepped back from the opened door. Grant walked toward it and entered into what he assumed was the club's meeting room. Seven bikers sat around an old oval shaped table. They all stared at him, and Grant felt about as welcome as a Satanist at a gospel convention. One of the Fortunates, the biggest in the room, who sported a complete face tattoo of a skull, stood up and spun his chair around, slamming it back onto the floor, and then sitting back down so he was leaning over the back of the chair with his back turned to Grant.

"Take a seat," the man who had opened the door to him said.

Grant did as he was told and sat on one of the two chairs that were empty, taking a chance that it wasn't the chair belonging to the man who Grant guessed was the club president. It was hard to tell, as the oval table had no obvious head place. The president of the Fortunates sat down and looked at Grant.

"Firstly, thank you for not bringing your colours into our clubhouse, which at least shows your respect for us and our ways," he said. "I am Stretch, and I assume you are Grant."

"Well, as of today I am Nameless," Grant replied.

Stretch looked confused, and asked, "What do you mean?

You have no name?"

"No, I mean my road name is Nameless," Grant responded.

"Makes sense," the biker who had turned his back on Grant said. "They never name the afterbirth."

Grant so badly wanted to respond, but decided better of it.

"The fact that I reached out to you, I believe, demonstrates that I have the respect and knowledge required," Grant said to Stretch. "I, we the Nameless Ones, don't want to fall out with you, The Fortunates."

"Satan's Fortunates," one of the bikers around the table said. "At least have the respect to get our name right."

Stretch held up his hand asking for quiet.

"There is no disrespect in referring to us as The Fortunates, but as you can see, many of my brothers do not believe you should be sat among us. In fact, most of them want me to feed you to my wolves in the room on the other side of the door," Stretch said. He paused for a few seconds, and then added, "I, though, am intrigued and want to hear what you have to say."

"Simple really," Grant replied. "I need your permission to have our clubhouse in your territory."

Stretch stared at Grant, as if he was studying the man, and then placing both of his large hands flat on the table, which Grant noticed for the first time that one was missing the little finger, and said, "Is it not customary to make this request, before your club members start moving in?"

"That is why I am here today," Grant replied, slightly confused by the question. "Granted one of my people have been there for a while, but they have been doing some work to the place and have stayed there for security purposes. I am sure you can understand the need for that. Other than that, only me and a brother have been there, and that only

103

happened today, just to visit and see the place for the first time."

"I thought you came here to show us the respect we deserve?" Stretch asked.

"I have, and I don't understand where all of these questions are leading, or why they are necessary. I have explained the presence of my people," Grant replied, who was genuinely confused by the line of questioning he now faced.

"And yet you blatantly lie to my face," Stretch responded, his tone becoming more serious.

"What lie have I told you?" Grant asked, becoming more and more uncomfortable with the way this meeting was going.

"I have been informed that a fourth member of your throng arrived just a short time ago," Stretch replied.

"I know nothing about this matter, but I will look into it and address the matter when I return to my clubhouse," Grant said.

"If you get back," Stretch replied menacingly.

Grant decided enough was enough, and stood up looking around the table at all of the bikers. The biker who had turned his back on him, reacted by also standing up and turning around to face Grant.

"Listen well, brothers. My bike club will be set up in your territory, whether or not you decide to grant your permission. I came here out of respect, and I believe that is what I have shown, but what you lot need to understand, is that the people who I am bringing in, are a collection of fucked up individuals who, to be honest, I'm not sure I can even control." Grant stopped talking and looked directly at the president.

"Between them, they are responsible for causing more chaos than you could dream of doing in a thousand pox ridden lifetimes, and if I don't return to my club by tonight, a horde of maniacs will come looking for me and tear you, limb from limb, just for the fun of it. We don't want any trouble. We have come here to get away from the rules of civilian life, to remove ourselves from a population that doesn't understand, or accept us willingly, to come together as a group of like-minded people. So, give your permission, don't give your permission, I really couldn't give a rat's ass, but you do need to accept that we are coming and then learn to live with it." Grant stopped speaking again and waited for the inevitable reaction, which much to his surprise, did not initially come from the club president.

The biker who had stood up as a show of strength, took a step in the direction of Grant.

"Take one more step this way, and I will strip that tattoo off your face and use it as a face mask, you cunt," Grant threatened.

Stretch stood up, and Grant immediately reacted by adopting a defensive position, ready to dish out as much pain as he could, before he succumbed to the beating he now fully expected.

"Skull, sit your bony ass back down," Stretch ordered. He looked at Grant and smiled, holding up the hand that was missing the little finger.

"Do you want to know how I lost this finger?" he asked.

Grant didn't respond. His attention was focused on every other person in the room. Stretch continued speaking.

"I started to hang around with this club when I was just fifteen years old," he began. "I would serve behind the small bar, fetch and carry food from the kitchen, and help the men to fix and tinker with their bikes. It was a great life, and I found a family who loved me, unlike the one I had living back at home. Eventually, after a few months, I moved in here permanently, and found that I suited the lifestyle very well. Just before my seventeenth birthday, the president at the time, called me into a meeting of the top table. I remember him inviting me to take a seat and patting me on the back, calling me his brother, and it was a great moment in my life. Then, he placed a large machete on the table in front of me, and said that if I wanted to prospect, I would need to prove that I was willing to make sacrifices, and instructed me to cut off my little finger. At the time, I was in total shock by this instruction, and all that I could think about was that I had just spent a great night with a biker groupie by the name of Mandy, and that little finger had been up her ass just a few hours before." He waved the first two fingers of the hand missing the little finger. "And these two had been up her tight snatch. Those were my last thoughts, before I swung the machete down on my little finger and separated it from my hand." He paused, slightly rubbing at the stump of his longtime severed finger, and then continued.

"A couple of days later, I returned here from the hospital. There was another meeting going on, and to the surprise of everyone, I walked into the middle of that meeting, and taking my little finger out of my pocket, I grabbed the president's throat, forcing his mouth open, and stuffed my finger inside his mouth and told him to eat it. I punched the fuck out of his face with the only good hand I had at that time, breaking four knuckles in the process. His face was a bloody pulp by the time I stopped. The brain damage he sustained ensured that he would never ride again, and was subsequently booted out of the club. Two months later, I was patched in as a full member of the club."

He looked at Grant, his silence an invite for his guest to speak.

"Well, that is some story—a tale of romance, pain and loss. Talking about romance and pain, is Mandy still around?" Grant said.

Stretch laughed, and replied, "Unfortunately not, but the point of my story is that it took balls to do what I did, and it has taken exactly that for you to turn up here and speak to us like you just did. That level of balls gets my respect, and so you and your gang of rejects can move into our territory, but it comes with conditions."

Skull started to speak, to voice his objection, but his president stopped him immediately.

"Skull, you are my number one brother. You are my sergeant at arms and we have known each other for more years than I can remember, so you, of all people, should know not to question me when I have made my decision."

Skull sat back down in his chair, this time facing the table. This alone, Grant thought, was an improvement in the relationship at least.

"What are the conditions?" Grant asked, eager to bring this meeting to a close and get himself out of there.

"Firstly, none of you ride in your colours within ten miles of our clubhouse, and secondly, you never return to this clubhouse," Stretch responded.

"Sound like conditions we can easily adhere to," Grant said.

"Make sure you do, Nameless, or you will find that you lose more than just a little finger," Stretch said. Grant didn't need any confirmation about what part of his body the club president was referring to.

The two men walked out of the meeting room, followed closely by Skull and the other top table members.

"The Nameless Ones are welcome additions to our area," Stretch announced to the people sat in the bar area. "They will not be harmed or interfered with, unless I say otherwise."

Shaking Grant's hand, he asked if he would stay for a drink.

"No thanks, brother," Grant replied, even more eager to get away from this situation than before. "I need to get back to my clubhouse and find out who has unexpectedly arrived, and make sure that they know never to place me in an embarrassing situation like this again."

"Sometimes, a strong pack leader has to chastise their puppy dogs in ways that many do not understand," Stretch responded, slapping Grant on the back several times. "Now remember, those colours of yours do not go on, until you are at least ten miles away."

Grant gave an understanding nod to Stretch and walked out of Satan's Fortunates' clubhouse, grateful for the natural light and fresh air. From behind him, a voice spoke.

"The next time we meet, he may not be around to protect you, Nameless," a pissed off Skull said.

"Have you ever thought that it wasn't me he was protecting?" Grant warned.

He got on his bike and rode away, hoping that he would never have a reason to return.

The Nameless Ones

Grant spent that night discussing what had happened at the clubhouse of Satan's Fortunates with Stacker over a few drinks. Double D had walked into the bar, having stowed away her few belongings in her room, and having a much-needed sleep.

"Hi," she said, holding out her hand to greet Grant. "You must be Grant."

"And you must be early," Grant replied, deciding not to accept the hand being offered.

"And when did arriving early become a problem?" she asked defensively.

"The moment it puts me in an embarrassing and potentially hazardous situation," Grant replied, picking up his drink and emptying the last of the brandy from it. He slammed the glass back down on to the bar.

"Now, if you have a problem with that, I can always find someone else who is capable of applying a sticking plaster," he said, glaring at the woman.

Double D raised her hands in the air, and sarcastically replied, "Hey, fucking shoot me, but at least get me a drink first."

Stacker, feeling uneasy, walked behind the bar and picked

up a glass.

"What's your poison?" he asked, raising the glass in the direction of Double D.

"Vodka, double," Double D replied, not breaking the eyeball standoff that was taking place between her and Grant.

"Anything with it?" Stacker asked.

"Yeah, another fucking vodka," she replied, refusing to lose the battle with Grant.

Grant slid his glass across the bar toward Stacker, saying, "Stick as much brandy in there as you can, without spilling any." Then breaking the deadlock between Double D and himself, he held out his hand. "Let's start again. I've had a stressful day,"

Double D took his hand and shook it briskly.

"And somehow my arrival added to that stress level?" she asked inquisitively.

"It created a small bump in what was already a bumpy road," he replied, smiling at last.

"I've got a shitload of medication that can make your day better, if you like?" she replied, relieved that the tension had gone.

Grant picked up his glass of brandy that Stacker had filled to the brim, and took a large gulp of it. He raised the glass and tilted it in the direction of Double D and then Stacker.

"This will do the job for now," he said. "Anyway, welcome to The Nameless Ones."

"When do we find out what the job is?" Double D asked.

"When the whole team is here, and let's hope they are all as prompt as you," Grant answered. "We have a lot to do."

"Talking about that," Stacker said, "the cuts will be ready tomorrow, and they are going to deliver."

"Great news," Grant replied, happy to hear some positive news. "Now let's get drunk, It may be the last time we will be able to do it for some time." He downed the rest of the brandy in one gulp, and said to Stacker, "Don't bother filling her, just pass that bottle over here."

"This could get messy," Double D said laughing, and then noticing the dirty smile on Stacker's face, she added, "Has the swelling gone down already?"

Stacker winced, as he remembered the pain that had resonated through his groin region following the very effective knee strike. Both he and Double D started to laugh, as they shared this private joke. Grant joined in even, though he didn't know what the pair were going on about. He was just grateful for the opportunity to relax and be normal for a change.

* * *

The following morning, as Grant raised his head from his pillow and looked, with disbelief, at his watch that was telling him it was 10:40, Shuffler was walking into the small dock-in court room number two of the local magistrates' court. The magistrate entered the courtroom and everyone stood, except for Shuffler.

"Stand up," the court custody officer stood next to Shuffler whispered.

"Go fuck yourself," Shuffler replied loudly and remained seated.

The magistrate sat herself down and looked over her glasses

at Shuffler.

"Any repeat of that type of language in my courtroom, Mr. Dawson, and I will be making arrangements for you to have your very own room, courtesy of Her Majesty's pleasure."

"Well, that will be a fucking first. I never had the pleasure of a member of the royal family," Shuffler replied, and was immediately filled with guilt for saying such a thing about an institution that he had the utmost respect for.

"Heed my warning, Mr. Dawson. I am not in the mood," the magistrate warned sternly.

"I bet I know what you are in the fucking mood for," he replied defiantly, wondering how much more of this behaviour he had to dish out, before the judge lost her patience, and did what he needed her to do.

"This is your last chance." The magistrate was now clearly vexed by this strange man's behaviour. Her voice strained as it rose by an octave or two.

Shuffler slowly stood, and unseen by the custody officer, he pulled down the zipper of his jeans and quickly pulled out his penis. Twirling his hips, he swung it around and around, repeatedly.

"Sounds like an offer to me, bitch. Come jump aboard this helicopter ride, you little slut," he shouted across the courtroom, and started to laugh hysterically.

The judge, initially shocked by the outrageous behaviour in her courtroom, stood up from her chair and screamed her instructions to the custody officer, who was now trying to stand in front of Shuffler to hide what was happening from the occupants of the courtroom.

"Take that man down, officer. You will serve six weeks for contempt of court, or until you can return here and apologise to me personally for this inexplicable display of public disrespect."

As he was being dragged away and out of the dock, to be returned downstairs to the holding cells, Shuffler gave his answer to the judge.

"Sorry, missus. I didn't think seeing my dick would upset you so much. You must be a fucking rug-muncher or summat."

* * *

Grant reached for his phone and saw that he had no missed calls, but had received three text messages from three different people, informing him of the imminent arrival of three of his new crew. He quickly got off his bed, and sniffing his armpits, knew that a shower was called for, but deciding that it could wait, as he wanted to personally greet the people turning up. Pulling on the jeans and T-shirt he had been wearing the day before, he thought, *I'm the leader of a fucking bike gang and that has to be the best excuse ever for being a smelly bastard.* He left his room and walked into the bar area, where the two empty bottles of vodka and the same number of empty brandy bottles still sat on the bar were evidence of the night before—to say nothing of the numerous empty beer bottles that were laying on the floor around the sofa, where the still unconscious Stacker had decided to spend the night.

"Wake up, you drunken bum," he called to Stacker. "They are on their way."

Stacker shot up to a sitting position, almost falling onto the floor in the process.

"Who are?" he asked, as the full force of the headache hit his brain.

"The fucking Nameless Ones, who do you think?"

"Fuck me, Grant, don't do that. I thought you meant the Fortunates or the coppers, and I am in no state to have a fight," Stacker replied, falling back onto the sofa in an effort to stop his heading spinning.

"Get your lazy ass out of your sack," Grant said to Stacker, tapping him on the head with one of the beer bottles that he was now picking up from the floor. "And from here on in, it's Nameless, not Grant." A quick thought flashed through his head ... *how many more names am I going to have in my life?*

Stacker groaned, as the bottle tapped against his head, and he got himself into a sitting position, holding his heads in his hands.

"How much did we bloody drink last night?" he asked.

"Enough to ensure you will have to restock," Grant replied.

"Please tell me you fucked her," Stacker said, raising his head from his hands and smiling at Grant.

Grant shook his head in disbelief.

"Oh come on, mate. Don't tell me you wouldn't, and definitely don't tell me that one of us can't."

Grant placed the dozen or so empty bottles that he had retrieved from the floor onto the bar next to the others that were already there.

"Can you think about nothing else, bro?" he asked Stacker. "She is an integral part of this team, and one day, she just might save your life."

Stacker held out his hands in front of him, in an attempt to look like the innocent party, similar to the pose you would normally see a five-year-old child adopt when trying to convince a parent that they don't understand the point being made.

"Hey, I have a reputation to uphold," he said. "I am the man who can get you whatever you want, no matter how difficult that request is."

"Good," Grant replied. "I want you up and active, and manning that gate. See if you can meet that request."

Stacker rose to his feet, rubbing his hands roughly through his hair, and immediately regretting it, as the pain of the headache struck again.

"I hope one of the new arrivals is the chef. I could eat shit right now," he said.

Grant couldn't help but think about what he had read about the team's chef, and what he had done to get himself booted out of the forces. *Shit could prove to be the safest option*, he thought.

* * *

As Grant and Stacker were getting themselves sorted in readiness for the arrival of the new cohorts, and Shuffler was sat in the court cells pondering what laid ahead, the young man who felt nothing but contempt and hatred for Grant and his Nameless Ones, was putting himself through his daily rigorous exercise regime that kept him in such great shape.

A well-equipped multi-gym unit was located in one of the corners of the large living area of his apartment, and it was here, that the man now sat on one of the exercise benches, breathing slowly and bringing down his already low heart rate, despite having just completed a two-hour workout.

He walked the length of the large room to a table where a glass of freshly squeezed orange juice sat, of which he took a much needed couple of gulps. He placed the glass back on the table so he could take the call coming through on his mobile phone.

"Good morning," he said.

"I hope it is, Sean. Progress report, please," the male voice on the other end of the call said.

"Inside man has been secured, and I am moving location today to be nearer to the target," the young man named Sean replied.

"Good news. I will call again in a few days' time," the caller said.

"Fine," the young man replied. "And when you do, please call me Cutter. I have asked you once to do this, and this is the second and final time I will ask you."

"No problem, but before you start to threaten me, just remember who is signing the cheques," the caller responded.

"And you remember who is doing your dirty work," Cutter replied, ending the call to ensure he got the last word in.

※ ※ ※

Agent Fox placed the encrypted GPS phone back into its charging unit. He was fully aware of what Cutter was capable of, so he did not want to push the wrong buttons too often, but at the same time, he needed to maintain some control over the situation, to ensure that he was able to decide when, where and how Grant was to die.

* * *

Stacker and Grant approached the large compound gate. The steady rumble of bikes could be heard from the other side.

"Sounds like some of the gang is here, bro," Stacker to Grant said, who nodded his head indicating to Stacker that he could open the gate.

Opening both gates, Stacker watched as four bikes rode past him. He gave it a few seconds, and when happy there were no more, he began to close the gates shut again, when a loud blast of a horn sounded from the street outside. He stopped the movement of the gate and popped his head out to see who had blasted the horn, ready to give them a piece of his mind for causing the pain of his alcohol-induced headache to increase. To his surprise, there were no more bikes outside, but there was a dirty black van stationary, just a few feet from the gate. The driver waved his arm to tell Stacker to open the gate. Stacker looked over toward Grant, asking him if he knew the van driver. Grant looked beyond the gate and instantly recognised Frank Magill.

"Yeah, that's our pickup. Let him in," Grant told Stacker reluctantly. He was still not sure about his decision to include Magill.

Grant turned his attention back to the four bikers who were all now parking their bikes in position alongside the three belonging to him, Stacker and Double D—two Harleys, a Bandit and a Café Racer style bike that he wasn't familiar with. He stood back and watched as all four bikers got off their bikes and removed their helmets, one by one, revealing their identities.

Grant recognised two instantly, those being Dave Silcoe, otherwise known as Ordnance, the man who Ian had turned to for the incendiary devices when they had been in conflict with The Crippens. The second recognisable figure was Tony Carr, who while not known to Grant personally, was memorable from the information that Grant had read about him. Tony Carr was chaos on two legs, and had proven it throughout most his life, both civilian and military. Grant searched his memory banks, flicking through the mental information he had stored away from his selection of the individuals from the list provided by Magill. He was fairly certain that the other two were Mick Maloney and Shane Greenway.

He walked over and greeted the four new arrivals in the same traditional way—a handshake and a one-armed hug, followed by a couple of slaps on the back.

"Welcome to you all. Let's go inside and get the introductions done," Grant said, genuinely pleased to see them.

He led the way, followed closely by the huge frame of Ordnance, who the other three had decided should be allowed to follow first. Tony Carr, who was the smallest of the other three, stared in awe as Ordnance walked past him.

"I bet that fucker would crack paving stones if you managed to floor him," he whispered to the other two.

"You wouldn't be able to reach his chin, you fucking shortarse," Shane Greenway replied.

"Yeah, you're right," Carr said. "But I bet I could give his balls a nasty bite."

As Carr, Maloney and Greenway fell into line behind Ordnance, Frank Magill quickly pulled his van up alongside the bikes and jumped out of the van quickly, wanting to join the other new arrivals now disappearing into the clubhouse. As he approached the door, he was met by Stacker, who stood in the doorway, having secured the gate once again.

"No bikey, no entry, dude," Stacker said. "Who are you, stranger?"

"Frank Magill, I'm the pickup guy," Magill replied, trying his best to look over the shoulder of the taller man still blocking his way into the clubhouse, in an effort to see where the others had gone.

"Well, if you are the pickup guy, you and your van belong in the garage, my friend," Stacker said, pointing at the metal building on the other side of the parking area.

"No, you don't understand," Magill protested, but before he could add any more, he was gently, but firmly, pushed away from the door by Stacker.

"You and your van to the garage," Stacker instructed. "Do you understand that?"

Reluctantly, Frank Magill turned away and walked slowly back to his van, muttering insults and threats under his breath, so Stacker wouldn't hear them. Stacker, while not being able to hear what Magill was saying, was not willing to let this little jumped-up snotbag have the last word, even if those words were being spoken almost silently.

"You also need to understand that I have the hearing of ..." Stacker couldn't think of the right ending, but was determined that he was going to make his point to Magill. "...a bat," he eventually said.

Magill stopped and look around at Stacker with a quizzical look on his face.

"I thought them fuckers were deaf?" he said to Stacker.

Stacker pointed determinedly in the direction of the garage.

"Garage, now!"

Inside the clubhouse, Grant led the new arrivals into the bar area, where they were met with the sight of Double D sat at the bar, nursing a cup of coffee and a headache. She looked the worse for the wear from the night before, and was seriously considering self-prescribing some of the strong painkillers that were part of her medic's kit. The first to react to seeing a woman sat at the bar was Ordnance, who said quite excitedly, "Fanfuckingtastic … didn't know you were going the full hog, Grant, and providing biker chicks, too."

Before Grant could turn and inform Ordnance of his mistake, and despite Double D not being in the mood, she provided the four men with all the evidence they needed as to why she had been given her nickname, as she stood up and gave Ordnance both barrels.

"Listen up, and listen good, you oversized wankstain. I am not here for your pleasure, I am not something you can ride when your bike will no longer take your fucking weight. I have two skills, saving life and taking life, so think hard, before you decide on your next action, because that will dictate which skill I will use on your ass."

From behind them all, Stacker warned, "She can damage your marbles fairly well, too."

"Will sorry be enough to ensure you save my life"" Ordnance asked Double D.

"No," she replied quite harshly. "But it does mean I won't take it."

Tony Carr walked past Ordnance and held out his hand, which Double D took willingly.

"Chaos," he said, introducing himself.

"Double D," she replied, watching the biker's eyes, and happy to see that they didn't drop to take a look at her breasts.

"You are the perfect example of why I never got married," Chaos said, and then asked, "Drink?"

"Probably never again," Double D replied and sat back down at the bar, feeling pleased that she had made some headway in this male-dominated world—not the first that she had worked in.

Maloney and Greenway made their way around to the other side of the bar, asking each of the others what their poison was. Grant stood at the back of the room, where he had positioned himself during the verbal altercation, watching as his forming team started to develop and bond. Like many previous coming together of military and ex-military folk, this one quickly developed into a healthy swapping of tales and banter, mixed together with drinking. He smiled, as he observed this healthy behaviour, which was a good sign that this band of strangers could become the strong loyal team he needed. His mood changed when he saw Magill enter the room with the speed of an eager puppy dog looking to please his master. This individual was going to be a problem, but he was confident that his decision to have the problem on the inside, rather than on the outside beyond his control, was the right one.

"I'll have a drink, too," he heard Magill call out, trying to make himself heard over the buzz of the ongoing conversation. The only response he got was from Stacker, who by now, was the only one behind the bar, comfortable in this position of authority. A glass filled with ice slid down the bar toward Magill, who stopped it in its tracks.

"What the fuck is this?" he asked Stacker.

"The strongest thing that the pickup is allowed to drink," the tall barman called back, tossing a bottle of water in Magill's direction. "Add that to it, and turn it into a double, if you like."

Everyone laughed in good humour, except for Magill, who stormed out of the clubhouse.

* * *

Handcuffed to the custody officer, Shuffler stepped off the meat wagon, and placed his foot onto the concrete floor of the secure prison reception area. He stood still for a few seconds, looking at the building in front of him. A solid door with a barred gate in front of it, and a sign above it with the word Reception, was being opened by a prison officer. He watched, as the officer slotted his key into the lock of the barred gate and push it open, stepping out into the open area, and standing next to the gate, the key attached by a chain to his belt still in the lock.

"How many you got for us?" the officer called across to the custody officer.

"Including this one, just two for now. Bit of a slow day, thankfully," the custody replied, and tugged at the cuffs to indicate to Shuffler that it was time to move again.

"Bring the guest in," the officer said, clearly bored with the monotony of his job.

Shuffler followed the custody officer into the building, and continued to watch the prison officer, as he secured the gate and door. He felt the cuffs being removed from his wrists.

"I'll get the other one and put him in the holding area for you," the custody officer told the prison officer.

"Let me process this one first. Get yourself a cuppa, and I will be with you in five," the officer replied, walking behind the reception desk, upon which sat a number of official looking forms.

The custody officer walked away, to find the staff tearoom, leaving Shuffler and the officer to get on with the business of processing the prisoner.

The prison officer perused the paperwork in front of him.

"Confirm your name for me, please," he asked Shuffler.

"Shuffler, 364," he replied.

The officer let out a sigh of frustration.

"Real name, not the pathetic biker boy name your little leather clad gang of cocksuckers call you," he replied.

Shuffler smiled and repeated the same answer given seconds before.

Looking over the paperwork, the officer saw that in the box where the prisoner's name should have been, were written the words "Not Known." In a box below this, it said AKA Shuffler. The officer looked up at the prisoner in front of him, and more sternly, he said, "Look, I need you to confirm your actual name. It's a requirement of the process. I don't care about you pissing off a couple of coppers, and I care even less about you winding up a judge, but pissing me off is not your next best move. Let me help you. My name is Officer Marshall, but my colleagues call me Lock On, that is my nickname. Now, when somebody asks me what my name is, I answer Officer Marshall, I don't say Lock On. Does that make it clearer for you?"

"I want to go to the block," Shuffler replied.

"You see, there you go again, not answering the fucking question, lad," Officer Marshall replied. "Now, I will give you one last chance to confirm your real name, otherwise, I may have to show you why they call me Lock On." His voice was now slightly more raised than at any other time of the conversation.

"Shuffler, 364. Now, take me to the seg unit," Shuffler replied, not raising his voice at all.

Officer Marshall walked around from the back of the reception desk, and stood himself in front of this annoying little old man, who he had decided was now about to be put on the floor and receive a certain amount of pain. He was more than confident that he was capable of dealing with this insignificant old man right, up to the point when Shuffler head-butted him straight across the bridge of his nose, and he staggered backwards, falling to the floor and covering his now bleeding nose with both hands.

The impact of the attack had split open the skin just above Shuffler's nose, as he had applied the head-butt slightly wrong, mainly due to the difference in height between the two men. However, he didn't let this faze him, as he moved quickly toward the floored prison officer, unclipping his keys from the chain, and using it to unlock the door of the holding room. Returning to Officer Marshall, Shuffler began to kick him around the stomach and chest area, and telling him to get into the room.

As he kicked, Shuffler saw the officer trying to reach for a small box attached to his belt. It was clearly a personal alarm, and the officer was trying to activate it. Shuffler reached forward and grabbed the officer's flailing hand, and started to drag him toward the open doorway, but only managed to pull the heavy man a few feet, before the effort proved too painful for him, so he returned to the kicking tactic, after ripping the personal alarm off the belt of Officer Marshall.

"Get in the fucking room, you daft prick. I don't want to hurt you too much," Shuffler demanded, as kick after kick impacted on the officer's stomach.

Officer Marshall pulled and pushed himself, using his arms and legs across the smooth floor, into the holding area room, and felt the door slam against one of his boots, as Shuffler pushed the door closed and locked it, leaving the key in place.

"I really didn't want to hurt you," Shuffler said to Marshall, who was now beginning to get to his feet, wiping the blood away from his eyes.

"Unlock the door. Don't make this situation any worse than it is," Marshall called out from inside the room, knowing that it was going to be as bad for him as it would be for the prisoner.

The trapped officer looked through the glass-fronted door at the smiling prisoner with blood dripping down his face, who now began to remove all of his clothes, until he stood in front of him totally naked. He watched in utter amazement, as Shuffler squatted down and produced a huge shit on the floor, and then scooped it up with both hands. He remained transfixed for the first few seconds, watching Shuffler begin to spread his own excrement over his face and chest. At that moment, Officer Marshall began to call for assistance as loudly as he could, and violently kick the inside of the holding room door.

By the time Shuffler heard the approaching thuds of boots, he had managed to spread his body waste over his face, upper torso and arms. Surprised at how much coverage you could get from one average size shit, he slowly dropped to his knees and knitted his fingers together behind his head. As the first two staff members arrived at the scene, stopping rapidly in their tracks as they were faced with the kneeling man covered in his own faeces, Shuffler quietly and calmly said, "Shuffler, 364. Now take me to the fucking block, you motherfucking bunch of cunts."

* * *

By that evening, all except two of the newly formed Nameless Ones, were present in the clubhouse, the obvious absentee being their Vice President, Shuffler. The clubhouse was filled with chatter, as the club members renewed old friendships and made new ones with people they had never met before, but had a common history and purpose with, even if most of them were not, at this stage, fully clear on what that common purpose was.

Grant had busied himself, with Stacker's help, introducing himself and showing the people around the building, those people subsequently making claim to a room, and stashing away their belongings, before returning to the bar to continue the bonding process.

At 9 p.m., Grant asked Stacker to get the attention of everyone, which he did by ringing the bell behind the bar. Having got their attention and silence, Grant began his first address to his team.

"Good evening, and welcome to your new home, gentlemen." He nodded in the direction of Double D, and said, "And lady. We appear to only have one member unaccounted for, but I have no doubt that he will arrive later tonight, or tomorrow at the latest. I appreciate your prompt arrival, something that does not surprise me. Your military training has clearly stayed with you, as we were all told at some stage, five minutes early is arriving on time."

"Yeah, and five minutes late is rewarded by seven days in the guardroom," someone shouted out from the back of the room, which was followed by a short burst of group laughter.

Grant smiled and continued to speak.

"Well, you will find no guardroom here, but that does not mean that discipline is no less important. I invite you to continue getting to know each and taking advantage of Stacker's warm welcome and bar service, but I ask one thing…," he said and paused briefly. "Tomorrow morning at ten-hundred hours precisely."

"0955 hours," came the shout from the back of the room.

Grant continued without acknowledging the confirmation of the time, although not annoyed by the minor interruption.

"Every one of you will be expected to be present in the briefing room, in a proper state, capable of starting our mission. Until then, enjoy yourself, but not too much. We may not have a guardroom, but we do have Ordnance, and trust me when I tell you, that seven days in the guardroom will seem like a holiday in paradise, compared to what he will do to you if you are late."

Ordnance held a clenched fist up in the air and then brought it down heavily onto the table he was sat at.

"The head crusher," he shouted and laughed, which every-one joined in with.

The multitude of conversations immediately recommenced, as Grant walked over to the bar and leaned over it toward Stacker.

"Any contact from Filston?" he asked quietly.

"Nothing, gaffer," Stacker replied. "You worried?"

"No, I am sure he will arrive by tomorrow. The instructions were to arrive by tomorrow, so let's give it until then, before we start to worry," Grant replied.

Grant left the bar and entered his room, closing the door behind him and sitting at the table. He pulled out the personnel information and began to read a bit more about Terry Filston, but could find nothing that could raise any concerns about the man. *Probably just running late,* Grant thought to himself, and began to prepare to get a good night sleep. Climbing into his bed, he took a mouthful of water from the glass that sat on the small bedside table to help the two Zopiclone down, and slowly fell asleep to the sound of the buzz of conversation coming from the bar.

* * *

Shuffler sat on the floor of the dirty protest cell in the segregation unit. The journey from the reception building to the Care and Separation Unit, to give it its correct name, had not been as painful as he had expected. The staff had not used restraint techniques to move him, primarily because he offered no violence and complied with every order given to him, and probably more because he was covered in shit, and none of the staff members had wanted to make any contact with him whatsoever.

The dried excrement was making his skin itchy, and every time he moved, it pulled at his skin, especially where there was a good covering of hair. The smell was overpoweringly disgusting, but it had ensured that his aim to not be located in the general population, had been achieved. A shaft of light pierced through the darkness of his cell, as an officer opened the observation panel cover and looked through the slit of glass.

"You okay?" the officer asked.

"Shuffler wants a shower," he replied.

"Not going to happen until tomorrow, if it happens at all. You will be seen by the duty governor first," the officer replied.

"Shuffler want shower, now," Shuffler replied.

The officer slammed shut the cover, and could be heard saying, as he walked back down the landing, "Great, another fucking head case. That is all this place needs."

The noise of the observation panel cover slamming shut reverberated down the landing of the quiet unit, which immediately ceased to be silent, as several other occupants of the unit began to shout.

"Keep the fucking noise down, screw."

"Hey new boy, what's your fucking problem?"

"He's covered in his own shit, dirty fucking bastard."

"See you on the yard, shitboy. I'm going to cut your throat open."

The officer walked back to his office and sat down to complete the prisoner observation sheet, knowing that he had very little chance of having a quiet night shift, and as if to confirm his thoughts, he heard the new arrival scream loudly, "Shuffler want shower, now!"

Initial Briefing

Grant woke early and got out of bed, immediately grabbing his towel, and wrapping it around his waist. Taking his wash bag with him, he made his way to the communal shower area, dropping his towel on the floor and taking his wash bag with him into the shower. He turned the shower on and immersed himself under the warm water, placing the wash bag on the floor next to him just outside of the tiled area being showered with water, and pulling out a bottle of shower gel. He rubbed the gel harshly over his body, covering himself in an ever increasing coating of foam, enjoying the feeling of freshness and cleanliness. After ten minutes of showering, he turned off the stream of water and walked toward where he had dropped his towel, bending down to retrieve it from the floor—a habit of his that his wife had often chastised him for. He sharply returned to an upright stance and looked toward the door of the shower block.

"I never thanked you for the ride," Double D said, standing in the doorway wearing a long vest type top.

It was obvious to Grant that she was wearing no bra, and he could only assume that no other kind of underwear was being worn underneath her choice of sleeping attire.

"I am guessing you are talking about the bike I got you, so no problem. Couldn't have a biker medic with no bike," he replied, still totally naked in front of the woman.

Double D's eyes moved up and down, taking in the sight of Grant's nakedness.

"Yeah that's right, however, I just wanted you to know that if you ever need a different type of ride, I am able to return the favour," she said smiling.

Grant picked up the towel and wrapped it around his waist, deciding to dry himself off later. He walked toward and then past the female biker, knowing that he needed to nip this situation in the bud and quickly.

"What's wrong?" Double D asked. "Shocked by the offer?"

"No, not at all," Grant replied. "I'd just rather have a wank."

He didn't bother looking back, because he knew those words of rejection would have hurt Dee. He returned to the privacy of his own room, and started to dry off his damp body, suddenly remembering that he had left his wash bag in the shower room. He decided to leave it a while, as he didn't want to come face-to-face with Dee again for a while. She needed time to get over his hurtful words.

Outside, Stacker was leaning against the frame of his room door, having heard every word of the conversation between Double D and Grant. He walked over to the woman and put his arm around her shoulder, casually, but intentionally, allowing the tips of his fingers to rest at the top of one of her breasts.

"He is one fucked up individual, darling," he said to her. "Got a lot going on inside that head of his, and not in touch with the right emotions at the moment."

Double D lightly grabbed Stacker's lingering hand and

slowly removed it from her breast, lifting it up so the man's draped arm moved away from her shoulders, and then walked forward and away from the friendly embrace. She turned to face Stacker, and quietly, but firmly, said, "You ever touch my tits again, you pervert, and I will shove them so far up your arse, you will be able to tickle your own tonsils."

Down the corridor, Grant's door opened slightly, just enough for his hand to appear through the gap and drop a piece of paper onto the floor.

"Stacker, give Thunderbox a call and find out where he is. His number is on the sheet."

His door shut again.

"See," Stacker said, "totally emotionless."

Double D shook her head in disbelief at this man, who seemed to have the ability to be totally unaffected by what she had just said to him.

"Is it the lonely existence of being a store man that makes you so weird?" she asked, as she walked back to her room, still feeling embarrassed for her behaviour.

Stacker watched her walk away, admiring the outline of her naked body under the thin vest top.

You have no idea how fucking weird I am, he thought, as he returned to his own room, retrieving the piece of paper from the floor before doing so.

As the doors of Double D's and Stacker's rooms closed, Grant's mobile phone began to ring. He stopped the process of drying himself, and once again, dropped his towel to the floor and picked up the phone. A voice he didn't recognise spoke.

"Hey, is that Grant?"

"Yeah, who is this?" Grant asked.

"Hey brother, it's Filston, sorry I mean Thunderbox. I've dropped my bike, bro. Any chance of a pickup?" he asked.

"Fuck, you okay, and where are you?" Grant asked, genuinely concerned about the condition of his absent member.

"Yeah, yeah, shoulder and chest a bit banged up, but nothing more than mildly walking wounded," the stricken biker replied.

He told Grant where he was, and Grant assured him that he would have the pickup driver to him within the hour, and without another word, the call was ended by the caller.

Grant popped his head out of his door and shouted down the corridor.

"Stacker!"

Stacker stuck his head out of the door in response to the call.

"Yes, boss," he replied.

"Thunderbox has dropped his bike and needs a pickup. Wake Magill and tell him to do his job. Tell him to come to see me, before he leaves, so I can give him Thunderbox's location."

At the top of his voice, Stacker bellowed an instruction up and down the corridor.

"Right you lot, hands off cocks and pull on your socks. Magill, my room now, you fucking waste of space. Got a job for you."

Grant smiled as he shut his door once again.

Just like being back in Army training again, he thought.

* * *

The man who had made the call to Grant, placed the phone on the ground inches away from the lifeless hand of the biker lying dead on the road. His bike lay a few feet away on its side. He got back into his car and drove it about a quarter of a mile up the quiet narrow country lane, switching off the engine after bringing it to a stop. He got out again and checked the paintwork down the driver's side of the vehicle, just to confirm that he had made no contact with the bike when he had run it off the road. He had steered it closer and closer toward the biker, before the biker had run out of road and crashed his bike into the grassy verge.

As the biker lay on the road dazed, but not badly hurt, he had quickly got out of his car and made his way toward him, before he could get up, and stuck the needle into the side of Thunderbox's neck. He watched, as over the next few minutes, the fallen biker twitched and struggled with his breathing, as the lethal dose of Tetrodotoxin coursed through his bloodstream. Paralysis soon kicked in, and within four minutes, the inevitable heart failure occurred.

He knew it wouldn't take long for the biker to die, because he had witnessed it work before, a few months prior, when he had used it on the greed-driven scientist, who had provided him with the venom of the blue-ringed octopus.

Satisfied that there were no incriminating scratches or dents on his car, he returned to the driver's seat and waited. He selected a radio channel playing classical music, and leaned the chair back a few inches, relaxing into it and closing his eyes, as the stirring sound of Vissi d'arte from Tosca filled his ears. His head swayed, and face contorted with the rise of and fall of the music, as he immersed himself into it, now totally removed from the cold-blooded crime he had just committed.

* * *

After passing on the location of Thunderbox's accident to Magill, and telling him to get there as quickly as possible, without attracting attention from the coppers, Grant finished off drying himself and dressing. He could hear the bustle of people getting ready for the day, mixed in with the banter you would expect from people with military service. He was happy that he could not hear any reference to the conversation that had happened between him and Double D, which meant Stacker had kept his mouth shut, but that didn't mean she wasn't the target of any of the banter.

He walked down the corridor toward the welcoming smell that could only be produced from the ingredients of a British breakfast being prepared, and allowed himself to enjoy the ongoing banter that many civilians would find outrageous and absolutely not politically correct.

"Hey split-arse, get yourself in here! There are two showers available for both of your barrels."

"You wash that cock for much longer, and it will officially be called wanking."

"Who the fuck has left their wash bag in here? You have two minutes to come get it, before I dump a turd into it."

"Fucking hell, look at the cock on this boy. You must pass out when that gets hard."

"I'd rather have one this size, than that little thing you've got. I've seen bigger clits."

Each comeback was met with raucous laughter and more banter.

"Hey, is that breakfast I can smell?"

"Either that, or someone has just produced the best smelling fart ever."

Grant entered the bar area and was pleasantly surprised to see the tables laid out for breakfast. Paper place mats, cutlery, salt and pepper pots and a variety of sauce bottles finished the ensemble, making Grant think that maybe his choice of chef had been a good decision. At that point the chef, Hammer, appeared from the kitchen.

"Morning, Nameless. Breakfast?"

"Absolutely, bro. Is there a choice?" Grant asked.

"Sure is," Hammer replied. "Full English, or fuck off."

"I'll take both, chef," Grant replied. "One full English, and I'll fuck off outside for a smoke. In fact, when it's ready, bring it outside to me. I'll eat it at one of the bench tables out there."

Grant walked outside and immediately lit one of his miniature cigars, inhaling the intoxicating smoke and holding it in his mouth for a few seconds, before exhaling. His breakfast was brought out, with a set of cutlery, before he had finished his cigar, and with a nod of his head, he indicated to Hammer to place it on the picnic style bench table nearest to him. Hammer did as he was bid and returned silently to his kitchen, getting the impression that Grant wanted some alone time.

"Tell that lot I want them in the briefing room for a ten o'clock briefing, will you?" asked Grant, who appeared to be preoccupied with something.

Grant finished his cigar and stubbed it out on the wall, allowing the stubbed out remains to fall to the floor. He sat on the bench table, picked up the fork and began to eat. Hammer had been correct in his assumption that Grant had other things on his mind. Grant did not cope well with a change to a plan that he had no control over, and relying on others so much was just not his style. Being a self-admitted control freak, he wondered why he had decided to set up this bike gang scam, instead of just turning up at the door of Kelvin Armstrong and stabbing him in the eye. Ever since his revenge attacks against The Crippens, and before that episode in his life, he had been a lone wolf, a maverick.

Throughout the period when the organisation had entrapped him they thought that he was under their control but he never had been. In fact, way before any of this, going way back to his military days, and his entire prison service career, he had bent the rules, and on occasions, broke them, to ensure that he remained in control of whatever situation he had found himself in. On many occasions, control had not meant success, but to Grant, even controlled failure was better than chance success, and he had never been a willing leader—a reluctant one often, but was never comfortable with the role of leadership and responsibility to others. He preferred responsibility for others.

For some reason, the late arrival of Thunderbox, even though it was clearly because of unforeseen circumstances, did not sit comfortably with him, and neither did sending Magill out to pick him up. The inclusion of Magill was a regret, but one that he could do nothing about at the moment. Grant looked down at his plate, and realised that after the initial mouthful of food, he had done nothing but play with his food, merely moving it around the plate. He could almost hear his maternal grandma calling out to him, *"Don't play with your food, John. I cannot afford to waste good food."* The thought made him smile. He had loved his Nana Smart, a well-built, no-nonsense woman, who had fed him with good advice throughout his childhood, without even realising she was doing it. One of these that he had stuck by his entire life, had been, *"Don't follow others, John, because most of them don't know where they are going themselves. Follow your own path—it might be the wrong one, but at least it was your own choice."*

He had stayed in his bedroom for two days following her death, not eating or drinking, just crying, until another piece of her advice had popped into his head. *"No use in crying, John. It won't change a thing, other than to waste water."* He picked up his cup of coffee, and after taking a mouthful of the warm liquid, he raised it to the sky silently thanking his grandma for all of her wisdom.

He looked at his watch. Over an hour had passed since he had risen, but it was still early, so he decided to go to the briefing room and make sure everything was set up and ready for the first meeting of The Nameless Ones. Even though he knew that everything was as ready as it was ever going to be, *"You can never take the need for control out of the control freak,"* he thought to himself, as he stood and made his way back into the clubhouse, leaving the full plate of food and still half full cup of coffee on the table.

* * *

Following the directions of his sat nav system, Magill arrived at the location that Stacker had given him in just under forty minutes. Or to be more exact, he had come to a screeching halt about four-hundred metres before his preset destination, in order to stop himself from crashing into the lone figure standing in the middle of the country lane—a man he recognised immediately.

"I could have fucking killed you," he shouted at the man as he got out of his van.

"Shut up, you fool. You couldn't kill me if I was in a drug-induced sleep, you fucking moron," the man replied.

Magill went quiet. This individual scared the shit out of him. He could never be described as the brightest button in the box, but Magill recognised a person who was clearly driven by an anger so deep that it hurt to the core—and this man was being driven by an anger more forceful than that.

"What are you doing here?" Magill asked. "I am supposed by picking up one of their crew."

"It is time to implement the next stage of the plan," the man replied.

"But you told me to wait until Grant had explained everything, before I got in touch with you," a confused Magill explained.

"Yes, and now I am telling you that it is time to implement the next stage of the plan," the man replied, already feeling the frustration of repeating himself building up inside.

"So, I'm not collecting a biker?" Magill asked, now even more confused.

The man, an individual by the name of Sean Cutter, clenched a fist instinctively, and squeezed it tight, as a physical reminder for him not to punch Magill.

"Let me explain this simply for you, as if you were a brainless fart," replied Cutter, who was now seriously contemplating punching the shit out of this idiot, and at the same time, telling himself that he needed him for a while longer. "Down the road, about a quarter of mile away, is a motorbike and a dead motorbike owner. Your job is easy. Leave the bike and move

139

the body. About a hundred metres farther down the road, is a deep ditch. Dump the body into it."

Cutter was hoping that even if someone found the bike, it would be a while longer, before anyone started to look for the biker who had, for some reason, left the bike. By the time it was found, any faint residue of the poison inside his system would have dissipated enough for it to be overlooked during the inevitable post-mortem procedure. Tetrodotoxin was difficult enough to detect, and left the obvious signs of a heart attack, which he hoped would be good enough for a busy pathologist. He knew that there were potential flaws in his plan, but this was a calculated risk he was willing to take.

"Do you want me to stand the bike back up?" Magill asked, which did not improve Cutter's mood.

"Did I say to move the bike?" Cutter asked.

"Err, no," Magill stuttered. "I don't think so."

"Move the body, don't move the bike," Cutter responded. "Is there any part of that you find confusing?"

"No, no ... got it," Magill replied, now just wanting to get away from this psycho.

Cutter waited for Magill to move, but it didn't happen.

"What are you waiting for?" he asked. "Well, then what?"

Cutter's patience broke. He grabbed the neck of Magill's T-shirt, and pulled the man toward him, so their faces were millimetres apart. Magill could smell the fresh minty breath of Cutter, as he spat out his instructions into his face.

"You return to that rat's nest that they call a clubhouse, and you explain that you went where you were told to go, and there was no sign of their brother." The last word was spat out with an extra feeling of contempt. "You say you searched around the area, but still couldn't see him, so you returned to find out what to do next. Is that clear enough for you?"

"But … but don't you think they would expect me to call them, instead of going back there?" Magill asked.

"No," Cutter replied. "Because, like me, they will have realised by now that you are a useless, stupid piece of fucking cat vomit." Cutter pushed Magill away, releasing his grip on him at the last moment. Magill staggered backwards and fell to the floor.

* * *

Grant stood alone in the briefing room. He began to stick up photographs of the Armstrong family, and pieces of paper that gave the basis of the job ahead. None of this was for his benefit, as he knew every detail. It was purely for the bikers who would be entering the room in the next hour or so.

He could hear the chatter of those very people coming directly from outside the room, as they tucked into their breakfasts. As he looked at the photographs of the Armstrongs, which had been provided by Lambden, his determination to do this job properly for his friend David, made the slight guilt he felt disappear rapidly. The guilt was caused by the knowledge that it was almost guaranteed that some of those people, who were at that very moment thoroughly enjoying the first meal of the day, would not be around to see the completion of the job.

Having finished the task of pinning up the pictures and information, he sat down in his chair and looked up at the wall directly opposite to him—the wall on which were hanging the three skull banners.

Surdux was the connection between matter and spirit. He stood for money, power, ambition and strength—all of the negative attributes of the Armstrongs, but he also represented pride, intolerance and impulsiveness which, as far as Grant was concerned, were some of the attributes of The Nameless Ones, especially himself. He cast his eyes slightly right to take in the middle banner, Sputux.

Sputux was the symbol of great ambition—a visionary genius who strives for great achievements, but is also the creator of excess stress, depression and self-destruction. Grant saw this character as a blend of the mission ahead and his negative characteristics.

Finally, the last banner showed Caecux. His eyes covered as a warning not to be blinded and deviate from the path you have placed yourself on, to not allow the extraordinary ability of your enemy to use their skills of smooth talking and fake warmth and hospitality, to fool you into believing that they are not your enemy.

There was plenty of other information on these characters, if you could be bothered to read about numerology analysis, which Grant couldn't, because he was more interested in the symbology of these creatures. It was this, that he planned to use to fire up his team into a frenzy of focussed hate against the Armstrong family, which he hoped would increase the chances of a successful conclusion.

The greatest symbol that Grant planned to use was the very look of the three skulls, which said, no matter what, The Nameless Ones would forever have heard nothing, seen nothing and would never speak of anything—unquestionable loyalty to the team.

Grant relaxed back into his chair, and closing his eyes, he

waited.

* * *

The duty governor sat in the segregation unit office in deep discussion with the junior psychologist from the Personality Disorder Assessment and Therapeutic Unit.

"He is a nobody, serving six weeks for contempt, because he got mouthy with a judge. Please tell me why he warrants a place on your unit?" he asked the young psychologist.

"Stephen, I have been instructed by Ms. Wolstenholme to come across here and merely assess this man. I do not know why she wants me to do that, and I will admit that he does seem to be a strange choice for an assessment of this kind," she replied.

Stephen Watson shook his head. Only his bewilderment outweighed his confusion of this whole situation. Referring to the Ms. Wolstenholme who the junior had previously mentioned, he asked, "How is the chief shrink justifying wasting your time and mine on a prisoner who does not meet the first requirement of a place on the assessment unit? That being, a convicted prisoner serving twelve months or longer."

"All she has told me, is that this prisoner has demonstrated all of the behaviours that would indicate that he is potentially a danger to others and himself, and wanted me to emphasise that she includes staff when she talks about others. She also asked me to remind you that as the senior psychologist, her final decision holds a lot more weight than that of yours, or even the number one governor's."

The junior, a young lady named Melanie Ash, who had recently graduated and was very grateful to be given this job by Jenny Wolstenholme, when there had been much better candidates for the position, repeated the words of her employer to the letter.

"She actually said that, did she?" the operations governor asked.

"Yes sir, exactly that, and also said that she is in her office, ready to take your inevitable phone call," the now increasingly nervous young junior replied.

"She is, is she?" It was a question more for him than it was for Melanie.

Stephen Skelton looked at the phone sat on the desk in front of him and contemplated his next move. He really wanted to call the head of psychology and give her a piece of his mind. He really disliked the woman, but at the same time, was aware of the power she wielded in this particular field, and had the ear of many influential people, including the prison governor.

Skelton knew that he had very little choice but to go along with Wolstenholme's request, but as a last attempt to show some level of power, he said to Melanie Ash, "You can return to your nut job unit and tell Ms. Wolstenholme that I will allow the assessment interview to take place, but not this morning, due to the fact that we do not have enough staff required to safely monitor that interview and run the normal daily regime of my unit. I am certain that she will understand this, due to the behaviours demonstrated by this particular prisoner." He smiled, as he allowed himself the pleasure of using Jenny Wolstenholme's own words to justify his own conditions.

Melanie Ash stood and made her way to the office door.

Just before opening it, she turned to the governor, and said, "Jenny did say that is what you would probably say, and so I have arranged for the additional staff to be made available to your unit this afternoon at 2 p.m. for one hour, sir." Without a further word, or allowing Skelton to respond, she closed the office door behind her, just as her boss had instructed her.

Skelton shouted for his unit supervising officer to come to the office. SO Davidson arrived promptly after hearing his name being called out.

"Yes, sir," he said to Governor Skelton as he entered the office.

"Get me two staff members, Mike, to accompany us to the door of our new mystery guest, would you?" Skelton instructed more harshly than he had meant to, due to still feeling quite angered by the words of the junior psychologist, and more by the fact that he had not been given the time or respect to give a response.

"Three of us to open the door of that little short arse runt, sir?" Davidson enquired.

Governor Skelton stood to his full height of five-feet-five inches.

"Never underestimate a short arse, Mr. Davidson," he responded.

SO Mike Davidson turned sharply on his heel and left the office, to find the two staff members required, with a smirk on his face.

Five minutes later, Stephen Skelton joined SO Davidson and two officers, Mr. Alan Sharpe and Miss Shelley Morgan, at the door of Shuffler's cell.

"Open the door please, Mr. Sharpe," Skelton instructed the tall and well-built, muscular male officer.

"Are you sure, sir?" the officer asked. "He is covered in his own shit."

"Open the door, now," the governor instructed again.

As the officer looked inside the cell through the observation window, he knew that the smell was going to be bad, and as the door was cracked open, it proved to be much worse than even he, a seasoned dirty protest officer, had anticipated.

Despite having not had anything to eat in more than twenty-four hours, Shuffler had managed to produce another fresh turd, and used this one to write the word "SHOWER" on the one of the cell walls. All four of the prison staff members visibly screwed up their faces, as the smell of the freshly spread human faeces hit their noses. Shuffler was sat in the centre of the cell, his legs now covered in the remains of his chosen artistic material. He looked toward the now fully opened door at the three uniformed and one suit wearing staff members.

"Shuffler want shower … and breakfast," he said in a low voice.

"Well, Mr. Shuffler," the prison governor replied, "your request for a shower will be met when we have the staff to facilitate it, which is in accordance with this prison's dirty protest protocols, however, your request for food will not be met for as long as you insist on continuing with said dirty protest."

Shuffler did not move a muscle—his legs bent up to his stomach and clasped hands resting on his knees.

"Shuffler knows his rights. Shuffler not get breakfast, so he want food now."

Officers Sharpe and Morgan, who were stood shoulder to shoulder in the open doorway, noticed the slight movement of Shuffler's hands, before the governor did, and anticipating what was going to happen next, managed to duck slightly, just seconds before Shuffler unclasped his hands and hurled the lump of shit in his right hand, directly toward the open cell door. Some of the excrement left small splatters on the shirts of the two officers, as it flew over the top of them and hit the governor squarely in the face, who at the last moment, had managed to close his mouth, but not his eyes. SO Davidson reacted quickest, stepping forward and grabbing the door handle, pulling the door firmly shut.

"Fucking hell, he's quick for an old guy," he exclaimed.

"Yeah," added Officer Sharpe, who was now looking at the prison governor. "A bloody good shot, too."

Governor Skelton was slowly wiping the human waste away from his eyes and nose. He did not say a word, being obviously reluctant to open his mouth.

Officer Morgan gently took the governor's arm, saying, "We have a shower upstairs for such occasions, sir. Come with me."

In total silence, Governor Skelton allowed himself to be led away from the cell door and toward the unit office, from where a set of stairs that led to the staff restroom and shower area was located. The voice of Shuffler followed his progress down the landing.

"Shuffler will see you later, shit face."

Even the two officers who remained outside of the cell door, quietly joined in the laughter coming from inside Shuffler's cell.

* * *

The members of the newly formed Nameless Ones, began to enter the briefing room, one by one, led by Stacker and Ordnance, at exactly 0955 hours. Grant slowly opened his eyes and nodded his head at Stacker, grateful to the man for ensuring their timely arrival.

"Find your seats, people. They can be identified by the cuts hanging on the back of each of the chairs." Grant asked each member's rank and file, as the last of them entered the room. Chaos closed the doors behind them all.

Without further instruction, each of them located their chair, and pulled on their cuts, before taking a seat.

"Best uniform I have ever put on," Hammer said, as he took his seat and looked down at his road name and service number patches.

Reckon did a full 360-degree twirl, and then continued the turn, so he ended up with his back facing the rest of the team.

"Check out the artwork on the back, real fucking bikers, or what?" he asked like an excited child.

Grant brought the banter to a standstill by standing up, leaning forward and resting his fists on the table, before saying, "People, for those of you who have never been involved in a covert operation, let me inform you that these cuts are just a small part of this façade, as is the clubhouse. They are all just part of this simple, but effective, cover. In fact, the only real things are yourselves and your bikes that sit outside."

The occupants of the briefing room instantly went quiet, and those who had not already taken their seats, did so immediately. Grant continued with his short speech, which was designed to do one thing—to remind his team of the reality of the situation, and keep their feet planted firmly on the ground.

"None of you are real fucking bikers. In fact, the only one who is, isn't actually here, and he is the only current active member of this group, so please let us all remember who we are, and why we are here." Grant waited, and was happy to hear no response.

"Now, down to business," he said, as he made his way around the table to the wall, where he had placed the photographs and sheets of paper.

"Most, if not all of you, have at some point, asked about the job I have brought you together to do." He pointed at each of the ten photographs on the wall, slowly—one by one—as he walked past each one of them.

"These are the job. These are members of the Armstrong family," he stated. "They are not the whole of this family. If I were to put up a picture of every member of this family, I would be able to decorate every wall of this room. They are, however, the most important family members, as far as everyone in this room are concerned." He looked around the table and was content that he had the attention of everyone.

"Study their faces, get to know their names, better than you know your own, and never underestimate any single one of them." He paused as he made his way back to the first photograph and stood next to it, placing a finger adjacent to it.

"Especially this one."

Every man and woman sat at the table looked at the photograph of the partially burnt face of a man as yet unknown to them.

"This is Kelvin Armstrong and he is, hopefully, the only person who will end up dead as a direct result of our actions. Every person on this wall is indirectly responsible for the death of a poor unfortunate woman, but he," Grant struck the face of Kelvin Armstrong with his finger, "he is directly responsible for the horrific murders of three innocent young girls, and we are going to make him pay for it through the suffering of these family members, and the ending of his pathetic putrid waste of an existence." Once again, Grant paused, this time for slightly longer than before, waiting for any reaction from his team. He was about to begin speaking again, when Reckon spoke up.

"Now, I am not the most clever of people, but ...," he was interrupted by Ordnance.

"No shit, mate. When you filled in your application to join the recon unit, you wrote, 'I think I would be a good candidate for the reckon unit,' hence your fucking nickname." A few around the table, who were also familiar with this story, joined in with Ordnance's laughter. In response, Reckon curled the thumb and fingers of his right hand around each other, and moved his hand up and down in the direction of Ordnance.

"Now, you are either telling me to move rapidly ...," Ordnance said, referring to the military use of hand signals to communicate, and this hand signal or particular, "... or you are suggesting I am a wanker."

"He's bunked up in the room next to you, Ordnance," Hammer said. "I don't think there is any doubt that he has already worked out that you are a wanker." This time, everyone around the table laughed.

Undaunted, Reckon continued speaking. "As I was about to say, or in fact, ask for clarification. Is what you are saying, that the job you want us to do, is basically to cause pain and suffering to nine of these people, and kill one of them?"

"Yes," Grant replied firmly. "Do you have any other questions, or do you just want to leave now?" he asked Reckon, although the question was intended for all of them.

Reckon shook his head. "No, I don't want to leave, but I do have one question. Why aren't we killing all of them?" he asked.

"Because these nine did not kill anyone," Grant replied. "They simply inflicted so much suffering to one woman, that she decided to take her own life, so we will make them suffer just as much, but the real suffering and torment will be experienced by Kelvin Armstrong himself, as he watches his family members put through the same level of suffering, and more, if necessary, before he suffers an equally horrific end, as the one he put his victims through."

"An eye for eye, so to speak," Syco said.

"So to speak," Grant replied.

"Why?" The question came from Double D.

"Why what?" Grant asked in return.

"Why are we doing it?"

"Because nobody should suffer like the victims of this family suffered," Grant replied, surprised that the question had been asked.

"Oh, that bit I agree with," Double D said. "But what I mean is ... why? What is so special about these victims? What are they to you, or any of us come to think about it?"

"They are, were, the family of a good friend of mine. A friend I owe. A friend I let down once and don't intend to let down again." Grant's response was said with a sombre note to his voice and a lump of guilt in his heart.

"All you had to do was say that at the start, would have saved you a lot of time." This response from Double D was tinged with the hurt she still felt from her earlier conversation that day with Grant.

The tension in the room between Double D and Grant could be felt by everyone, although, only Stacker had any idea why it existed, but before anyone tried to ease this tension, it was broken by Magill, who suddenly, and unexpectedly, burst into the room.

Grant did not acknowledge Magill, as he was more interested in who should have been following him into the room, but nobody did.

"Where's Thunderbox?" he asked.

Magill looked around the room at the occupants, and suddenly, his only concern was their attire.

"Where's my cut?" he shouted.

"I asked first," Grant said, raising his voice, so Magill was left in no doubt that he was being spoken to.

"Couldn't find him. Searched for ages, but couldn't see him or his bike. I assumed that he had managed to get his bike upright and had made his way here." Although Magill had answered Grant's question, he was still focussed on the cuts being worn by everyone. He stared intensely at the back of the cut being worn by Chaos, who was sat directly in front of him, and stroked his finger over the large centre patch. Feeling the contact, Chaos slowly stood and turned to face Magill, dropping his right hand into the front right pocket of his cut.

"Don't ever touch me again," he told Magill. His voice was hateful, and the look on his face turned vicious, even more malevolent looking, as the pupils seemed to increase in size, to the point where you could hardly see the colour of each iris. In a flash, his hand moved from the pocket in which it had been placed, and ended up adjacent to Magill's left eye. With a deft downward flick of his wrist, Chaos inflicted a small cut, approximately half an inch long, from the outer point of the eyelid.

"That's the only cut you're ever getting out of this club," Chaos informed Magill, as blood started to stream down his cheek.

Magill instinctively raised his hand to his eye and face, and only when he looked at his blood covered fingers, did he realise he had been cut. Then the stinging pain kicked in.

Double D raced around the table to go to the aid of Magill. Whatever the level of his popularity within the group, she could not stand by and watch him bleed.

"Come with me," she said to him, and glaring at Chaos, she yelled, "Don't you think there is going to be enough blood shedding in the weeks to come, without attacking each other?"

Chaos didn't react, other than to sit back down and put the small sharp blade back into his pocket.

"Get him out of my briefing room," Grant ordered Double D. "And when you have been patched up, get your blood cleaned off my floor."

Magill looked quite shocked and merely gazed silently at Grant.

"After you've done that, we will talk, and you had better have a better explanation," Grant said to Magill, showing no sympathy toward the injured pickup guy.

Grant cast his eyes over the remaining bikers, now all sat once again at the table. He waited for Double D and Magill to leave the room, before speaking again.

"Anybody else want to draw blood?" he asked the group of men. The question received no response. He walked over to where Chaos was sat, and leaned in toward him.

"Don't ever think I am not capable of leaving you in a state where you are capable of nothing more than sucking your food through a straw, you hearing me?" he asked him.

Chaos simply nodded his head.

"Good," Grant continued. "I am aware of your reputation, Chaos, and it doesn't scare me. One more attack against any member of this team, and I promise you, that you will spend the rest of your life having your arse wiped by an underpaid carer, who gives less of a shit about you than I do."

He instructed the group to leave, by loudly announcing, "Briefing over. Go and make sure your bikes are sound." Looking at Stacker, he further announced to everyone, "and the bar is closed for the next forty-eight hours. Focus your minds, gentlemen, because from this point onwards, every single one of you needs to be on point, twenty-four, seven."

Everyone stood and silently left the room, with the exception of Stacker, who remained seated.

An Unexpected Protector

Shuffler sat upright quickly, as he heard the key rattle inside the lock of his cell door, and was on his feet, ready for a fight, before the door had been opened.

"Chill, prisoner," the officer said, as he opened the door farther and planted his foot firmly against the bottom of the cell door. "You have a visitor, and she doesn't want to speak to you in your cell. So, first thing's first ... let's get you cleaned up, shall we?"

Shuffler studied the officer in front of him, and immediately came to the conclusion that he seemed to be a decent bloke for a screw. He had enough experience to work out screws fairly quickly and usually accurately. In addition to all of that, he was also desperate for a shower, because his dry excrement was now making his skin extremely itchy.

"I'll need shower stuff, boss, and a towel and stuff," Shuffler replied.

"All waiting for you in the shower room," the officer said.

Shuffler walked toward the door as the officer backed away, not wanting to get too close to this prisoner. Shuffler stepped out onto the landing and stopped, looking left and right. There were no other screws waiting for his appearance, with the exception of one at the end of the landing, leaning against the door frame of the unit office, watching proceedings intently.

"Taking a chance opening me by yourself, aren't you guv?"

"No, I don't think so. I am a good judge of a man, and you seem like a decent fella who just wants to be treated with a bit of respect and decency."

Shuffler looked at this member of the segregation unit team, and thought to himself how much he reminded him of Grant at their first-ever meeting on a prison wing.

"And I am confident I could kick the shit out of you by myself if you tried anything," the officer added.

Yeah, definitely just like Grant, thought Shuffler and smiled at the screw.

"What's your name, guv?" Shuffler asked.

"Sir, boss, guv, or Mr. Walpole ... you choose," Officer Walpole replied, smiling back at Shuffler.

"Well, Mr Walpole, let me try to get this shit off me with soap and water, before you try to kick it off me," Shuffler said.

Officer Walpole gave a quiet laugh.

"Good decision. Good for your body, and my nice, clean white shirt. Down the landing, second door on your left," Walpole said, pointing down the landing away from the office.

He fell in behind Shuffler at a safe distance, who now had his mind on the reason why Officer Walpole had opened him up. He came to the conclusion that the best way to find out would be to ask.

"Who is visiting me, guv?"

"A young lady," the officer replied, as Shuffler arrived at the open door to the shower unit.

Shuffler turned around to face Officer Walpole, and stepped backwards into the shower room saying, "Best I clean behind my foreskin then, eh?"

Officer Walpole's expression changed, as he replied to Shuffler's course question.

"The only reason you are not flat on your arse right now, is because you are covered in your own shit. I have shown you nothing but respect and treated you decently, so I ask that you show the same to all of my colleagues. Is that clear?" He locked the door without waiting for a response from the stinking excrement covered prisoner, now safe and secure in the shower room.

From behind the door, he saw Shuffler nod his head and give him a thumbs up. Had he not turned away so quickly to make his way back to the unit office, he may have seen Shuffler silently mouth the word "Sorry."

* * *

Stacker stared in the direction of Grant, who stood in front of the photographs on the wall, his attention totally focused on the picture of Kelvin Armstrong.

"Grant, my friend, you need to tone it down a bit with the lads. It appears to me that you are close to breaking point for some reason," he said to Grant, whose gaze did not break away from the photograph.

"They need to be kept in their places," Grant replied, without turning to look at Stacker.

"Fair do's, but there are ways and means, bro, and your way ain't gonna cut it, if you want my opinion," Stacker responded.

"When I want your opinion I ….," Grant started to say,

before being interrupted by Stacker.

"If you are about to say that you will give it to me, I promise you, I will walk. I am here for one reason, Grant, because I respect you and our friendship. Those people," Stacker said, pointing at the photographs, "mean nothing to me and neither does your mate, his dead missus or those poor unfortunate kids."

Grant broke his attention away from the picture of Kelvin Armstrong, and turned to face Stacker, taking a deep breath, before speaking.

"Most of this lot will be nothing more than observation scouts and snatchers. Only a small handful of us will actually be involved in the dirty work of this job," he said. "I could replace each and every one of them with trained chimps if I had to."

"If that's your opinion, Grant, then so be it, but I think it is my place to point a few things out to you," Stacker replied thoughtfully. "Firstly, yes I am sure most of these people could be replaced with ease, but could they be replaced with people who you trust? Because let's face facts, bro, trust is the main issue here. Secondly, they are all ex-military people. They have had their fill of being shouted and yelled at, or being told what they have to do without a reason being given. What they need and want, is a leader who they can respect. Not another jumped-up Rodney, who is here because his birth-right somehow gave him that position."

Grant listened carefully and begrudgingly, although silently agreeing with everything that his friend was saying.

"Finally," Stacker continued, "in my limited experience, chimps—trained or not—are really shit when it comes to riding motorbikes."

There followed a few seconds of silence, before Grant quietly and humbly responded.

"Tell them to all work on their bikes for a couple of hours. Grab a bite to eat, before being back in here at 1300 hours."

"Will do, Prezzo," Stacker replied with a beaming grin on his face.

"And tell Magill to get back in here immediately," Grant said.

"Will do again. And there is one untrained chimp who proves my point," Stacker replied, once again leaving the briefing room with a bounce in his step.

Grant sat at the table, looking over at the position he would normally be seated at, and contemplated the type of person he would like to see sat there, It certainly would not be the person he had just been during that briefing, if that is what it could be called. Stacker had hit the nail on the head.

Even Grant felt that, at times, he was nearing breaking point. He thought about the last few short years of his life, the loss of his family, and the subsequent brutal acts he had committed in the name of love, loss and grief. The most recent time, included the close brush with death, and then, finding himself alive, but badly broken and under the control of an officially unofficial organisation, through which he had discovered that he had not, in fact, lost his wife. After coming through all of that, and finally coming face-to-face again with Mortimer Church—this time winning—and most crucially, getting his wife back into his life, only to lose her once again. The most painful and confusing element of all of what had happened was the final loss of Julia, because Grant still did not know if his wife had taken her own life, because of what she had been through, or because she could not live with the man her husband had become.

He reflected on his life before any of these events had occurred—a good and trustworthy member of a forgotten service, who had stood shoulder-to-shoulder with some brave men and women, who had taken crap on a daily basis, and sorted it out in his own unique way … then devastation. False accusations and a kangaroo court, all arriving in his life at the end of one of the worst years of his life—the tragic and unexpected loss of a close colleague, and the expected, but no less painful loss of his father-in-law. It all broke him eventually. He had walked away battered and bruised, but the most difficult aspect of it all, had been the lack of support from colleagues he once thought close. That had hurt him deeply. He hid his anger—a deep resentful dangerous anger—but all that did was make it ferment inside him and grow into a caged beast—the catalyst for its release, being the attack on his family.

He thought that the anger had, over the years, been replaced with disappointment and regret, but the news of his childhood friend, and the brutal deaths of his daughters, had shown him that his anger had just been hidden away in a deeper and darker place inside him, and it had matured into something that he feared he could not control.

His thoughts were interrupted by the door being pushed open, and Magill entering the room for the second time that morning, his face now repaired by a couple of nicely applied stitches.

Looks like Double D has a deft touch, he thought, and then shook his head to rid his mind of such thoughts.

"Do you ever fucking knock, before entering a room?" he snarled at Magill.

"But Stacker said you wanted to see me," Magill replied, not quite understanding what point Grant was trying to make.

Grant was no longer surprised by the stupidity of Magill, but he wanted to keep him close for two reasons. Firstly, he could keep an eye on him, and secondly, for some unfathomable reason, he had contacts and that was what Grant needed right now.

"With the unexpected failure of Thunderbox joining our throng, I need a replacement," Grant said. "And to be perfectly honest, nobody else on that list you gave me can fill the gap left by our absent colleague. So, my question to you, Magill, is do you know of anyone else?"

Magill took his time in answering Grant's question, as if thinking for a few seconds.

"There is one bloke I know of, but I didn't put him on the original list, because he isn't ex-military, so to speak," he eventually replied.

"How do you mean? You are either ex-military or you are a civvy," said Grant, who was not in the mood for games with his pickup man.

"Well," Magill said hesitantly, as if already knowing that Grant was not going to like his next few words, "he's ex-mercenary."

Grant's gut tightened as he heard the word. He did not have much personal experience with mercenaries, but he knew a few who had, including a couple of The Nameless Ones. Generally, the consensus of opinion tended to be negative. He also knew that a mercenary was always a mercenary and never an ex one.

"What do you know of this individual?" Grant asked.

"He did some security work in Afghanistan, and more

recently, was involved in something somewhere in Somalia—hand-to-hand combat specialist and sniper quality shooter," Magill replied swiftly, as if he had rehearsed the response.

"Neither of those skills are any use to me," Grant said.

"General all-rounder is what I would describe him as," Magill quickly replied. "Exactly what Thunderbox was."

Convenient, thought Grant, who was not a man to normally like convenient situations, but he needed a replacement and quick.

"Trustworthy?" Grant asked.

"As much as the others I recommended," Magill replied dishonestly.

"And does this mercenary have a name?" asked Grant.

"They call him Cutter," Magill said.

"Sharp," Grant replied, and instantly wished he hadn't wasted his breath, as what he thought was a witty response, flew clear of Magill's thick skull. "Reach out to him and ask him if he is interested and available," Grant instructed Magill.

Magill left the room, already reaching for his phone, and already knowing that he didn't need to ask his real boss either of those questions.

Grant started to rearrange the photographs on the wall, and pin up a few other sheets of paper, in readiness for the return of his team for what he hoped would be a more successful and peaceful briefing. His mind flitted between the earlier conversation with Stacker and this Cutter character, and in particular, he wondered how he had got his nickname.

* * *

As Grant was preparing for his briefing, DS Bradley was reading through an email with interest. He got up from his desk, and opening the door, popped his head out and shouted across the main office.

"Woody, my office now,"

Bradley had not even sat back down behind his desk, before his office door flew open and in walked DC Pete Wood.

"Yes, boss," he said enthusiastically.

"Shut the door and take a seat," Bradley replied, sitting himself down. "And then tell me what you know about the content of the latest briefing update email. And before you say what email, I know you have read it, because you are the only sad fucker in the office who reads every email you receive."

"Oh, I read it, boss," Woody replied smiling. "But there was a bit in there, so which part in particular would you like my analysis on?" he asked.

"Guess," Bradley replied sarcastically.

DC Wood knew which part of the email his superior was referring to. It was no secret in the department of DS Bradley's unhealthy interest in gangs, and in particular, bike gangs. Mike Bradley, aka Boomer, because of his incredibly loud and deep voice, was the younger brother of DS Richard Bradley, and was currently eight years into a life sentence for the murder of a woman who frequented the clubhouse of the Satan's Fortunates, the bike gang that Boomer had been, and effectively still was, a full member of.

"New bike gang in the ghetto, boss. Not a great deal known about them, but I expect, like you, I am wondering how they have been allowed to set up in what could be construed to be the territory of Satan's Fortunates," the young DC answered.

"Yeah, my thoughts exactly," Bradley replied, He was distant for a few seconds, as his brother briefly entered his head.

"Tell you what, Woody, things are a bit quiet, so let's make our acquaintance with these new brothers," Bradley said, standing up and putting on his suit jacket.

"Yes sir, boss. I'll get the car and meet you out front," Woody replied, leaping to his feet, thrilled to be going out on a job with the boss.

"And don't tell any of the team where we are going, if they bother to ask," Bradley added.

Woody tapped the side of his nose with one finger.

"Just going for a coffee and a doughnut, boss," he said, giving a cheeky wink toward his boss, and instantly regretting it, as Richard Bradley glared back at him.

"Err, how about going to have a chat about my future?" Woody asked, and disappeared out of the office, but not without hearing DS Bradley's response.

"Yeah, that would be more believable."

* * *

Shuffler sat on a chair secured to the floor by four bolts, inserted through its metal feet, and looked over the narrow desk at the woman on the other side. The office was sparse—two chairs, one desk and an empty pin board on the wall. The whole front wall of the office was reinforced glass, which allowed the two officers stood outside the office, to observe every move that the occupants made, without being able to hear what was being said.

"Hello, Mr. Dawson. I hope you are well," the attractive middle-aged woman sat opposite to him said.

Shuffler was immediately confused, because nobody in this prison knew of his real name. The police had not been able to find out anything about him. His fingerprints had not shown up on any database, and he knew that he had been processed by the police, the courts and the prison authorities as Mr. J. Doe. He was confident that this information could not have been breached, because Grant had told him that his *unofficial friends* had seen to it that none of The Nameless Ones effectively existed.

"Who you talking to lady?" Shuffler asked. "I don't know no Dawson."

"Stanley Dawson, aka Shuffler," the woman replied. "Other than that, the man you know as Grant, has told me very little, other than you are to be looked after, during what he hopes will be a very short stay with us."

When Grant had informed him that he would be looked after while he was inside, Shuffler had assumed that it would be a screw who was the inside man.

"You a governor?" Shuffler asked.

"No, Dawson," the woman replied, a short burst of laughter escaping from her mouth, which she cut short and returned the professional look to her face, as she saw the two officers look at her through the windows.

"My name is Jenny Wolstenholme, and I am the senior psychologist in this prison," she replied.

"Why you helping me and Grant, then?" Shuffler enquired. "You an old fuck buddy of his?"

"Mr. Dawson, the reasons for why I am doing what I am doing, are none of your business," the psychologist replied curtly. "However, if you suggest anything like that again, I will show you how quickly I am willing to drop you. Do I

165

make myself clear?"

"And I am guessing that when you say drop me, you are referring to withdrawing your assistance, rather than dropping me in the way that those two Neanderthals outside would?" Shuffler replied, in an equally curt manner.

"It would appear that we now understand each other, Mr. Dawson, so pin back those monkey ears of yours, and listen to what is going to happen next," Jenny Wolstenholme instructed in a tone that Shuffler had not expected. It had become abundantly clear why she and Grant had got on during his previous career.

The senior psychologist quickly explained to Shuffler that he was going to be transferred to her specialist unit, so his mental health could be properly assessed. She further explained that she would work to keep him on that unit for as long as possible, but could not give any promises to how long that would be.

"You do not meet one criteria for assessment, other than the behaviour you demonstrated on your arrival into the prison, and from what I hear prior to that also," she told him. "And that is a tentative reason for assessing you."

"And while I am there, will I be given the freedom to do what I am here to do?" Shuffler asked.

"You will be treated the same as every other patient. What you get up to, and how you conduct your business, is exactly that, Mr. Dawson, your business. I do not want to have any further part in it. I have done what I told Grant I would do, and that is to gain you access to the people you need access to," she answered.

"Tell me to fuck off if you like, but I have to ask … Why are you doing this?" Shuffler asked.

Jenny Wolstenholme chose her words carefully.

"The man you know as Grant, the man I once knew as Senior Officer Andy Richardson, was treated appallingly by this service. At the end of an exemplary career, when he needed the same level of help that he gave his employers on many occasions, he was let down. In fact, no, he was dropped into the bin like a piece of rubbish. I admitted into evidence that he was suffering from a mental illness, and that I had previously indicated that he had a multiple personality disorder, following his removal from the Close Supervision Unit that he had been working in at that time. That evidence, along with every other piece of evidence, was at the very least, mitigation for what he did." She took a brief moment, before ending with, "I told him at the time he was dismissed, that if he ever needed my help with anything, that I would be there for him. So deep was the shame I felt about the way he had been treated by an organisation that I had been, up to that point, very proud to be associated with."

"What the hell did he do?" Shuffler asked.

"If he hasn't told you, then he obviously doesn't want you to know, and I don't believe it is my place to tell you. What I will tell you, though, is that the service was changing, and Andy wasn't. He had served his purpose, and his kind wasn't wanted anymore," she replied, and Shuffler detected a hint of sadness and shame in her reply.

She stood up and walked toward the door. Before opening it to speak with the officers, she addressed Shuffler again.

"I have done my bit now and cleared my conscience. I would ask that you don't let him down, because I don't know if he could handle that again."

"He is my brother from a different mother, and I have no

intention of letting him down, now or in the future," Shuffler replied, as he watched the senior psychologist open the door and tell the prison staff that they were to transfer the prisoner to the PDAT unit immediately.

Interference and the First Guest

The group of military veterans and bikers filed, one by one, back into the briefing room, and sat quietly in their seats, waiting to see what Grant had to say. Grant could feel the uneasy atmosphere, but a confident nod of the head from Stacker in his direction, settled him down and he began to speak.

"Gentlemen, and lady, of course," he began, nodding toward Double D. "I would like to begin by asking for your forgiveness for my earlier behaviour. I allowed my emotions to take control, because of the personal nature of this whole situation."

"How do we know that won't happen again?" Alec White, aka Chalky, asked.

"Because I give you my word as a man who has served this country of ours," Grant replied.

"Good enough for me," Andy Southall, aka Disposal, called out.

"Maybe it is for you, bro, but behaviours usually stay the same, don't they?" Chalky asked in response.

"So, we can expect you to draw white lines around the bodies of anyone you kill, like you did with the Taliban fuckers out in Afghan, can we?" Disposal asked, referring to the reason behind Alec White's road name.

"That wasn't a behaviour, that was my way of preserving evidence," Chalky retorted.

"The military thought it was the behaviour of one sick fucker," Disposal replied, looking pleased with himself, as all of the occupants of the room joined together in laughter at this reply—ripple of laughter that helped to ease the tension in the room, and one that Grant quickly took advantage of.

"Chalky, I understand and appreciate your concern, but I can assure you that I won't allow emotion to cloud my behaviour or judgment again, and I am asking you to trust me," Grant asked the concerned member of his team. Addressing the whole team, he then said, "I ask for the trust of you all, the same trust you have given many, during your military service, and I promise that you will receive the same level of trust from me in return."

Stacker smiled to himself, as he watched Grant taking his place as the leader of this group of people.

"I also ask for the same level of commitment, bravery and ability to follow orders, even when you don't fully understand the reasons behind those orders, which you have all demonstrated in the many past situations you found yourself in. Those missions were no different than this one. There is one enemy and that enemy needs to be brought to task to answer for his crimes, with the least amount of collateral damage as is possible." Grant stopped speaking and hoped that the silence would be filled with the right response.

Chaos filled that silence.

"Least amount of collateral damage?" he exclaimed. "I didn't sign up for that kind of pussy operation."

Laughter filled the room, and Stacker could see Grant fully

relax. He stepped forward, and said to the group, "Right folks, from this point, we are no longer military veterans. Our pasts will not be spoken about outside of this clubhouse. Your real names will no longer be used—road names only, please. We are The Nameless Ones, and we wear our badge with pride and honour—the same as we have worn our individual badges before. Now, let us hear what our president needs us to do."

Grant approached Stacker and held his right hand in the air, which Stacker duly grasped.

A loud cheer erupted from around the large table, and Chaos yelled at the top of his voice, "Fuck yes! It's going to get FUBAR."

Grant waited for the noise to abate, before speaking again. When eventually it did, he once again addressed them.

"Syco, will you join me, please," he asked one of the bikers sat at the table.

The biker, who up until recently, had been named Pete Johnston, stood and quietly joined Grant.

"This is Syco. He is our intelligence officer, and for the past few weeks, unbeknownst to all except myself, he has been collecting information about our targets." Grant swept his arm below the photographs behind him. "All of the information about these people is contained in files that will be issued to you, following this briefing. You will have one night to digest the information in those files, before handing them over to Disposal tomorrow morning, who will arrange their destruction. You will be working in teams of two. Each team will have a target, and you will only have access to the information relevant to your target. You will not discuss each other's target with the other teams, unless it is deemed necessary by Syco."

171

A voice interrupted Grant, who allowed it to happen without question.

"Question, boss … if we are allowed to ask any during your briefing?" MadDog asked.

Grant nodded his head to show MadDog that questions were allowed, and the biker continued.

"Can Syco assure us that the targets have no idea that they were being observed?"

Before Syso could respond, Grant answered the question.

"Stacker has correctly said that our military pasts will not be discussed outside of this building, and I will add a bit more to that order. Our pasts will not be discussed, even inside this building, unless it is relevant to this mission. However, your question does require a relevant response," Grant replied. "Syco spent six years in Northern Ireland, working for 14 Intelligence Company, otherwise known as The Unit, before working out in Iraq, prior to the conflict, collecting information about the Iraqi regime. During all of this time, the information he collected was absolutely accurate, and his position as an intelligence officer was never compromised."

"Yes, would have done, boss," MadDog replied, with a hint of sarcastic humour.

"Syco, the audience is yours," Grant said with a smile.

"Thank you," Syco replied. "As already said, you will be working in pairs. Stacker will let you know what pairs at the end of this briefing, and each pair will be working on one target. Target Alpha is Kelvin Armstrong, and all other targets are to be utilised to persuade Target Alpha to disclose the truth."

"For the truth will set you free," Chaos called out.

"Or, in Armstrong's case, the truth will get you a life sentence, during which you will be passed around the wings like a groupie on a rock band's tour bus," Syco replied, before continuing with his part of the briefing. "The targets are all members of the Armstrong family—the inner circle so to speak."

Ordnance held up his arm like a young child in school.

"No need to raise your arm if you have a question, Ordnance," Grant said.

"Yeah, you only need to do that if you need to leave for a piss," Fixit, the team's mechanic, called out. This was followed by more laughter, which added to the comfort zone that Grant now found himself in.

Ordnance ignored the friendly banter and asked his question.

"Well, I realise that I ain't the brightest button in this here box," he said, and raised two fingers in the direction of Chaos, and then closing the two fingers together, pressed them against his temple like the muzzle of a pistol. Chaos, who had been about to throw some more abusive banter in the direction of Ordnance, decided better of it, and kept his mouth shut. "But I see nine targets, not including Target Alpha, and assuming that the boss will not be in one of the teams, and seeing how Shuffler is somewhat otherwise engaged, I can only count enough people in this room to work on six of those targets, and that is assuming that Thunderbox eventually turns up." Ordnance finished speaking, and looked around the table for some sort of signal that his numbers were correct.

People spoke to each other in hushed tones for a few seconds, while others silently did the math in their heads to confirm Ordnance's observation.

Once again, Grant stepped in. The role of leader sitting more comfortable with him, as each question was raised.

"Ordnance, you are correct, sort of!" he answered and then gave a short explanation. "I am working with Magill on a replacement for Thunderbox, as I can only assume that he has his own reasons for not turning up, and for not reaching out to any of us to explain those reasons."

There was a collective groan from around the table, upon hearing Magill's name. Grant held up his hand for silence.

"Once I decide on that replacement," he said, emphasising the word "I" in order to highlight the fact that Magill would not be making that decision. "That will leave twelve of you available to work on six targets. The two Armstrong brothers, Michael and Harry, are currently residing at Her Majesty's pleasure, where a colleague of ours is, as we speak, hopefully close to keeping an eye on them. A third brother is also in prison, but he is not one of our current targets, as he was in prison during the period that his family was committing their reign of terror against my friend and his family. Does that answer your question, Ordnance?" Grant asked.

Ordnance smiled a huge great grin, pleased that his original observation had been accurate, and gave a thumbs up to Grant.

"Syco, is there anything else you want to add at this stage?" Grant asked.

"No," Syco replied. "All the required information will be in the files that Stacker will hand out soon." He quietly returned to his seat without any fuss, and it was easy for everyone to see why this man made a good convert intelligence officer—he went about his business, almost without being noticed.

"Right, one last thing, before you are dismissed," Grant

said. "The observant among you will have noticed a map pinned to the wall, and on that map, an area has been coloured orange. That area is out of bounds to us when we are on club business. We will not ride anywhere within that area wearing our colours. This area is the territory of another group of bikers, and we will observe a level of respect for those people." Grant intentionally over emphasised his last words, in order to get across their importance. "It is imperative that this is adhered to, no matter what."

"Sounds a bit like the good old Northern Ireland days," MadDog said.

"Just the same, bro, and with the same end result, if you ignore the order," Grant replied, with a hint of seriousness to his tone.

Grant allowed the silence to roam around the room for a while, and when no one seemed interested in saying anything, he concluded the meeting, or at least attempted to, before once again, Magill burst into the room.

"Right, gentleman, take your files and embed the information into your minds. We will meet again tomorrow morning at …" He had almost finished, when a flushed looking Magill shouted, "We have a couple of visitors, boss. They say they are coppers."

Grant looked around the room, as if searching for some explanation for this unexpected interruption, but the occupants of the briefing room all appeared to be as confused as him.

"Did you check their IDs?" Grant asked.

"Yeah," Magill replied. "They look kosher."

"Please don't tell me that you have let them into the compound?" Grant asked..

"Do I look stupid?" Magill asked, and instantly regretted it, as many around the room muttered comments ,such as "yes" and "fucking A you are." "They are outside the front gate, and none too happy that I told them to wait there."

To the people sat around the table, Grant said, "Take all your information with you and stash it away in your rooms, away from prying eyes, please. Fixit, go the garage, mate, and a couple of you make your way there, too. Make it look like you are working on your bikes. Magill you, too, in the garage working underneath the van. I can't risk you opening your gob."

He turned to Stacker, and said, "Stacker, clear this room of all of the info and photos, please, bro. Put them downstairs." Stacker nodded and started doing as he was asked immediately, as Grant noticed a few faces of the people now leaving the briefing room look once more confused, as he remembered that except for Stacker and himself, nobody else knew about the underground part of this complex so far.

He played it cool, as he made his way through the crowd and out of the room. Looking over his shoulder, he looked for Chaos, and once his eyes had located him, he said, "Chaos, once you have got rid of the file, I want you at the gate with me. I could do with a crazy fucker at my side. It will help to convince these nosey bastards that we are what we are masquerading to be."

Chaos held up his right hand, the first and little fingers raised in the familiar rockers "horns" sign. Grant was happy to hear a bit more laughter in the crowd of bikers, and the looks of inquisitive confusion disappear from their faces. He thought that he had managed to get away with his earlier slip of the tongue.

176

* * *

Making his way across the open compound toward the gate, he slowed his pace and watched Fixit enter the garage. He stood next to the gate, and saw two of the guys running in the same direction. He allowed them a few extra seconds to reach the garage, before sliding open the panel in the large gate, allowing to see who or what was on the other side. Two suited men stood outside the gate, one a few paces behind the older of the pair, who Grant assumed was the more senior.

"Can I help you, gentleman?" Grant asked.

"Yes, you can open this gate and let me and my colleague in," DS Bradley replied, holding up his warrant card. "Before I start to think you have something to hide."

"Now that would suggest you are here to look for something, Officer Bradley, so I do hope you have the necessary paperwork to give you the authority to search our property," Grant replied, noticing the name and rank on the detective's warrant card.

"It's Detective Sergeant Bradley," the copper replied. "I haven't been a plod officer for some years and this is just a friendly visit. Welcome you to the neighbourhood, so to speak."

Grant smiled, happy that his intentional use of the word officer had received a reaction.

Chaos appeared over Grant's shoulder, or rather Chaos's head and face appeared over his shoulder. He filled the open observation hole with his face, and in a deliberate crazy voice, said, "Man you must be busy fuckers if you give a welcome visit to every bastard who moves into your neighbourhood."

Grant gently pushed Chaos back away from the gate, glad that he was playing his part as requested, but then thinking he wasn't actually playing at anything, other than being his normal self.

"I'll open the gates, detective. Bring your vehicle and your quiet colleagues with you. I wouldn't want any of them getting hurt while they wait out there for you," said Grant, still smiling and sliding the panel shut, without waiting for a response.

He and Chaos opened the gates and then closed them, as the unmarked police car drove through and parked up next to the three bikes adjacent to the clubhouse.

As Bradley opened the passenger door and began to step out, Grant called over to him.

"Not there, please, detective. That is a motorbike only parking area. Ask your driver to park it over by the far wall." He pointed directly ahead of him to show where he wanted the car to be parked.

Bradley tuned his head to face inside the vehicle.

"Do as this muppet requests," he said to Pete Wood.

"But…," Woody began to argue.

"He's just being a smartarse, letting us know who is in control here," Bradley replied, holding up his hand to calm his junior. "Let him think that way … for now." He got out of the car, and reluctantly, Woody reversed the vehicle away from the bikes and in the direction indicated by Grant.

DS Bradley walked toward Grant, holding out his hand, which Grant did not take.

"This way, detective," Grant said and then told Chaos to wait for the other copper and bring him into the clubhouse.

"He is also a detective," DC Bradley said, already becoming a bit fed up with the man's little power games. "Detective

Constable Wood, to be precise."

Grant ignored the detective's words, and led him through the door and into the clubhouse bar area.

"Would you like a drink, detective?" Grant asked.

"Not when I'm on duty, thank you," Bradley answered.

"I actually meant a tea or a coffee. I never would try to entice one of our finest to partake in an alcoholic beverage while on the lookout for bad guys."

"No, I'm fine, thank you," Bradley replied. "Introductions would be nice, though."

Grant smiled at the detective.

"Excuse my bad manners. What would my good mother think of me?" Grant replied. He held out his hand and it was taken by DC Bradley. A firm handshake was exchanged, and Grant said, "I'm Nameless."

* * *

Shuffler stood in the middle of the open and brightly lit atrium that was the assessment unit of the larger PDAT unit. Apparently, the other part was the treatment unit. The staff members were a mixture of hospital staff, nurses, healthcare assistants and prison officers, all of whom wore a uniform comprising of light blue polo shirts and dark blue trousers. Embroidered on the shirts, were the names of the staff members wearing them—no rank, just names, which included their first names.

"Bit on the relaxed side, ain't it?" Shuffler asked the member of staff stood with him, who according to his shirt, was named

Alex Woodside.

"All helps to break down the barriers, so assessment and treatment can be achieved," Alex Woodside responded.

"And what are you, a screw or a scablifter?" Shuffler asked him.

"I'm a prison officer," Woodside replied, politely without correcting Shuffler on his use of slang.

"And how do I tell the difference between you lot and the scablifters?" Shuffler asked.

"Well, the nursing staff, or scablifters as you call them, are the ones who carry the syringes," Woodside replied with a smile, in an effort to show the new prisoner that he was joking.

"So what do I call you?" Shuffler asked.

"Alex, of course," the officer replied, as if it was the normal thing to do for prisoners when addressing prison staff.

Shuffler inwardly shuddered at the thought of addressing a screw by his first name, but before any more conversation could take place, a young woman called across the atrium.

"Harry Armstrong, would you come to assessment room two, please?"

Shuffler watched as a kid walked out of one of the cells and over the subtle yellow atrium floor toward the member of the staff who had just called his name.

"See you later, Harry," shouted a slightly older kid, now leaning against the doorframe of the cell that Harry Armstrong had just vacated. Michael Armstrong glanced over toward Shuffler and the screw, but paid no more attention to them than he would a flea.

Shuffler's eyes flitted between the two men—the two Armstrong brothers he had been given the responsibility of dealing with when the time was right.

"Which cell am I in, guv?" Shuffler asked the officer.

"That one over there," Alex Woodside said, pointing toward the cell adjacent to the one that Michael Armstrong was now walking back into. "And please, just call me Alex".

Two thoughts went through Shuffler's head. The first was how lucky it was that he had been located right next to one of the Armstrong brothers, and the other was that he would rather slam his dick in a drawer, than call this over-caring fucker by his first name.

* * *

As Grant walked behind the bar and grabbed a bottle of beer for himself, he heard DS Bradley ask, "Sorry, you are nameless, as in you don't have a name?"

"No," Grant replied, holding the bottle top against the side of the bar and slamming his hand down on top of it. The bottle cap flew through the air a few feet, and then skipped and skitted across the floor, making a faint tinny noise. "My name is Nameless, and my friend's name is Chaos," he said, pointing to the door, just as Chao entered the bar area with DC Wood in tow.

"Either you both have very cruel parents, or I am guessing these are your biker road names," Bradley replied.

"Road names," Grant responded.

"Although my parents were a pair of cruel bastards, too," Chaos said, as he walked past Bradley and sat down in one of the sofas.

"So, may I ask what your actual names are?" Bradley asked.

181

Grant's response was delivered in a tone that suggested that the detective didn't ask that question again, unless it was during an official police questioning session.

"As far as you are concerned, they are our real names, and I thought this was a friendly visit?" Grant said and nodded in the direction of DC Wood, who was sat on one the bar stools, beginning to make notes in his police notebook.

"Woody," DC Bradley called out, "put it away."

DC Wood looked up, finished off writing the word Chaos, and put his notebook back in his jacket pocket.

"Sorry about that. He's new and eager to please," Bradley told Grant.

"So, as I say, a friendly visit," continued the DS. "Why have you all of sudden arrived here and what are your intentions?"

"Who said anything about having any intentions?" Grant asked the DS back.

"Look, let me put my cards on the table for you, err ... Nameless," Bradley said. "The locals have every right to be worried when a gang of bikers park up on their back doors, no more than a stone's throw from another biker gang, which has been troublesome in this area in the past. To be honest, it stinks of potential trouble."

"Let me put you at ease, and correct some of the assumptions you are making, detective," Grant said, taking a gulp of beer from the bottle, before placing it on the bar, and then leaning his elbows onto the same wooden surface. "We are not a bike gang. We are a collection of military veterans, who all happen to enjoy the freedom of a motorbike, and have decided to form ourselves a little bike club, which will allow us a bolthole away from our troubles of civilian life, and mix once again with likeminded people who don't get offended by the slightest whiff of a swear word or threat delivered in friendly banter."

"And what about the concern of the other biker gang in this area?" Bradley asked.

"We have reached out to the Fortunates and all is well between us. I do not anticipate any problems," Grant replied.

"Let's leave anticipating problems to the professionals, shall we?" asked Bradley, who was slightly annoyed by what could be construed as well thought-out answers from this bike leader, who did not behave or talk like any bike gang member Bradley had come across before.

"What are you really here for, detective?" Grant bluntly asked Bradley. "And please, don't give me any more bullshit about a friendly visit."

"Okay, let me say it straight, Nameless," Bradley said, with a hint of sarcasm, as he spoke Grant's road name. "I don't believe your sudden appearance has been caused by a desire for a bunch of delinquent adults to get away from it all. I'm neither blind, nor stupid, and this compound of yours has taken some planning—weeks, if not months."

Grant remained silent.

"Whatever your plans are, I would suggest that you and your comrades in arms all keep your noses clean. Otherwise, I will be all over the lot of you, like a dog over leftovers, you get me?" the now straight-talking detective asked Grant.

Before Grant replied, a hand touched his shoulder. He had not seen Reckon enter the bar area and walk to the bar to stand alongside him, such had been his focus on DS Bradley. Reckon quietly said, "Me and MadDog are going out for a ride, bro. Might take Magill with us to pick up some supplies on the way back."

"Yeah," Grant replied, his focus still almost entirely on

183

Bradley. "Just keep it shiny side up and ride clean."

"Always, boss," MadDog said, as he walked past the front of the bar, brushing closely by Bradley and DC Wood. As he walked past the latter, he whispered, "Woody, eh? What do your friends call you? Peckerhead?"

The two bikers left the building, and one could be heard calling for Magill, "Get your van, you good for nothing piece of shit."

The next noise was the roar of their bikes, as they were revved into action.

"I think your time is up, detective, and if I may suggest something to you, it would be this—no more friendly visits. So the next time you feel like making an appearance, make sure you have all the correct paperwork with you. Do you get me, officer?" Grant asked, and without waiting for a reply, he walked over to the opening of the corridor that led to the bedrooms, and at the top of his voice shouted, "Can someone come up here and kindly show these detectives the way out?"

A few seconds later, Double D sauntered into the bar area, and looking at the two policemen, said, "This way, officers."

The look on the faces of the two detectives gave away that they were surprised by the appearance of a woman.

"What's wrong, gentleman? You never seen a woman with a large chest and a mouth to match it?" she asked them.

"Be seeing ya, guys," Grant said to the two detectives, who were now standing up and turning to follow Double D, who was holding the door out to the compound wide open for them. "And make sure the gate is shut firmly behind them, D," he said to his biking sister.

It was about five minutes later, when Grant heard the gate slam shut with a metallic clunk, followed by the sound of it rattling in its holdings. He had no idea why that visit had just taken place, but as he was confident that their cover and real identities could not have been discovered by a standard issue police detective, he put it down to DS Bradley just wanting to throw his weight in their direction, and shake the tree a little to see what fell out.

Double D returned with a huge smile on her face.

"Where have Reckon and MadDog gone?" Grant asked her.

"No idea, they never said a word. Spent a while holed up in MadDog's digs together for a while and then left together," she replied. "In fact, until you just asked me where they went, I just assumed they had gone to the garage to do some work on their bikes, or simply gone out for a smoke. Is there a problem?" she asked.

"No," Grant said, shaking his head unconvincingly. "They're just out for a ride and blowing away the cobwebs, I guess. I just thought they may have told someone where they were heading."

He headed down the corridor to his room. On the way, he popped his head into the rooms of Stacker and Hammer, asking them both if they had asked Reckon or MadDog to get in some supplies. Both gave him the answer he was expecting, which was that there was no need for supplies at the moment, since both the bar and kitchen were well-stocked. *So, why did they need to take Magill with them,* Grant thought, as he entered his room and laid himself down on his bed.

* * *

"Pass me your notebook," Bradley said to Woody, as the young detective steered the car back to the police station. He did as he was told without saying a word. You didn't have to be a police detective, to work out that DS Bradley was not in a happy place. He reached into his jacket pocket, retrieved the small black notebook and handed it to his boss, who snatched it from his hand.

Flipping through the pages, he asked Woody what he had written when he had been in the clubhouse. His words were short and snapped out of his mouth.

"The two names I heard mentioned," Woody replied, "were Nameless and Chaos."

"And what is the point of doing that?" Bradley asked, finally reaching the page containing the two names, just spoken by the young detective, who by now had decided to focus fully on the road, and let his boss's words float straight over his head. He was going to be a kicking board for DS Bradley, just because some low-life biker boy had got the better of him.

"They obviously aren't their real names," Bradley snapped again. He was now getting angrier at himself for letting his anger and frustration get the better of him.

"Then add the name Magill to that short list of names," Pete Wood replied. "Sounds a bit more real than the others, don't you think?"

Richard Bradley pulled a pen from his inside pocket, and wrote the name Magill below the name Chaos.

"Yeah, you may be right," he said to DC Wood, which was the nearest thing to an apology that the young detective was going to get from DS Bradley that day, or probably any other.

* * *

Reckon and MadDog sat on their now still and quiet bikes, side by side, slightly back from the corner of a street that joined a busier, but still quite small road, certainly not what you would describe as a main road.

"Are you sure we are in the right place?" Reckon asked his accomplice.

MadDog raised his visor so it fully opened and looked at Reckon through slitted eyes.

Why did I have to get paired up with this thick shit? he thought.

"Look, Reckon, the file said the girl worked at a greasy spoon, called The Spitting Sausage on this road. Just across the road, there is a café with a sign above its window with that very name written across it. How many spitting fucking sausages do you think there are on one fucking road?"

"Why does everybody call me Reckon, when they know my road name is Recon?" he asked, totally ignoring MadDog's sarcastic question.

MadDog pulled his visor down so is returned to its previous, almost fully closed position. His muffled words could still be heard though.

"Kill me now, Lord. Kill me fucking now."

Fifty or sixty metres behind the two bikes, Magill sat behind the steering wheel of his van—one eye on the bikes, and the other on his mobile, as he typed a text message.

You are in, what now?

He typed quickly, before hitting the send key. A reply was quickly received.

What did he tell you to do?

Magill typed his response, and once again pressed the send key.

Told me to reach out to you and invite you to the clubhouse.

The receiver of Magill's text messages grimaced, as he read the last text.

"What is it with these bikers? Reach out to him," he said, "Why not contact him or speak to him, but no, they have to have their own fucking language, along with their back slapping manly hugs and fucking biker handshakes," he said to nobody but himself in an almost hysterical voice. "And now, everyone is speaking the fucking same. Good God, I heard the actual resident of the United States say on television that he would reach out to the Palestinian leaders to discuss a peace deal." His fingers hit the mobile's screen keyboard with the same level of anger as his voice portrayed.

Tell him I will be with him tomorrow, not sure what time yet.

Magill switched off the mobile, and reaching down below the driver's seat, stuffed it back into the hole, returning it to its hiding place in the inners of the seat. He grabbed his other mobile from the dashboard of the van, and sent a text to MadDog.

Anything yet?

Another response, not as fast as the one from Cutter, told him to *FUCK OFF.*

* * *

MadDog put his phone back into the front pocket of his jeans, pleased with his witty and direct response to Magill, and looked up, just in time to see the girl he had been hoping to see, walk out of the café door and head down the pavement, away from where they were parked up. He waited a few seconds, watching the girl walk away from the café, and turn right down a side street, before starting up his bike. Reckon followed suit and tucked in behind MadDog, as he slowly pulled away. Behind them, Magill started up the van, and keeping a comfortable distance between himself and the two bikers, he pulled his van away from the kerbside.

The convoy of two bikers and a van followed the route taken by the girl, who very quickly, was back in sight, and immediately, MadDog saw an opportunity. The side road was empty of people, other than the Armstrong girl, and she was about fifty feet from what looked like a narrow alleyway, probably one that led to the rear of the businesses on the same road as The Spitting Sausage café. He let go of the left handle, and lowered his hand to the level of his knee, and waved it slowly up and down, hoping Reckon would understand that he wanted him to slow down and back off. At the same time, he gave his bike a bit more throttle, and pulled ahead of the girl, and pulled up at the side of the road adjacent to the alleyway entrance. Putting his bike into neutral, he reached into his jacket pocket, and pulled out a piece of paper. It was nothing more than a petrol receipt shoved into his pocket after his last visit to fill his tank up, but the girl wouldn't know that. He heard the shuffling walk of Courtney Armstrong getting closer, as he pretended to be studying the blank reverse side of the petrol receipt.

As the younger Armstrong daughter approached the area directly between where MadDog was parked and the alleyway, he called out to the girl.

"Excuse me, love, I'm looking for Burnham Street," he said, doing a very good impression of a lost traveler.

"Sorry, I've not heard of it," Courtney replied, her sweet voice not in fitting with her large frame and face, which could only be described as ugly, even by the kindest of people.

MadDog reached into his pocket, making out that he was finding it difficult to retrieve what he was looking for.

"Hold on a minute," he said, getting off his bike. "These damned pockets are so small. I have the name of the building I need to find written down on a piece of paper. Maybe you will have heard of that."

He didn't wait a further moment, as he stood just feet from the young girl. His right hand wrapped itself around her throat, and his left hand covered her mouth, preventing her from screaming, as he pushed her back into the covered area of the alleyway, slamming her body against the brick wall.

"You scream, bitch, you even let out a whimper, and I will mess you up bad," he snarled, his voice clear, even through the slight gap left by the slightly raised helmet visor. He eased the pressure over the girl's mouth, but slightly tightened his grip on her throat.

"Don't hurt me, please," Courtney whispered, the words muffled by MadDog's large hand.

"Oh, don't worry, I won't," he replied. "That's not my job."

Back on the street, Reckon remained where he was, acting as watch-out, while Magill casually parked his van up just in front of MadDog's bike. He got out of the cab and walked to the back and opened the back doors.

MadDog let go of Courtney Armstrong's throat and spun her around by her face, so he now ended up behind her, his hand once again tight around her mouth, and his arm curled around the side of her neck.

Magill looked at the girl and performed a low bow, while sweeping his right arm toward the inside of the van.

"Walk," MadDog instructed, and with no other choice, Courtney did as she was told.

He glanced left and right down the street, and once happy that it was clear of people, he forced his body forward, pushing the girl toward the rear of the van. Using the small metal step at the back of the van, he climbed inside with her and forced her to kneel down. Magill climbed in behind them, grabbing a roll of thick silver tape from a box that had been secured to the inside panel by two elastic bungee cords.

To Magill, ModDog said, "Pass me two cable ties while you are there." Magill grabbed them out of the box and handed them to MadDog, who then told the girl, "Arms behind your back."

He secured the girl's wrists tightly with both cable ties, as Magill ripped off a piece of the sticky tape.

"You said you weren't going to hurt me," she said, a bit too loudly for Magill's liking.

"Trust me, you fat fucker, that will come later," he said and placed the tape over her mouth tightly, then slapped it hard twice with his hand.

191

MadDog gently spun her around on her knees and helped her to sit back, pulling her legs out to allow her as much comfort as possible. For the first time during the whole event, he fully opened his visor and looked at the petrified girl's face.

"Sit still. Don't create any problems for us and you will be fine," he said to her with a gentle voice.

Courtney looked at her assailant and was surprised to see a pair of kind eyes looking at her. She nodded her head, and the tears began to trickle down her cheeks.

MadDog stood up as much as the confines of the van would allow, and without any warning, threw a punch that landed squarely on the midriff of Magill's body. He fell immediately to the floor of the van, struggling to breathe, winded.

"You speak to her, or any other woman disrespectfully again, and I will force feed you my boot, is that clear, you fucking bag of wank?" he asked his gasping unwanted colleague.

Unable to talk, all that Magill could do was nod his head to show MadDog that he understood, before the huge biker decided to hand out some more of his type of justice.

"Good," MadDog said. "Now, get your scrawny fucking body behind the wheel and drive this girl back to the club-house. Do not speed and do not use your mobile while driving. In fact, imagine you are taking your driving test again, because if you give the coppers any reason to stop you, I will give them a reason to transport your broken body to a morgue."

Magill rolled over and got onto all fours in an effort to get up, despite him finding breathing still quite difficult. As MadDog moved past him, he couldn't resist kicking Magill's backside, forcing the kneeling man to hurtle forward, sprawled out on his front. Courtney, knowing it was probably a risky thing to do considering her current situation, kicked out her leg and caught Magill in the ribs with her foot.

MadDog laughed loudly.

"You should have called her a feisty fucker, not a fat fucker," he said, exiting the van and making his way to his bike.

Magill got to his feet, but before leaving the van and angrily slamming the doors firmly shut, he lowered his face to within a few millimetres from Courtney's.

"When these animals have finished with you, I am going to take what is left for a short walk into the woods, and only one of us will be walking back, you ugly fat whore."

Courtney Armstrong cried for the entire duration of the uneventful journey back to the clubhouse of The Nameless Ones.

A Message of Intent

Grant was sat in one of the soft sofas, sending and receiving texts, when Stacker entered the clubhouse. He was rubbing his temple with his fingers and thumbs, and slowly drew them down the side of his face so his first finger and thumb of his right hand met just below his bottom lip, before speaking.

"Boss, we have an unexpected problem."

Grant looked up from his phone. He remained silent as he waited for Stacker to explain the supposed problem.

"MadDog and Reckon have just returned from their little ride out," he continued.

Still there was nothing but a wall of silence from Grant.

"Magill is with them. He said they have a large feisty package in the back of the van."

Now Stacker got the reaction he had been expecting.

Grant jumped to his feet, asking, "Explain what he means by package."

"Err ... Courtney Armstrong boss," Stacker replied.

"You are shitting me!" Grant exclaimed, as he stormed toward the door and out of the clubhouse.

MadDog and Reckon were leaning against the side of Magill's van, looking very proud with themselves as Grant walked out into the daylight. The minute they saw the look on their leader's face, they knew it was misplaced pride. Grant did not say a word as he walked briskly past them and opened the back doors of the van. He briefly looked inside, and shaking his head in disbelief, he slammed the doors shut.

Standing directly in front of the two bikers, Grant began to speak, quietly and slowly at first, but that didn't last more than a few seconds, before he was spitting with the force and anger of each word.

"What part of, 'read the file and await instructions,' was not quite clear enough for you two fuckheads to understand? Which part of Lokie's madness did you insert into your information package that helped you two partially brained pieces of camel shit to think, 'hey fuck, it let's go out and get us a girl'?"

MadDog began to speak, but was halted by Grant as he raised one hand.

"I haven't finished," he stated. The two bikers waited, but no more words came out of the mouth of the now speechless and furious Grant.

"No," he eventually said, "I cannot think of anything else to say."

MadDog now took his chance to explain. "Boss, we went for a ride, just to do a bit of a recce."

"My area of expertise," Reckon said, with pride in his voice.

"An opportunity arose, so we took it, boss," MadDog finished off.

"You just went for a ride, did you?" Grant asked sarcastically. "You just went for a ride ... do a little recce did you?" And yet you took the pickup with you?"

Both bikers took a few seconds to think. MadDog knew

instantly that his lie had held no credibility with Grant, while Reckon was still wondering which parts had been questions, and which were statements.

Grant turned to face Stacker, and lowering his voice, said, "Make sure the garage is empty. I want everyone, except for you and Chaos, in the briefing room … now. When that is done, you and Chaos transport the package to the holding area using the tunnel you built from the garage. Get her prepared, understand?"

"Yes boss," were the only words Stacker said, before quickly moving away to do as he had been told.

Returning his attention to the three instigators of the unsanctioned kidnap, Grant said, "Leave the van where it is, and all three of you go to the briefing room. Do not leave there. In fact, do nothing but sit down and silently discuss a reason why I shouldn't kill each and every one of you."

He returned to the clubhouse as fast as he had left it just a few moments ago, and made his way to his room, slamming the door behind him and letting out a scream of anger and anguish that could be heard all the way to the garage, which was across the car park area.

Fixit looked up from where he had been working on Double D's bike, and said, "Call me psychic if you want, but I think we are all about to be on the receiving end of an ear bashing from hell."

After about thirty minutes, Grant entered the briefing room, where every member of The Nameless Ones—with the exception of Stacker and Chaos—had been sitting in silence for about twenty of those minutes. He made his way to the head of the table, and without sitting down, began to address the group of bikers.

"Many of you will have noticed that I choose not to wear a badge of rank. I have not bestowed upon myself the visual indication of being the president of this club. In the past, I have never been able to hold onto a badge of rank for too long, so I didn't bother with one on this occasion. However, it would seem that some of you need that visual reminder, so as of later today, you will all see that my cut will have had sewn upon it, the president's patch." The group of people listened in complete silence, all looking intently at Grant, except for MadDog and Reckon, who were both looking down at the table top.

"With that patch, will come a change in leadership style—one that is more befitting of my role, one that will see mistakes punished, and one that will see disobedience managed swiftly and brutally. When I brought you all together, I mistakenly thought that your previous military experiences and discipline were still well and truly engrained into you, but clearly this is not the case." He made his way around the table, and stood still between and slightly behind Reckon and MadDog.

"I have always adopted a one-strike-and-out policy, but that policy is no longer applicable. From this point forth, the new policy is one strike," and with those words, he placed his hands on the backs of the heads of the two bikers in front of him, and slammed them simultaneously into the table. The crunching and cracking of their noses as they hit the firm wood floated around the room. He grabbed the necks of the two bleeding bikers, and pulled them backwards, to show off their damaged faces to the rest of the group. Blood trickled down both of their faces.

"This is a warning. Each future mistake will receive an

increasing level of punishment, and if any of you are even thinking that you will fight back if something similar happens to you, think on, because I have a gun in my room that I am more than willing and very capable of using."

There was nothing but silence—no arguments, no sarcasm, no banter—just pure, screaming silence.

"Now, get out," Grant ordered them all. "Feel free to leave if you want, and those who make that decision, take this warning with you: Any payment you have received so far, will be removed from you, your identities will be returned to you, but may have some additional information added that may attract the attention of the police, and if they don't want you, just remember to spend the rest of your lives looking over your shoulders. It is time to get with the program or get off the rollercoaster. I personally couldn't give two flying fucks what you do."

He sat down in his chair, and waited for the room to be vacated.

* * *

"Who are you?" Courtney asked, as she was escorted down the underground tunnel by Stacker and Chaos.

"What have I done? What do you want with me?" she asked again, but received the same response she got to her first question—nothing.

She stopped walking, and turned around to face the two men behind her. For the first time, she saw biker cuts. Stacker and Chaos name patches were etched into her memory banks.

"I don't recognise you as any of The Fortunates. So who are

you?" she asked again.

"We tell you, we kill you," Chaos replied chillingly. "You ask again, we kill you," he added.

"I don't think you have gone to all of this effort, just to kill me," Courtney Armstrong replied bravely.

"You are right. We are hungry, too, and you look like you would sustain us for about a week," Chaos said with an insane look on his face.

Stacker intervened with a few short words, because he just wanted to get this girl locked away in a room, where any noise from her, would not be heard. Down in this tunnel, there was the danger of echoing.

"You will leave this situation alive, as long as your family does the right thing, and the right thing for you to do right now, is shut up."

"What does my family have to do with this?" were the last words Courtney Armstrong said for the rest of that day, as Stacker muffled her screams effectively, with a firm hand across her mouth, as he ripped out one of the girl's earrings.

* * *

The clubhouse bar area was empty, except for Hammer, by the time Grant walked out of the briefing room.

"I'm making sausage and egg banjos all round, boss, if you are interested?" he asked.

"Sounds like a grand plan, bro. How are the troops?" Grant asked.

"Pissed off, angry, some want to kill you, and others want

to shake your hand," he replied. "A typical response from a group of veterans to a bollocking."

"How are the two walking wounded?" he asked, trying not to sound as concerned about the situation as he actually was.

"Surprisingly chipper, boss. I think the fact that I told them that the injured get double portions helped a bit," Hammer replied, smiling a huge beaming grin across his face.

"Any of them planning on leaving?" he asked.

"No, but I think some are planning to hold you down and spin a rear tyre across your face for a few minutes at about sixty miles an hour," Hammer replied still smiling.

"Do I get to live if I eat one of your banjos?" Grant asked finally.

"Oh yes, boss," Hammer said, walking into the kitchen. "You didn't bust my nose!"

Reaching the door of the kitchen, Hammer turned round, as he heard another question from Grant.

"Do you have a maggot I can borrow, bro?"

"In my room," Hammer replied.

"Thanks, I'm going for a ride. Tell the others that I will be back soon, if any of them are even bothered."

※ ※ ※

It was more than an hour, before anyone asked about the whereabouts of Grant. Stacker, his forehead beaded in sweat from his exertions, had emerged from the room below the complex, and after looking in almost every room, he walked into the bar to find most of The Nameless Ones sat around chatting, the remains of egg sandwiches and cups of coffee and tea spread across tables. Hammer was in the process of beginning to tidy the place up and return dirty dishes back to his kitchen.

"Hey, Hammer, have you seen our illustrious leader?" Stacker asked.

"He went for a ride about an hour ago," the biker/chef replied, with his hands filled with a precariously balanced pile of plates and cups.

"A ride to where?" Stacker asked.

"No idea," Hammer replied, heading back to the kitchen. "He borrowed my sleeping bag and went. Told me to tell anyone who asked that he would be back soon."

Stacker hid his immediate concerns caused by this news. He had become increasingly worried about Grant. Maybe all the hurt he had been through over the past two to three years was now proving to be too much for one man.

* * *

Sticking to the main routes, motorways and major A-roads, Grant had ridden for just over eight hours, when he finally arrived at his destination. On the way, he had stopped on three occasions, but only for fuel, to have a smoke, and on one occasion, to grab a coffee of which he only drank half of the cup's contents. He now sat on his idling bike, looking at the white lighthouse in front of him, illuminated in the darkness of the early hours by the bike's headlamp.

The far Southwest tip of Cornwall had been a favourite holiday destination for him and his family for years. Pendeen lighthouse and its rugged coast had always been his place to go for peace and tranquillity—a place he could be alone in his thoughts. His wife had once said to him that this was the place where he found spirituality.

He steered the bike to the right and carefully manoeuvred his way down the wide pathway, which was strewn with large rocks and natural potholes, until he reached a stony parking area. Parking his bike so it faced the ocean, he got off it and stretched his aching body, before reaching for the sleeping that he had strapped to the back seat at the start of his journey. Making his way over a stile and climbing down large rocks, he found himself at the top of a steep grassy drop down to the ocean's shore. He rolled out the sleeping bag, climbed inside it and propped himself up against a large stone. Zipping the bag up to his neck to keep out the early morning chill, he sat and looked out over the ocean, listening to the sound of its waves crashing against the rocks below. *His wife had been sort of right*, he thought. This was where he found his heaven, which he continued to gaze at, until he fell into a peaceful sleep.

Dawn broke and Grant slowly opened his eyes, as the warming rays of the emerging sun cast a glow over him. He clambered out of the sleeping bag and immediately felt the chill of the morning. Leaving his temporary bed where it lay, he walked carefully down the dew covered slope. As he reached the bottom, he came to an abrupt stop and held his breath. The grey seal sat on the large rocks, just feet from the water, stared at him.

Once again, he heard the wise words of his wife, spoken to him the first time he had found himself in this very situation.

Approach it carefully, love. You need to learn that sometimes to get what you want, you need to change the way you handle the situation.

On that occasion, he had listened to her and managed to get within a few feet of the seal. He decided to listen to her again.

When he was little more than four feet from the seal, he lowered himself to a sitting position on a flat rock. He looked into the deep large eyes of the animal, who did not look away. He felt no fear from it, just curiosity and, as daft as it sounded, a connection between them.

"Do I walk away?" he asked quietly, speaking to the seal, but mentally asking the question to his dead wife.

"Do I leave a friend? Is that your advice? You know what that will do to me," he said, his words spoken gently.

For thirty minutes, he and the seal sat and shared this moment, before without warning, it slid from the rock and disappeared into the waves.

Change the way you handle the situation, the words repeated themselves, over and over again, inside his head.

He climbed to the top of the grassy cliff, rolled up the sleeping bag and walked back to his bike. Retrieving his mobile from his jacket pocket, he made a call. He had not spoken to this friend he had met through his wife for years, and the conversation lasted almost an hour. Returning the mobile to his pocket, he smiled and took one last look out over the shimmering ocean. The bobbing head of a grey seal could be seen about thirty feet out. It could have been any seal, but Grant decided that it was the same one that he had just made a connection with.

"Thanks, Jay," he yelled.

"Now it's time to get back into the action and get this job back on track," he said to himself.

* * *

Despite riding for about sixteen hours, broken only by a few hours' sleep, and his time spent in the company of an aquatic animal, Grant rode into the yard of the clubhouse with vigour. Stacker had quickly opened the gates to let him in, and just as quickly closed them again, so he could seek an explanation from Grant about his sudden disappearance.

"Where the fuck did you go?" he asked, watching Grant dismount his bike stiffly.

"Had to clear my head," Grant replied smiling. "I also needed to reach out to a seal, and a person you will never meet."

"What?" Stacker exclaimed. "Did you say a fucking seal?"

Grant waved his hand, swatting away Stacker's question.

"Doesn't matter, all will become clear."

He walked toward the garage with Stacker in pursuit. The garage was empty.

"Where is everyone?" Grant asked.

"Most are lounging around the bar; others are packing up their stuff. They think it's all over, Grant," Stacker responded.

"Never mind. Come on, let's take advantage of the opportunity and get downstairs."

Walking and talking as they proceeded through the underground walkway, Stacker found it difficult to keep up with Grant. Entering the large cavernous room, Stacker eventually grabbed Grant by the shoulder and spun him around.

"Enough, Grant. Tell me what the fuck is going on, and please, tell me why you are so hyper?"

Grant didn't answer any of the two questions.

"Where's the girl?" he asked.

"Prepared, as you ordered," Stacker replied.

He walked over to the corner of the room and pulled aside a sheet of thick industrial plastic. Holding it open, he extended his arm into the area concealed behind. Grant could not believe what he was looking at.

"I said prepare, as in, get her ready. What the fuck have you done?" he asked.

Lying face up and strapped to a framework of wooden struts, Courtney Armstrong was pale faced, and on first inspection, she looked dead. A frothy line of saliva extended from the corner of her mouth down to her chin. Her eyes, despite her situation, remained open, the pupils dilated and the eyeballs rolled upwards. She lay totally naked, her ample body on full display to both men.

Grant stooped down to see beneath the body of the girl. The sight of the thick, hard branches of bamboo, congealed in a mixture of dry and wet blood, shocked him, despite the fact that this torture was one that he had devised.

"Your research into that particular bamboo was spot on, mate. Grows at a spectacular rate and is as strong as steel. Nothing gets in its way," Stacker said with a hint of pride in his voice.

"How is … why is she not screaming? She must be in agony," Grant said, lowering himself even more, so he was able to see that the tips of the bamboo shoots were growing into the body of the Armstrong girl.

"Mogadon," Stacker replied. "Got it from the medic."

Grant shook his head in disbelief, as he tried to imagine the conversation between Stacker and Double D, where one had asked for some Mogadon, and the other had willingly given it without question.

"It works really well, puts her in a kind of zombie state," Stacker began to explain.

"I know what fucking Mogadon is," Grant replied loudly. "I worked in prisons for years, bro. Who the fuck injected her? Please tell me it wasn't you? In fact, please don't tell me it was Double D either."

"Tablets, dude," Stacker replied, taken aback by Grant's reaction. "We crushed them and mixed them in some food. The one thing that girl cannot turn down, is the offer of food."

"We need to get her off there, now," Grant told Stacker.

"That is going to take some doing, bro," Stacker replied. "It took some effort for me and Chaos to keep her still while we strapped her down, but now that she is impaled on that bamboo … well, we are gonna need a bit more manpower."

Grant ran through names of the members of The Nameless Ones, trying to think who could be most trusted.

"Probably going to need the medic down here, too, to patch up the wounds," Stacker added, breaking Grant's thoughts.

"Go to the clubhouse and firstly, tell all those who are packing up to stop," Grant ordered. "Secondly, bring Chaos, Double D, Ordnance and Shovel back down here with you."

Stacker didn't move, but stood looking at Grant, his mouth slightly open and his forehead creased, as if confused by what Grant had just told him to do.

"Move it, soldier, before I kick your sorry ass back to the clubhouse myself," Grant shouted.

Stacker turned on his heel and left Grant alone with the girl.

Grant swept aside the plastic privacy sheeting, and knelt down next to Courtney Armstrong's head. He wiped away the sliver of spittle from her mouth and chin with the sleeve of his jacket, and stroked her cheek.

"Just one more thing I need you to do for me, and then we will patch you up," he said gently, getting no response from her.

He spent another ten minutes with Courtney, talking quietly to her, even though he suspected she could not comprehend one word of what he said. Hearing the footsteps and voices of people approaching, he stood and walked out of the makeshift torture chamber, allowing the plastic to close behind him. The five people came to a stop directly in front of him.

"What you see from this point, you discuss with nobody. You do as you are told, without question or judgement, is that clear?" Grant asked.

Five heads nodded in acknowledgement of the question.

He turned and pulled back the plastic sheeting. He heard a couple of gasps from behind him.

"Holy fuck," Shovel said.

The only two not to react, were Chaos and Stacker, as it was them who were responsible for the girl being in the state she was in.

"Is she dead?" Double D asked.

"Amazingly, no," Grant replied. "But she is not in a good place."

Grant instructed Double D to move a table away from the wall into the centre of the room, while he and the others loosened the straps. The makeshift shelf she was secured to stood about four feet off the floor. The space beneath it had given the bamboo the room they needed to grow thickly. Once completely removed, Grant took hold of the girl's hands, and Ordnance grabbed her ankles. Stacker, Chaos and Shovel arranged themselves around her body and placed their hands beneath her.

"Lift," Grant ordered, and together, they all began to pull the limp body upwards. A strange squeaking noise could be heard, as the bamboo shoots slowly slid out of the flesh. The tops of the bamboo could now be seen clearly, sharpened to a deadly point. Grant had to assume that this had been done by Stacker, as he was the only one who had access to them during their growing process.

Having moved the table as instructed, Double D returned to the corner of the room and held open the plastic as wide as she could, allowing the men to carefully carry the girl over to the table. They lifted her slightly higher, to get her over the height of the table, and as they were about to lay her down upon it, Grant issued the instruction to lay her face down.

With much effort, the five men laid her initially face up, and then rolled and shuffled her, so she was eventually face down, her head lying to one side, giving full view to the wounds caused by the strong fast-growing bamboo. Holes going into the flesh of her back, shoulders and legs to varying depths—between a centimetre and almost an inch—were congealed in blood, evidence of the body's repair system attempting to battle against the persistent growth of the unforgiving bamboo.

Shovel stood back, and half-concealed his face with one hand, which he used to rub his forehead, his eyes firmly closed.

"Get the camera, Stacker," Grant said.

Stacker did as he was told, without question, and returned to the table.

"Take a few photographs, but make sure that you can clearly see her face and her wounds," Grant instructed.

Once again, Stacker did as he was told.

"Can I do my job now?" Double D asked.

"Yes, please do," Grant replied. Double D was sure she detected something resembling regret in his voice.

He took the others over to the far end of the room, where the opening of the corridor was located.

"Gentlemen," he said quietly. "Return to the clubhouse and get everyone together in the briefing room. Do not let any of them leave. Let them know that I will be there soon, and will explain everything with absolute transparency."

They walked away, leaving Grant alone with his thoughts. *Well not absolute transparency*, he thought.

He returned to where Double D was now starting to clean the wounds on the body of Courtney Armstrong.

"Is she going to be okay?" he asked.

"Well, let me think about that," Double D responded angrily. "She has at least a dozen open wounds, she has been bleeding for God knows how long, and she has been doped up on enough Mogadon to floor a horse."

"Yeah," Grant replied flippantly. "I have eyes, but I don't have the medical knowledge … so how about just answering my goddamn question."

"Probably," Double D replied curtly. "What are the photographs for? Your memory album?"

"No," Grant responded. "They are to prove our intent."

With perfect timing, Stacker walked over to where the pair were stood, and said, "Ready to send, boss."

Grant nodded his head and Stacker pressed the send button on the mobile.

He walked back over to Courtney Armstrong, and unaware whether or not she could make out what he was saying, he whispered, "Time to reconnect with nature, bitch."

He looked over at the people in the room and ordered them to place the girl back from where they had moved her.

"And place her so her head is where her feet were this time, and strap the bitch down nice and tight."

* * *

Kelvin Armstrong shifted in his armchair, trying to get comfortable. The burn wounds made this as impossible as always. Just as he found a position that caused him the least amount of discomfort and pain, his mobile vibrated with a buzzing noise, causing it to move slightly across the highly varnished dark wood table top. Three times in succession, it made the annoying noise.

"Fucking hell, what now?" an exasperated Kelvin Armstrong asked, as he leaned forward to retrieve his mobile.

Cutter

E veryone was waiting for Grant, as he walked into the briefing room, and he immediately felt the animosity toward him.

He walked to the wall where all the papers and photographs were still pinned, instead of to the head of the table, as most of the room's occupants had expected. He proceeded to rip down the pieces of paper, leaving only the photographs of the Armstrong family.

He turned around to face his audience, and began to speak.

"Right, I owe you all an explanation, and to offer some clarity, so we can make some forward progress. However, firstly, I offer you my apologies." He immediately had their attention and could feel the atmosphere in the room change.

"Too right, you fucking do," Chalky exclaimed.

"Let the man speak," Syco retorted.

"Thank you, Syco," Grant said. "But Chalky is right." He paused and was glad that silence prevailed, so he continued speaking.

"My recent absence was necessary. I had to clear my head, get my thoughts organised, re-evaluate what we are doing and how we are to go about doing it. The desired outcome has not changed one bit, but the method has changed considerably.

The thing is, I need your trust, even more because most of you will have no idea why you are doing what I ask you to do, and that is for your own protection. I need to provide you all, well most of you, with plausible deniability for when this is all over." He paused yet again, giving everyone an opportunity to ask questions, but nobody broke the silence.

"The Nameless Ones are going to be exactly what they appear to be—bikers. And that means no rules, no areas we cannot ride into. Your targets remain the same, but I need them to be picked up when, and only when, I say. Stacker is the store man, so all deliveries will go directly to him. He will be ably assisted by Chaos. Onward transport and disposal will be headed up by Fixit and Shovel, with Magill driving the van. Syco, you will be the contact with Shuffler, and I need you to reach out to him over the next day or two. As for the rest of you, when you are not collecting your targets, I want you to be Nameless Ones. I want you to ride out, cause some concerns and have some fun … and all of that will be done wearing our colours. If you are picked up by the coppers, you will give them nothing but your name, your number and your club rank, along with a large dose of attitude."

A loud cheer went up in the room, along with fists being pumped into the air, some of them wearing the devil's horns.

Grant pointed at two of the photographs on the wall, and said to the group, "Chalky, Reckon, you will go with Syco and get these two. Prep your bikes for a ride out tomorrow. Stacker, stay behind for a few minutes, please."

The three bikers identified by Grant were the first out of the door, heading toward the garage to get their bikes ready for the hunt. They all knew that Alfie and Patrick Armstrong were not going to be easy prey.

Stacker stayed in his seat and waited for the room to empty. When it was just himself and Grant, he nodded his head in Grant's direction in an approving way.

"Nice, brother. You have them all back on board," he said.

"Yeah," Grant agreed. "Now we just have to keep them there, and keep them from going out of control."

"Can I ask, why did you place the girl back and turn her around?" Stacker asked.

"Killing them isn't enough anymore. They have to suffer, just like those three little girls," Grant replied.

Grant sat on the chair adjacent to Stacker.

"I need a favour, mate, and I need it quick," he said, moving on from the statement he had just made like it had been nothing more consequential than giving directions to a lost driver.

"Whatever you need," Stacker replied.

"I need you to construct me a room in a corner of the cellar room. It needs lots of plug points and a lockable door, and finally, a long work bench the length of the whole room. Think you can do that in the next day or two?" he asked.

"Yeah, what's it for?" Stacker replied.

"Who, and what it is for, is need-to-know, brother, and sorry, but you don't need to know," Grant responded, hoping his friend did not take umbrage.

"Suits me, man. The less I know, the less jail time I may end up doing," Stacker said laughing.

"Plausible deniability, my friend," Grant responded, slapping Stacker on the shoulder, as he stood up and walked out of the room.

* * *

Kelvin Armstrong stared at the screen of his mobile, unable to comprehend what he was seeing at first. The images of one of his daughters lying naked, face down with bloody holes in her back, would not compute in his brain for the first few seconds. He flicked through the four images that he had been sent from an undisclosed number, and by the time he stopped, the only question somersaulting through his head was, *is she alive or not?*

Using two fingers, he zoomed in on one of the pictures that showed Courtney's face, and saw a small tear falling from her right eye. Returning the image back to its original size, which allowed him to once again see all her wounds, he said, "Fuck me, this was done to her alive."

His thought was confirmed by the text beneath the image.

DO THE RIGHT THING OR SHE DIES.

He selected his favourite numbers, and pressed on one of the names. The phone was answered almost immediately.

"Patrick, I need you over at my place, now," Kelvin said to his cousin.

"Yeah okay, give me an hour, cuz," Patrick replied.

"Fuckin' now," Kelvin screamed. He ended the call, confident that his cousin Patrick Armstrong, the biggest animal the Armstrongs had in their family, would be knocking on his door very soon.

He stared at one of the images again, and said in a whispered voice, "You are dead, whoever you are, who did this. You are fucking dead."

* * *

Grant and Stacker were walking toward the hidden stairway that would take them to the room below, when a voice from the bar area called out to Grant.

"Stranger at the gate, Nameless." It was Fixit, who must have been walking across the courtyard as someone had announced their arrival.

"The person I don't need to know about?" Stacker asked.

"Too early. He ain't expected until tomorrow evening at the earliest," Grant replied.

"Them fucking coppers again," Stacker stated.

"He ain't no copper, fellas," Fixit interjected.

"Stacker, you go make a start on what I asked for. Fixit, introduce me to our unexpected visitor," Grant said, following the club mechanic out of the clubhouse.

Once outside, Fixit jogged to the gate and opened it up wide enough for an almost all black Kawasaki Z1000 R edition to speed through the gates and race toward the end of the short line of bikes still parked outside the clubhouse. Grant and Fixit watched on, as the rider came to an abrupt halt, sliding the backend of the bike around, and then rolling it backwards, through the rising smoke created by the dramatic wheel skid, to line it up with the other bikes. The green 'Z' design flashes on its front end and rear raised tail stood out from the matt black paintwork.

The rider, wearing a plain all black one-piece leather suit, black helmet with no insignia of any kind and a black visor, still in its closed position, dismounted from the bike and stood next to it. He did not walk toward Grant and Fixit. A couple of the other guys popped their heads out from the garage and watched the proceedings, although most of them were just admiring the new bike in the courtyard.

Grant was the first to break the stand-off and walked over to the stranger, stopping about four feet away from him.

"Nice entrance. Now, are you going to introduce yourself?" he asked.

The stranger slowly removed his gloves, before lifting off his helmet to reveal his identity. He was a couple of inches over six-foot tall. Dark brown hair that ended just above the collar of his racing suit, sat on top of a well-groomed face. Grant estimated his age to be late twenties to early thirties, and for a reason he couldn't put his finger on, he instantly didn't like him.

The stranger smiled, a well-maintained row of teeth shined toward Grant.

"I was told you were expecting me," he said to Grant.

"Son, I only ever expect one of two things. Trouble or shit. Now, you don't smell like shit ..."

The stranger responded with two words, not allowing Grant to finish what he was about to say.

"I'm Cutter."

Grant looked confused.

"And you say I am expecting you?" he asked the stranger.

"Yeah, I am your stand-in. Magill said he told you all about me."

"The ex-merc?" Grant asked.

"I would prefer to say, taking a short break to help you boys out," Cutter replied in a cocky manner.

Grant held out his arms at full length.

"Welcome to my world of steel. Let's see how long you last, son," he said, sounding for the first time like the president of a motorcycle club.

The two rows of perfectly set teeth gritted together as, for the second time, he heard Grant call him son.

"Please call me Cutter, but don't ever call me son again," the young, clean-cut biker replied.

"Or what?" Grant challenged.

Cutter's brain said, *Or I will rip your throat open and shit inside the hole you fucking skin crawler.* His mouth said, "Or I ride back out of here and find a war that pays better money than you."

Grant closed the distance between them and held out his hand, which Cutter took and shook.

"I'm Grant, but they all call me Nameless, or boss," Grant said, forcing a smile onto his face.

"Nameless seems appropriate," Cutter responded. Grant was sure he detected a trace of something distantly familiar in the lad's words. Unable to place it, he cast it out of his head, and placing a guiding hand on Cutter's shoulder, he said, "Come, let me show you the clubhouse and then you can stash away your gear."

* * *

Inside the clubhouse, Cutter asked if he minded if he stashed away his gear first, and then have a drink and a talk.

217

"No problem. Down the corridor," Grant said, indicating the direction with a pointed finger. "Find an empty room and claim it as yours."

Cutter made his way down the short corridor wondering where Grant's room was. He knew better than to ask that question, as it was likely to produce more questions and activate suspicious minds, rather than answers. The fourth room down on his left was unlocked and did not look to be occupied. He walked in and firmly closed the door behind him. Taking off the large rucksack that was beginning to cut into his shoulders and dig into the small of his back, he stretched out and put it onto the floor and against the closed door. He inspected the sparse furniture in the room, disappointed to find that both the small set of drawers, or the larger locker, could not be locked.

He reached into one of the angled pockets in the jacket section of his one-piece, pulling out a small, but extremely sharp knife, and he pulled the blade out of the handle. Returning to the bed, he pulled off the sheets and blanket, throwing them onto the floor. Lifting up the mattress, he sliced an eight-inch opening into the underside of the mattress, and lay back on the bed, slashed side up. Deciding to keep the rucksack up against the door as a bit of barrier, he removed a number of items from inside it and secreted them away into the inner part of the mattress. Inside, he put two pistols—the first a Glock .45 caliber G.A.P and the other, a brown Desert Eagle—four boxes of ammunition, three more knives, a push dagger held in a leather sheath, a SOG Seal knife 2000, this one housed inside a black nylon carry sheath, and finally, his pride and joy, a SOG Fixation knife, one of the finest weapons ever made. The last two items were identical—two lengths of garrotting wire with small plastic grips at the ends.

He turned the mattress back over and padded it over and over again, finally stepping back to ensure that no bulky items were bulging, causing detectable lumps in it. Satisfied that for now his trade tools were sufficiently hidden away, he made the bed, returning it to its original state. The final thing he did before leaving the room was to quickly change out of his leathers and into a pair of jeans, a T-shirt and a lightweight leather jacket.

He threw the rucksack on the top of the bed, and made his way back the clubhouse bar.

Grant had an empty glass set up on the bar, awaiting Cutter when he got there.

"What's your poison?" he asked, ending the question sharply, when he realised he was going to call him son again.

"A brandy would be good," Cutter replied.

"Nice choice, something we have in common already," Grant replied back.

"Whisky makes me feisty, but brandy makes me randy," Cutter said.

Grant paused pouring the drinks into the glasses on the bar, and looked directly at Cutter.

"That is fucking spooky. I used to say those exact words when I was a kid. Maybe late teens. I used it as a chat-up line to get into a bird's knickers."

"Did it ever work?" Cutter asked.

Grant continued, pouring the drinks. "Not as far as I can recollect," he answered and began to laugh.

Cutter raised his glass into the air, neither laughing, nor smiling. "A toast to those women who saw through your cheap chat-up line."

Grant raised his glass in response, adding, "And to those lucky whores who didn't." Grant laughed for a short while more, before drinking his shot of brandy in one gulp.

Cutter had finished his while Grant had been making his toast, and had already poured himself another. He drank this one slower, using the glass as a defensive implement to hide the anger that was fighting to show itself all over his face, hiding it from Grant, who was once again looking at him quizzically, before pouring himself another drink.

"Why don't you take a walk across to our garage and introduce yourself? I will join you in a few minutes," Grant said to the new arrival.

"Yeah, good idea. Will you be getting my cut ready to present to me during those few minutes?"

Cutter asked with a wry smile.

Grant raised his glass, before bringing it back down to his mouth and emptying it with one gulp.

"You have to earn that, son," he responded.

Cutter slammed his glass back down onto the bar. He looked up and saw Grant's reaction.

"Oops, sorry. One too many drinks for so early in the day. I don't know my own strength," he said quickly. Inside, the anger that was building up was almost impossible for him to hide.

* * *

Kelvin Armstrong sat in his chair looking intently at his

cousin, who in turn was staring at the image on the mobile that Kelvin had handed to him.

"Any idea who is behind this?" he asked.

Kelvin simply shook his head.

"What do they mean, do the right thing?"

"No idea," Kelvin responded.

"You must have some idea," Patrick replied.

"How many enemies do you think I, and this family as a whole, have built up over the years?" Kelvin retorted angrily.

"None that are capable of doing anything like this," Patrick replied.

"So they should be easier to find," Kelvin said. "Now, go find them and don't come back until you have."

The large man gently placed the phone on the table that stood between him and his cousin, and stood up. His immense frame seemed to completely fill the room.

"I will do as you ask, Kelvin, because you are family, and I respect your position as the head of this family. But if you ever speak to me like that again, I will snap your neck, rip off your crispy little head and feed it to my Dobermans. Is that fucking clear?" he said.

Kelvin Armstrong showed no fear, whatsoever. Reaching behind the cushion that supported his seated position, he pulled out an old military 9mm Browning pistol. He pointed directly at Patrick's groin.

"Before you ever get near my neck or crispy little head, I would have blown your ballsack to kingdom come. Is that fucking clear to you, cousin?"

Patrick did not respond, but simply walked out of the room and the house. At that moment, he had no idea that he would find the people he was looking for quicker than he ever thought possible.

Kelvin picked up his mobile and sent a text.

New enemy on the horizon. Whole family at risk. Beware of any approaches.

* * *

Michael Armstrong was sat in his cell, talking with his brother, Harry, when the mobile vibrated silently in his pocket.

"Keep an eye out, bruv," he instructed his brother.

Harry stood in the doorway and casually looked around the open atrium area of the wing. It was virtually empty. Only the new guy was visible, and he was sat at one of the tables at the other side of the atrium.

"All clear," he said to Michael.

Michael read the text message from his father, closed down the screen and placed the mobile back into his pocket.

"Do you know something, bruv?" he asked Harry. "Every time I use this phone, I cannot get it out of my head that it has been up your arse."

"Fuck off," Harry replied. "Who was the text from?"

"The old fella. Seems like he has made more enemies, wants us to be on the lookout for any interest in the family," Michael answered.

Harry returned his attention to the new arrival on the therapeutic unit.

Really, he thought silently.

Shuffler looked over in the direction of Michael Arm-

222

strong's cell, and seeing Harry stood in the doorway, nodded his head in his direction and smiled.

Harry nodded back in acknowledgement, and started to slowly walk over to where Shuffler was sat.

"Be back soon, bruv," he said quietly to Michael.

* * *

Cutter casually walked around the garage and introduced himself to all who were present, which was everyone, with the exception of Hammer, Chalky and Syco. Magill had quickly jumped into his van and left the garage within minutes of seeing Cutter walk in. He did a quick high-five with the new member of The Nameless Ones, saying, "Speak later, bro. Got a job that needs doing."

Cutter was much more relaxed about the face-to-face with Magill, than Magill was, who obviously did not want to be around, in case he gave something away about his relationship with this *stranger*.

He asked Fixit if he didn't mind giving a bike a quick once-over. Fixit said he would, despite the fact that he thought the bike appeared to be almost brand new.

"So, is this everyone?" Cutter was asking Fixit, when Grant walked in.

"Everything all right?" Grant called over to Cutter.

"Yeah, cool," Cutter called back. "Just asking if this was everyone. Seems like a small crew."

"Everyone who you need to know about at the moment," Grant replied. "You will meet the others as and when you need to." Grant was still being very cautious around the newest member of his team.

Cutter coolly nodded his head, as if to say that he understood, really knowing that he had to win the confidence of Grant, before he could do anything else.

"Anything I can do?" he asked.

"Just settle in and bide your time," Grant replied, at the same time thinking, *while I use that time to work you out.*

"No problem," Cutter responded. "Do you have a problem with me going out for a ride to get to know the area?"

"You have no colours. You are a free man, so go where you like," Grant answered.

"So, a patch imprisons me, does it?" Cutter asked sarcastically.

"No," Grant replied without a second thought. "It makes you mine, an asset, a piece of property." There was no smile on Grant's face to indicate that he was joking.

Cutter walked toward the garage exit. As he passed Grant, he slowed his pace and leaned in toward him.

"Let me be involved. I am very good at what I do," he whispered.

He walked to his bike, and after a few minutes spent putting on his gloves and helmet, he rode his bike to the gate. He didn't bother asking anyone to open or close the gate for him, doing it for himself, to prevent any further conversations with anyone.

Grant watched Cutter ride out of the complex and close the gate behind him, not bothering to slide the locking bar back into its securing position.

"Yeah, I wonder what it is that you are so good at?" Grant asked himself quietly.

Walking back to the clubhouse, he shouted toward nobody in particular, "Someone lock that fucking gate."

* * *

Harry Armstrong sat himself down at the table on the opposite side to Shuffler.

"Hi, I'm Harry. Thought I would introduce myself."

"Shuffler," was the response, as Shuffler held out an open hand across the table, which Harry took and shook.

"Strange name. Is it a nickname or something?" Harry asked innocently.

"Yeah, something like that," Shuffler replied.

Harry was used to people being cagey in prison when they first started to engage in conversation with people they didn't know, so he continued unperturbed.

"So, what's your angle then?" he asked.

"Don't know what you mean," replied Shuffler, who knew exactly what the Armstrong brother meant.

"Why are you here?" Harry asked, and before Shuffler could respond, he said, "And don't tell me any bollocks about seeking treatment or wanting help. Everyone on this unit has a personal reason for being here."

Shuffler sat silently looking over the table at Harry Armstrong.

"Well?" Harry asked after a few second of silence.

"Well, you told me not to give you any bollocks about wanting treatment and help," Shuffler replied.

"Oh, you are a sharp 'un," Harry replied laughing.

"So what's your angle?" Shuffler asked.

"Tell you what, pal. Why don't you come on over to my brother's cell, and I will make you a cuppa and get the biscuits out. I'll intro you to my brother, Michael, and we can get to know each better," Harry replied with a smile.

Shuffler looked hesitant.

"You need friends in this place, mate. Not everyone has an angle. Some of them are real proper nut jobs," Harry said, feeling the man's reluctance.

Shuffler stood and let Harry lead the way to his brother's cell. Harry walked straight in, but Shuffler hung around in the doorway.

"Come in, mate," Harry said. "Michael, this is Shuffler. He's new on the unit."

Michael Armstrong stood up from where he had been laying on his bed, and held out a bent arm, the hand held open and upright, in Shuffler's direction. Shuffler gripped it in the traditional biker's handshake style without hesitation or thought, as if it was a natural thing for him to do, which, of course, it was.

Shuffler spent the next hour or so passing the time of day with the two Armstrong brothers, drinking their tea and helping himself to almost the entire packet of biscuits they had opened in his honour. A few questions were asked, but none that proved difficult to answer with made up responses. He remained on his guard throughout the whole time and, not wanting to raise any suspicions at this early stage, asked nothing of the Armstrongs.

He left their cell and returned to his own, confident that he had not raised any suspicions.

Michael Armstrong gave it a few minutes, before retrieving the mobile from his pocket once again, and sending a text to his father.

Newcomer on the wing. No concerns at moment. His tattoos would suggest he is an ex-con, ex-military and a biker.

Kelvin Armstrong read the text message from his son, and immediately sent one to his cousin Patrick.

Check out any problems between us and the Fortunates.

It was a few minutes, before he got a response from his cousin.

Will do. Shall I check out the new gang of bikers who are in the old snooker hall building?

What new bike gang? Kelvin Armstrong mentally asked himself.

* * *

After riding around the local area for about thirty or so minutes, Cutter headed off in the direction of the territory that belonged to the Satan's Fortunates. It had always made him laugh at the way that bikers thought they owned territory and could have control over other bike gangs passing through it. A bunch of disorganised, alcohol soaked, gangbanging wankers, was what he thought about bike gangs, but he was also aware of their prevalence toward violence, to sort out any problem or issue.

He had parked up his bike in a secure car park about a half-mile walk from the Fortunates' clubhouse, and secured his helmet to the bike, happy that it would be safe enough for a short time. As he walked down the street, he tucked away his gloves inside his jacket and zipped it up high enough just to secure them into place against his body and keep them out of sight.

On the opposite side of the road to the Fortunates' clubhouse, and about fifty yards away, was an old café that had made an attempt to look more welcoming by placing three tables and half a dozen chairs outside the café front on the pavement. As the café was dark and filthy inside, Cutter decided to order a coffee and drink it outside, rather than sit inside at the window, where his view would have been hindered by the filth and grease on the inside of it.

He sat and observed the comings and goings of the clubhouse as he drank his coffee, which was better than expected, so he ordered another. His observations told him that the clubhouse was a busy place with, as expected, bikers arriving and leaving it mainly in at least pairs. He also saw plenty of skanky looking women, most of them scantily dressed, and the occasional visitor who did not meet any of these descriptions, but were non-descript at the same time.

It was while before he was distracted by the café waitress when ordering his second coffee, and he missed the arrival of Patrick Armstrong.

Mister Deception

G rant was awoken the morning, after the arrival of Cutter, by his mobile beeping, the noise that indicated that he had received a text message. Through bleary eyes he read the message.

Should be with you sometime this PM. Mr Deception.

Quickly rising from his bed, Grant spent a minimal amount of time in the shower block. Just enough time, in fact, to splash his face and armpits with cold water, spray on a bit of deodorant and brush his teeth.

On his way back to his room, he knocked on Stacker's door.

"Is that office space I asked for finished?" he shouted.

A half-awake voice answered back.

"What fucking time is it?" And then, "Nearly."

"Nearly isn't good enough, and it's time to get the fuck out of bed and get it done," Grant responded.

Grant heard the creaking of Stacker's door opening as his banged shut.

Dressing quickly, so quickly, in fact, that it was only when he zipped up his jeans, that he realised he had inadvertently gone commando. Not wanting to waste time taking his jeans off to put on underwear, he shrugged it off and slipped on a T-shirt.

Back in the corridor, he once again banged on Stacker's door.

"I'm still washing," came Stacker's voice from the washroom.

"You fucking RAF guys take your time," Grant called out, as he walked past the washroom to see Stacker in the middle of having a shave. "You ponce," he said smiling. Stacker responded by raising one finger of the hand that wasn't holding the razor.

"Join me downstairs when you are done preening, but tell the boys and girl to go for a ride this morning. See if they are interested in introducing themselves to the Fortunates, however, I want the two new packages picked up today."

"Colours off?" Stacker asked.

"No, full parade colours and if they feel the need, they can demonstrate to our hosts that The Nameless Ones are here to stay for awhile." Grant continued to walk down the corridor and into the bar area. Only then, did he realise how early it was when he saw that the kitchen was empty. Stacker was not going to be happy. This would be the first time in history that a RAF guy was up, before breakfast was fully prepared for him.

* * *

Bradley picked up his cup of coffee and raised it up to his mouth. The coffee that entered his mouth was cold and bitter, so he spat it back into the cup. He was dishevelled and bleary-eyed, having spent the entire night in his office, painstakingly going through the Warriner girl's case files. A4 sheets of paper lay all over the floor around and on top of his desk. A notebook lay next to his right hand. His scrawled handwriting had filled at least half a dozen pages with notes.

His tired mind could not get away from the one over-whelming thought that had developed during the many hours of trawling through the evidence of the case. The actual investigation had been minimal. It was as if every member of the investigation team for both crimes—the murders of the three young girls and the attack of Kelvin Armstrong—hadn't done much work, because they appeared so straight forward. Although the murder case remained open, it may as well have been closed. Everyone who had been involved, assumed that they had been done by the Armstrong family, but there was no evidence to tie them to the crime, and anyway, Kelvin had paid a good enough price. Justice had been paid.

Nobody liked working with Bradley, and for one good reason. He was a stickler for detail, for it was detail that solved a case and got a conviction—words that he was famous for around the station. But Bradley just knew that, in this case especially, things just didn't add up.

For a start, the Armstrongs were not master criminals and were not capable of leaving no evidence. Almost every single one of them had done time over the years. He knew that, because he had put most of them away, and in every single case, it was evidence such as fingerprints, footprints, and on one occasion, DNA, that had convicted them. Murder was a huge step up from their usual drug dealing, robbery and intimidation.

The new bike gang was also preying on his mind. The members weren't like gangs members he had dealt with before. These were not a bunch of misfits who had come together to party and earn from petty crime. This lot was organised, despite their efforts to appear otherwise, and that leader of theirs was too clever for his own good.

During the night, Bradley had made a number of calls to old contacts in various crime agencies. He had not been able to dig up one single fact about The Nameless Ones.

He stood up and poured himself a fresh coffee from the percolator that stood on the window sill. He looked out of the grimy window as he poured the strong black liquid down his throat, and then waited for the caffeine to kick in.

He came to the decision that Mr. David Warriner and Mr. Nameless were going to get a visit that day.

* * *

Using the hidden stairs, Stacker entered the clubhouse's basement. The first thing that hit his senses, were the screams and groans of pain coming from behind the plastic sheeting. The second thing, was how easily Grant seemed to be able to ignore them.

"We have to quieten her down, Grant," Stacker said.

Grant didn't say a word in response, but simply walked over to where the agonising screams were coming from, swept back the plastic sheeting and punched Courtney square in the face. The girl immediately fell unconscious.

"How's the crew this morning?" Grant asked, giving a

nonchalant shrug as he appeared from behind the plastic screening.

Stacker was taken aback by what he had just witnessed, but replied, saying, "Throwing platefuls of breakfast down their necks like it's their last ever meal. The three who have to pick up the packages are getting themselves organised."

"Good, good," Grant replied, his thoughts clearly elsewhere.

"What's the time?" he asked, realising that in his haste this morning, he had not put on his watch.

"It's seven-forty-five. Is everything okay?" Stacker replied.

"Yeah yeah, I just wanna check up on Shuffler, make sure he is okay, yer know."

Stacker didn't respond. He was becoming more and more concerned about Grant. It was like he was mentally falling apart at the seams, and after the things he had suffered over the past year or so, it was understandable. Losing his wife and daughter, the stuff with the Crippens, and then that secret agent shit, only to discover your once-dead wife was actually still alive. Add to that the recent actual loss of his wife. Stacker thought it was all too much for one man to handle.

"You joining us on our little soiree over to the Fortunates?" he asked.

"No, I'm going to give it a miss. Need to call Shuffler, and then pay a long-overdue visit to an old friend," Grant replied.

A low groaning noise from behind the plastic sheeting interrupted the conversation, and before Grant could move toward the girl again, Stacker said, "Grant, don't punch her again. I will get Double D to come down and give her a strong sedative or something."

"Yeah, whatever you want, bro," Grant replied, waving his hand in Stacker's direction.

"I'm going to grab myself a bit of breakfast, before it all disappears," Stacker informed Grant. He wasn't really hungry, he just wanted to get away from the horror that the Armstrong girl was going through, and away from the air of madness that felt whenever he was in the presence of Grant.

It was about ten minutes later, when Double D appeared, making her way into the basement via the corridor from the garage, which was the only way she thought existed. Her medical bag was slung over her shoulder.

"I understand there's a patient down here who needs my attention," she said.

Grant merely responded by pointing in the direction of Courtney Armstrong. Her groans were now louder, as her consciousness increased, and along with it, so did the pain levels.

Double D spent only a few minutes with the girl. Firstly, because administrating the sedative only took her a few seconds, but mainly, because she didn't want to be around what that girl was being put through for any longer than necessary.

"Do you need anything?" she asked as she walked over to Grant and dropped her medical bag to the floor.

"No, I'm sound," Grant said, his gaze remaining on the screen of his mobile phone.

"Expecting a call?" Double D asked.

"No," Grant replied, his monotone response not changing from inattentive. "Just keeping an eye on the time, as I need to make a call." He looked up at Double D for the first time since she had arrived in the basement and tapped his wrist.

"Forgot to put my watch on this morning," he said.

"Stacker is really concerned about you," she said.

"Ah, you know Stacker. He worries too much about everything," Grant answered, his eyes firmly trained back on the screen of the phone. He changed his body position so he could rest his butt against the edge of the table he was standing next to. Double D moved in close to him.

Grant felt her hand gently rub against the crotch of his jeans at the same time as hearing her words.

"You sure you don't need anything?" she asked, looking up at him and raising her eyebrows slightly. Gently squeezing him through his jeans, she felt him respond.

"Hmmm, nothing better than a commando," she said, a slight smile developing.

With every inch that his manhood grew, so did his guilt. Grant had not had sex since finding out about the attack on his family by The Crippens. In fact, the last woman he had had sex with had been the woman he had been having an affair with. The last time he was having sex, was at the same time his wife and daughter were being brutally abused.

He felt one of Double D's hands unzipping him, at the same time as her other hand was undoing the button of his jeans. He placed one hand onto her shoulder, weakly pushing her away. About to say something to her, he was stopped by her placing one finger over his lips.

"Don't say anything. You probably need this more than anything I have in my medical supplies," she said, as she gently guided his hand down from her shoulder and onto one of her ample breasts.

He squeezed it, gently at first, and then more firmly, but before he could go any further, she had hooked her fingers into the waistband of his jeans and in one deft move, dropped to her knees, taking his jeans down to his ankles at the same time.

She placed her lips around the tip of his extremely hard penis, and ran her tongue up and down the underside of it, before moving her head forward and gorging herself on his erection.

Grant's guilt was replaced with a pleasure that he had forgotten about, and he placed one hand on the back of Double D's head, and gently guided her deeper onto him.

He felt the woman's hands cup themselves around his buttocks and push him toward her mouth and then release slightly. She repeated this until he got the message, and began to move his hips back and forth himself, without any assistance.

As she sucked him, Double D felt Grant place his hand on her head and readied herself to be forced deeper onto his manhood. She was surprised when she felt her head being gently pushed away. She looked up at him, his face was pained with guilt.

Standing up, she asked him, "What's wrong with you?"

Grant didn't respond. His face was as guilty, looking as any she had ever seen.

"I'm just not ready for something like that," Grant said sheepishly.

The second rejection hurt her, just as much as the first one.

"I have never been able to work out your species, but you are a total enigma," Double D stated.

She picked up her medical bag and left the underground chamber.

Grant pulled up his jeans and tucked away his still semi-hard erection, being careful to pull his zipper up and not get any of his tackle tangled up in the metal teeth.

He picked up his phone and placed his finger against the screen to bring it to life. The white digital numbers told him that it was twenty minutes past eight.

He gave it ten minutes, before calling the number of Jenny Wolstenhulme's office. He smiled as the call rang out, thinking about what had just happened. The answering machine picked up his call, so he ended it. Deciding to call later, he made his way out of the basement, using the stairs that only he and Stacker knew existed. He slowly peered through the door at the top of the stairs that used to lead to the basement, and glanced down both directions of the corridor, grateful that it was empty. He entered the corridor and hurriedly closed the door behind him and disappeared into his room.

After a short wait, he made his way to the bar area and joined the others to have breakfast. He ate heartily, having developed an appetite that only a near sexual encounter can produce.

* * *

DS Richard Bradley arrived at the Greenhill Secure Mental Institution just a few minutes after nine that morning. He had decided to leave Woody at the station and go alone.

After going through all of the security checks, he was asked to wait, as Dr. Ainsworth apparently wanted to speak with him, before any visit with David Warriner could take place.

He sat waiting for almost thirty minutes, before Dr. Ainsworth graced him with his presence, and DS Bradley couldn't help but think that the length of his wait had been intentional. He stood as the doctor approached him and shook his hand.

"Thank you for your patience, Detective Bradley," Dr. Ainsworth said.

"Not a problem, doctor, although I am somewhat confused as to why you felt a need to speak with me," Bradley replied, keeping up a professional level of respect.

"Simple really, detective," the doctor responded. "I would like to know the purpose of you wanting to speak with one of my patients."

DS Bradley was confused by the question, but as the doctor had started his question with the word simple, he decided to keep it that way.

"David Warriner was involved in a murder case, a very brutal murder case. I have a few questions for him so the case can finally be closed."

"But surely, Detective Bradley, the case is closed. David was found guilty of the murders of his three daughters," Ainsworth replied. "What else is there to know?"

"Why?" Bradley replied bluntly.

"That, my dear detective, is my area of expertise. I think you will find that yours is how and if," Ainsworth retorted.

"With all due respect, doctor, I think you will find that all areas are mine. How, if, where, when and why," Bradley stated in a way that left the doctor with no doubts that the conversation was finished.

"In that case, Detective Bradley, I will allow you to continue with your work and wish you luck, because as I am sure you are aware, David has not spoken since the day he was arrested, and that stubborn silence continues."

Richard Bradley did not reply, but even his tired mind did

not miss the use of the word stubborn. It was not a word he normally associated with the chosen silence of the mentally disturbed.

"This way, Detective Bradley," Ainsworth called, as he unlocked the door in front of him. "I will escort you to the entrance of the secure wing where David resides, and then place you in the safe hands of Mr. Bailey, who is one of our most experienced orderlies."

* * *

Grant watched his biking colleagues getting ready for their ride out, and happy that they were too occupied with their bikes, he turned away from them and took his phone out of the back pocket of his jeans. Selecting the name of the individual he wanted to call, he placed the phone next to his ear, continuing to look at the ground, not wanting to give away the fact that he was aware that Cutter had been watching his every move since he appeared in the courtyard, while appearing to be tinkering with his bike.

The phone had barely started to ring, before the call was answered.

"Good morning, Jenny Wolstenholme speaking," the voice on the other end of the call responded.

"Good morning, Jenny. How is our mutual friend doing?" Grant asked.

"He is absolutely fine," she replied. "Do you ever wonder how I am?"

"No, not really," Grant answered honestly.

"Really? Not worried at all about the risks I am taking?" the senior psychologist asked.

"No, not one bit, because they don't come anywhere near the risks you subjected me to," he replied. "Now, what is he up to?"

Jenny Wolstenholme breathed in sharply and pushed out a breath of air, exasperated by this man. It was an emotion she had become used to over the years of working with him.

"He is playing pool with one of his new-found friends," she finally said, looking out of her office window across the open expanse of the unit, where she could see Shuffler talking with Harry Armstrong, who was playing his shot at the unit's pool table.

"Is he winning?" Grant asked.

"Is that bloody important?" Jenny asked.

"I wasn't talking about the pool game, for fuck's sake," Grant replied rudely.

"I have no idea. I haven't had a chance to speak with him."

"Well, make sure you do, and make it soon. One of my associates will be in touch with you soon. You will not be hearing from me again," Grant told her.

"And when you say associate, I assume you mean one of your biker buddies, who is probably twice as mad, but half as volatile as you?" Jenny asked, now getting very annoyed with a man she owed a great deal to, but wasn't prepared to be treated in the fashion he was treating her now. The line went dead, and after a few seconds, a long high-pitched tone was all that could be heard. She slammed the phone back onto its cradle, calling Grant a fucking prick under her breath.

Shuffler saw the angry movement of the psychologist putting the phone down, and could see the anger all over her face. He had no doubt that Grant had been responsible for this response.

* * *

Having been ceremoniously handed over to the orderly in charge of the unit for that day, DC Bradley was surprised to discover that he would be speaking with David Warriner in his room, and not an office or interview room.

"You will be closely monitored, detective," Bailey, the orderly, said in an effort to reassure the police officer. "It was Dr. Ainsworth's idea. He thought that being in a familiar environment would give you more chance of getting something out of David."

DC Bradley wasn't convinced or reassured. All he could see was that he was being put into an environment that Warriner controlled.

As he accompanied Bailey down the corridor, the unit was quiet, something that he had not expected.

"Where are they all?" he asked. "Watching TV, outside?"

"Neither," the orderly replied. "It's mandatory quiet time, so they are all in their rooms."

"Mandatory quiet time?" a surprised DC Bradley responded. "Does that actually work with people like this?"

"They know the outcome of not adhering to mandatory quiet time," Bailey replied.

DC Bradley felt the level of threat in Bailey's response.

"And what is that outcome?" he asked, but never got an answer.

Bailey came to a standstill next to one of the doors, and looked into the room, after unbolting the heavy steel cover and sliding it down to reveal a plate of thick glass behind it.

"This is David's room," he said, as he removed a key attached to a chain from his pocket.

Richard Bradley looked at the strange looking key, which was perfectly straight on both sides of its blade, unlike a standard key, which would have the cuts into it allowing it to turn in the lock that it belonged to. Bailey saw the detective looking at the key.

"Magnetised locks," he said. "They may be crazy, but some of them have photographic memories."

He unlocked the door and pushed it open.

"David, here is the visitor who we talked about earlier," Bailey said to the man who was sat on the floor at the back of the room, leaning against the back wall. David Warriner had his eyes closed, which he didn't bother to open.

"All yours, detective," Bailey said, standing away from the door to allow DC Bradley full access into the room. "I will be just outside, but this door will be locked behind you."

A slight panic rose up in Bradley, who couldn't help thinking that this situation had been set up purposely by Ainsworth. He walked into the room, and heard the door bang shut behind him and the bolt shoot into its locked position.

The detective decided that he should attempt to break the silence, rather than waiting for a man who had not spoken for months.

"May I sit down?" he asked, suddenly realising that there was no chair, which left only the bed to sit on.

As expected, there was no response from David. His eyes remained closed.

"I will take your lack of response as an indication that you don't have a problem with that," Bradley said, effectively answering his own question. He walked over to the bed, which stood against the wall on the left of the room, as you looked at it from the door. The headboard of the bed was against the back wall, so even sitting at the foot of the bed, only put about six-feet between him and the silent David Warriner.

"Morning, David," Bradley said. "I am DC Richard Bradley. I want to talk to you about what happened between you and the Armstrong family, if you don't mind."

He decided to open with the subject of Kelvin Armstrong and his family, rather than the murder of the three girls, thinking that it would have more chance of getting some dialogue from Warriner. There was no reaction whatsoever. Bradley pushed it further.

"I fully understand what you did to Kelvin. I would have done the same, given the circumstances."

Bradley often used the empathy approach when interviewing people, but never to this degree. However, as this was not being recorded and was technically off the record, it was a risk he was willing to take. Still nothing from Warriner. His eyes remained closed, his face relaxed. It was as if Bradley was not in the room with him.

"Why did you assume that it was Kelvin Armstrong who had killed your little girls? Why not one of the others?" he asked.

He noticed a slight movement of Warriner's eyes beneath his eyelids, a movement that could have easily been missed. It was his first reaction, and it had come at the mention of the girls.

"Can I talk to you about your movements, before you

243

discovered the bodies of Debbie, Karen and Amy?" Bradley asked, pushing it further, and without warning, he got a reaction. All that Warriner did was move to a standing position. It wasn't done quickly, or in a threatening manner, but that simple and unexpected movement, caused Bradley's heart rate to almost double.

Bradley suddenly realised that he had stopped breathing, so he took a few seconds to compose himself. He couldn't believe that such an innocent movement could have caused such a reaction, and he couldn't understand why, either. He decided to go back to referring to Warriner's daughters as the girls, rather than using their names.

"We still haven't been able to confirm who was looking after your girls that morning. We believe you had previously asked a number of girls who lived locally to look after them, but nobody we have questioned, have confirmed they were babysitting for you that morning. It would really help us if you could remember the name of the babysitter, David," Bradley said.

Whether it was a coincidence or not, the decision to not refer to the girls by their names seemed to have worked, because there was no reaction from Warriner.

Bradley took his time, thinking about his next question carefully. While he thought, David, eyes still closed, suddenly and slowly walked over to where the detective was sat on the bed, and sat down next to him. Now there was only inches between himself and a brutal child killer.

Outside, the orderly was texting his wife, asking her what she was cooking for dinner that night.

Richard Bradley could not prevent the natural reflex response to facing fear. He gulped, as if physically swallowing the fear he now felt.

"Do you want me to leave, David?" He heard his voice asking the question, which he didn't intend asking. It was as if his mouth had become temporarily disconnected from his brain.

David didn't respond.

DC Bradley fought against his body's desire to stand up and walk toward the door. He looked toward the door, hoping to see Bailey's face at the observation window, but was disappointed. All he could see was the corridor wall.

"David, I am just trying to tie up some loose ends, so I can mark this case as officially closed," Bradley lied. He watched as Warriner's hands moved from a flat open position on his thighs, to tightly clenched fists, and immediately decided that it was time to leave.

He stood up, and a split second after doing so, Warriner mirrored his move. He fought against another of his body's desires, this one to punch Warriner in the face and get the hell out of that room. Instead, he slowly made his way to the door and slammed his fist onto it twice. Looking over his shoulder, he saw that Warriner was once again sat on the floor in almost the exact spot he had stood up from just a few moments earlier.

The door was unlocked and Bailey pushed it open. If Bradley had not moved back as quickly as he did, the door would have struck him in the face.

"All done?" the orderly asked.

"Get me the fuck out of here," Bradley responded, his face pale from the fear he was experiencing.

He walked into the safety of the corridor and didn't start to relax until he heard the door behind him close. Bailey locked the door and looked through the observation window, before sliding the metal cover back up. Warriner sat on the floor, eyes closed, exactly like Bailey had last observed him, except for one difference. There was a slight smile on his face.

As the orderly and the detective walked down the corridor away from his room, Warriner's smile transformed into a large grin. The one thing he had learned since the day he was arrested, was that human beings were not comfortable with silence. In the right situation, consistent silence caused an irrational fear that could not be explained, or prevented.

* * *

Patrick Armstrong sat opposite to his cousin in the dark front room. Outside, it was quite bright for the time of the day, but the natural light was diminished by the thick net curtains that covered the window, and the fact that the curtains were drawn almost fully closed. Everyone in the Armstrong family was fully aware of the problem Kelvin Armstrong had with the heat of the sun, ever since being badly burned by Warriner.

"What did the Fortunates tell you?" Kelvin asked.

"Not much really," Patrick replied. "They don't appear to have a problem with us. They are satisfied with the money we are giving them from the selling of drugs and, to quote them, 'if they had a problem with us, we would know about it.'"

"Fucking bikers, they think they are masters of all they touch," Kelvin reacted angrily. "I would love to teach them a lesson they would never forget."

Patrick decided to move the conversation on quickly, before

his cousin's anger increased.

"As for the other bike gang, they reckon they are nothings and nobodies. A bunch of ex-military wankers who can't handle the chaos of civilian life."

"Ex-military, you say." Kelvin's anger immediately dissipated, as his interest levels increased. "Are they sure about that?" he asked.

"Yeah," Patrick replied immediately and confidently. "They said the bloke in charge of them told them exactly that."

"And does this bloke have a name?" Kelvin asked again.

"Yeah, he's Nameless," his cousin replied.

"How the fuck can he have a name and be nameless?" Kelvin asked, his anger beginning to rise again at the perceived stupidity of his cousin.

"No," Patrick replied defensively. "His name is Nameless. I'm guessing it's one of them road names they use."

Kelvin looked at him, his eyebrows raised. His expression asked the question, *are you taking the piss?*

Patrick picked up on his cousin's look, and said, "Nameless, leader of The Nameless Ones. Fits nicely, if you think about it."

Kelvin Armstrong didn't need to think about it anymore than he already had. His exterior may have been damaged, but his mind was as sharp as it had ever been.

"Go and find Alfie," he said to Patrick, referring to another of the many Armstrong cousins. "Hang around where these Nameless Ones live and see what you can find out. And be discreet."

He waited until Patrick had left the room, on the way out of the house, before picking up his mobile and sending a text to his son.

Mention the Nameless Ones to your new friend. Deal with it if you detect an association.

* * *

Detective Richard Bradley sat in his car outside of the mental institution's main building. He continued to try to compose himself and lower his heart rate to somewhere near normal, after his encounter with David Warriner. He had sat in the same room with many evil people, but for some unfathomable reason, this one had really got at him.

He attempted to place the key inside the ignition, and dropped it into the footwell area of the car. Reaching down and scrambling around with his hand, trying to find the damned thing, while silently cursing and berating himself for letting a clearly mentally disturbed man get at him so easily, his fingertips eventually came into contact with the plastic key fob, at exactly the same moment as the noise of a motorbike was detected by his ears.

Picking the key up and raising himself back into an upright sitting position, he looked out of the driver's window. The rider sat upon the almost all black bike, raised his hand and waved at him. The helmet visor was raised, and although Bradley could not see all of the rider's face, his eyes alone told Bradley that the helmet was hiding a large stupid smile.

Although surprised to the detective, Grant acted like he had expected to see him at the mental hospital. After delivering the hand wave, he removed his helmet, revealing the huge smile that Bradley had predicted would be present.

"Hello, detective," Grant said as Bradley lowered the car door window. "What are you doing here?"

"More importantly, what are you doing here?" Bradley replied.

"I've come to see what the requirements are for admission," Grant responded sarcastically.

"Mad, bad and fucked up," the detective replied.

"You've just managed to describe ninety-nine-point-nine percent of my friends," Grant said, continuing with the sarcasm.

"And there I was thinking it would have been all of your friends I was describing," Bradley said, adding even more sarcasm to this unexpected meeting.

"I count you as one of my friends now, detective, and I would never tag you with one of those labels. You being one of our police force's finest, and all," Grant was now not willing to lose in this battle of wit.

"Well, as I'm your friend shouldn't we start sharing, like what's your name, and what are you doing here?" Bradley asked, in an attempt to bring the conversation back to business.

Grant smiled, enjoying playing this game with Bradley, but now equally as bored with it.

"Nah, I don't mix well," he replied.

"Aww," Bradley replied, surprised at how easy it was returning to sarcasm when talking to this man. "Does the little biker not play nice?"

Grant jabbed his finger sharply in the air toward the face of the detective, who was now looking pleased with himself.

"No, he fucking doesn't, so don't do anything that would

cause you to find out how badly I play," Grant responded, as sharply as his finger movement. The warning not going unnoticed by Detective Bradley.

He watched as Grant walked away from his bike and entered the building that he had a few moments ago exited.

"One nil to the police force's finest, I think," he said to himself.

Following a few identity checks, Grant was directed to a comfortable visitors' waiting room. During those checks, he had inadvertently discovered the purpose of Detective Bradley's visit.

"Two visitors in one day," the receptionist had exclaimed. "That's more than David has received in the entire time he has been here."

Although she had not mentioned the detective by name, it was too much of a coincidence that Bradley had been leaving as he had arrived, for it not to have been him who had visited his old friend.

Before he could think about this any further, a door opened into the waiting room, and he was led through to a small, but again comfortable, visiting area.

"If you would like to take a seat at any of the tables, David will be along soon," the staff member instructed.

Grant looked around the empty visiting room and decided to sit next to one of the three windows that looked out over a grassed area. He sat and waited for about ten minutes, before he saw a face that he had not seen since he was sixteen years old. His best friend from his school days had not aged well, and the eyes that had once been full of the hope of one day being a rock star, were now empty and lifeless.

David looked across the room expecting to see a stranger.

When Bailey had come to his room, following the visit from the police, he was expecting the usual barrage of abuse about his behaviour, so he was surprised to be told that he had another visitor. Because of his self-imposed silent regime, he had been unable to ask any questions about who this unexpected visitor was. He allowed himself to be escorted to the visitors' room for two reasons. He was curious about the identity of his visitor, and he had never seen the visiting room, so it would be a welcome break from the normal monotony of his day. Despite the passing of years, the baldness of the head and the facial hair, David recognised his old friend immediately, but could not understand why, after so many years, John Richardson was here.

* * *

Disturbed from his cleaning of his kitchen, Hammer stormed out of the clubhouse to find out why nobody had gone to the gate to see who was persistently sounding their horn, and immediately realised that the yard and garage were completely empty. He had reluctantly decided not to go out on the ride with the rest of them. The thought of leaving a messy kitchen had not sit well with him, and after the amount of cooking he had done that morning, he had been left with one hell of a mess to clean up.

Already pissed off because of this, he walked angrily toward the gates, and without checking who was on the other side, unlocked them and swung them both open with such force that they bounced back on their hinges and began to close again. He walked a few feet beyond the gates and stood in front of the small van. The pressing of the horn stopped immediately.

"What the fuck do you want?" he shouted at the occupant of the vehicle.

"I want to come in," mouthed the driver. Although Hammer could not hear the words, he could see the mouth moving.

He walked to the driver's side of the vehicle, and once again shouted, "Open your window, you fucking idiot."

The window slid open, and once again, the driver said, "I want to come in."

"I want a million quid and a woman with huge tits who gives blowjobs on the hour every hour," he shouted back at the driver, despite the window now being fully open. "But it's highly unlikely to happen during this lifetime. Who the hell are you?"

"I'm not supposed to tell you," the driver replied in a quite effeminate tone. "I am only allowed to talk to John, apparently, or somebody called Stacky."

"Who the fuck is John?" Hammer asked, his volume now more appropriate to the conversation.

The driver became flustered.

"Oh damn it. Not John … Grant … no, Nameless. Oh bugger, I don't know what name he goes by anymore. The man in charge of you lot."

Hammer sensed that this was someone who was not used to being faced with, or shouted at, by a pissed off ex-Army cook, or an angry biker, so he softened his tone as much as he could.

"Oh okay, you mean Nameless. Stay there and let me push these gates open again, then drive in."

He placed his hands on both gates, and just before he pushed them open, he turned to the driver and shouted, "Who the fuck is Stacky?"

As the car drove past him, Hammer slammed his hand twice against the front passenger window. The driver applied the brakes so quickly that his face almost slammed into the steering wheel.

"Who the fuck are you?" Hammer shouted.

The driver opened the passenger window.

"They call me Mr. Deception, and will you please stop shouting at me," he answered, his nerves already on a knife edge.

* * *

David sat down on the chair opposite to his visitor. The man escorting him addressed Grant.

"Hi, I'm one of the nursing staff for David. They call me Bailey."

Grant nodded his head toward the member of staff.

"Just to make you aware that David does not speak, hasn't done since he arrived here, so don't expect much," Bailey advised him. "I will be just outside the door," he added, looking back at the door through, which he and David had just entered.

Grant waited for the orderly to leave the room and for the door to close. He noted that Bailey did not lock the door behind him.

He looked across the table at the man sat opposite to him.

"Hi Dave, it's been too many years. You're looking well," he lied.

David Warriner looked over his shoulder and saw Bailey watching intently through the glass panel of the door. He turned back to face Grant and said nothing.

"Come on, mate, I know that you have been through some shit, but I am here to help you if I can," Grant said, almost pleading with his friend to respond.

He noticed David's forehead clench, the lines across it became deeper, and in his eyes, he at last saw something other than lifelessness. He saw anger, intense deep anger.

"Silence will not help you, my friend," Grant said. "Trust me, I spent too many years not talking about stuff." Grant did not finish his sentence.

David rested his elbows on the table and cupped his hands, resting his chin onto them, and for the first time in what felt like an eternity, he spoke. His lips hardly moved and his words were spoken in a hushed tone.

Bailey watched from outside, intrigued by the sudden positioning of his charge. He wished he had insisted on David sitting in a position facing the door, so he was able to observe his face.

"Don't call me friend," David said. His voice was low and his lips barely moved.

Grant tried his best not to look surprised, as he was just as aware as David was, that they were being watched from outside of the room.

"Please, Dave," Grant replied. "I understand your anger. We parted on bad terms, but we were young"..

"Go away. Don't come back. Ever," David replied. Once again, his lips hardly moved as he spoke.

Outside, Bailey tried to read the visitor's lips, tried to work out if he was speaking to a wall of silence like everyone else did when they spoke to David Warriner, or if, in fact, he was involved in a conversation. He pressed the transmit button of the radio that was attached to his belt, not wanting to bring it up to his face, in case the visitor inside the room saw him speaking into it.

"Get Ainsworth down the visitors' room, now," he said. "Tell him it is important. Tell him it is about Warriner. Do not respond to this transmission." Bailey did not want the people inside the room hearing any response from the control room.

The control room operator picked up the phone and immediately rang the office of Dr. Ainsworth, passing on Bailey's message.

Inside the visiting room, the illicit conversation continued.

"Do you remember the good times, Dave?" Grant asked. "Do you remember listening to our music together, talking about forming a rock band and touring the world? How we joked about KISS eventually being our support band?"

The anger in David's eyes burned with an intensity that should have worried Grant, but he was too focussed on making a link with him.

"You know nothing about me. You walked away. You left me alone." The tips of David's fingers rubbed at his eyes, and then remained over them, keeping them closed. His hands were now fully covering his mouth, but Grant could still hear what was being said.

"Do not become my next victim," he told Grant.

Grant knew that he was referring to his act of violence against Kelvin Armstrong, and replied, "I would have done the same to Armstrong, mate. In fact, I would have done worse. I know what it is like to be hurt, to have your family hurt."

"You did the hurting. You are the cause of all my pain," David hissed back at him.

Dr. Ainsworth arrived at the door of the visiting room, and stopped short of the door, as Bailey held up his hand as he approached.

"Don't let them see you, doctor," Bailey said. "I don't want them to be aware of your presence, especially David. I think he is talking, sir."

It was as if the doctor had only heard the last part of Bailey's sentence, as he stepped toward the door and pushed at it, surprised, but pleased to discover that it had not been locked.

The next few seconds were a blur to everyone, except David Warriner, who looked over his shoulder as he heard the bang of the doctor's hand against it.

As Ainsworth entered the room, Bailey directly behind him, David Warriner leapt to his feet and flung himself across the table at Grant. They both crashed to the floor. Chairs and tables were clattered into each other, as the two men grappled with each other. David pinned Grant to the floor and positioned his face so his mouth was almost touching Grant's ear. In a hushed tone, inaudible to everyone except for Grant, David said, "Stay out of my life."

Grant thought he heard two more words, before David's teeth clamped around Grant's earlobe, and bit deeply into it, drawing blood immediately.

"Drawing blood."

24 Hours of Lost and Found

Hammer and the new arrival at the clubhouse sat opposite each other, Hammer staring intently at the man who called himself Mr. Deception, and Mr. Deception looking anywhere other than at Hammer.

Eventually, Hammer asked, "So why are you here?"

"I told you. I am not supposed to speak to anyone other than Grant," Mr. Deception replied.

"So, here's an idea," Hammer said. "How about I go to my kitchen and come back with my friend Neil the knife, and I ask you that question again?"

The man known as Mr. Deception went instantly pale in the face, and found himself asking the most ludicrous question, given the situation.

"Why would you call your knife Neil?"

"Because knife and Neil both begin with the letter N, you dickhead," Hammer replied.

At that moment, Mr. Deception decided he was in the company of a madman, who had a limited number of brain cells, which, in his opinion, was a very dangerous combination.

"My name is Will. Nobody calls me Mr. Deception, except for myself. I work, or I did work, in the film industry. I'm an expert in graphics, CGI, altering photographs. Basically,

I'm an expert in deceiving people, hence my nickname, which nobody else uses," he blurted out, each word tripping over the one before it.

Hammer smiled, and said, "See that was easy. Now, do you want something to eat or drink?"

"Coffee," Will replied. "Maybe with a brandy in it."

"Sure," Hammer said, reaching out his arm and playfully pinching Will's cheek. "Oh, and I know that knife doesn't begin with N, but it works so well."

He stood up and entered his kitchen, leaving Will alone to wonder what the hell he had got himself involved in.

* * *

Michael Armstrong lay on his bed, contemplating the text he had received from his father, when he saw Shuffler walk past his cell door, a towel hanging over his shoulder, and carrying a bottle of shower gel.

He got to his feet and slowly walked to his cell door, and watched Shuffler enter the shower room in the corner of the unit. The unit was empty, as it usually was following breakfast. Most of the cons went back to bed after consuming their morning meal, which was normally accompanied by morning medication, which helped with the desire to sleep.

He went back into his cell and picked up his Roberts Rambler radio from where it sat on his windowsill, placing it on the bed face down, so he could remove the back cover.

Removing the PP9 battery from the back of the radio, he placed it inside a pillowcase and spun it around, so the battery was tightly held into place. Finally, he wrapped the other end of the pillowcase around his right hand, and casually left his cell, making his way toward the shower room.

The journey to the shower room took a matter of a few seconds, and he quietly stood by the door. Shuffler was under the shower, his back to the door. Michael waited until Shuffler had foamed up the shower gel over his head and face, before speaking.

"Hey, bro, what do you know about The Nameless Ones?"

Two things raised the suspicion levels of the Armstrong brother, who was already suspicious enough. Firstly, the man in the shower continued to rub the bubbly foam over his head, and secondly, he paused as if trying to think of a suitable response to the question. As far as Michael Armstrong was concerned, the effort to remain cool and unaffected by the question posed, was almost palpable.

Shuffler eventually responded, but made the mistake of not turning around. A man with his experience of prison life should have known better.

"No idea what you are talking about," he said.

"Sure you don't," Michael replied.

This was point that Shuffler decided to turn around, but Michael Armstrong was already in full swing with the easily made prison weapon. The speed of the swing, and the weight of the PP9 battery combined, to strike heavily into the side of Shuffler's head. He fell instantly onto the water covered shower floor, his face striking the hard surface, cutting open one eye, the bridge of his nose and his chin. Luckily, he was already unconscious by the time the second strike buried itself into the back of his skull, and the blood began to pour out of his head, mixing with the shower water, making it look like a crimson sea.

Michael Armstrong walked out of the shower room, pressed the alarm bell that was located adjacent to the door, and casually returned to the lifeless body of Shuffler. He dropped to his knees and waited until he heard the heavy pounding of the prison staffs' boots approaching, before scooping up the blood filled water at the side of Shuffler's head, and pouring it into his mouth several times.

He spun around on his knees upon hearing the footsteps turn silent. He looked at the three unit staff members, who were stood in the doorway in utter horror and shock. The blood soaked water dripped from Armstrong's chin, who began to laugh, a crazy, evil, mad laughter that sent a chill through the prison officers. The sound broke the staff out of their temporary frozen reaction. They rushed into the shower room and took control of the prisoner, using their control and restraint techniques, with one in control of Armstrong's head and the other two controlling his arms. He lay pinned face down on the floor, breathing in water and sticking his tongue into it, attempting to lap up more of the bloody water.

One of the staff screamed the word "Medic" several times at the top of his voice, which only just managed to rise above the noise of Michael Armstrong's laughing and occasional screaming, as pain was applied through the arm locks being used to control him, not that it was needed, as he did not struggle one bit. As the madness took over the young man, all he could think about was how proud his father would be of him, having dealt with the biker, and guaranteed his place in Greenhill mental hospital.

The prison officer who was securing Armstrong's head looked up, noticing movement out of the corner of his eye.

The legs of the other prisoner began to twitch. He had no doubt that he was watching a man die.

* * *

The Nameless Ones rode out of the compound, minus three of their numbers: Hammer, Stacker and Nameless. They were glad of the freedom of the road again, and were all looking forward to introducing themselves to Satan's Fortunates.

Chalky, Reckon and Syco had decided to initially ride out with the others, before breaking away to search for the Armstrong pairing they were to pick up. Syco had briefed them and Magill to follow him no matter what, to stay close, and most importantly, to stay sharp.

The bikers, followed by two vans, all in formation, left the compound and turned onto the main road at the T-junction not far from the clubhouse grounds.

About half a mile up the road, in an unplanned manoeuvre, Syco, who was at the rear of the formation of bikes, along with Chalky and Reckon, did a slow U-turn in the road. Chalky, Reckon and Fixit, who was in one of the vans, reacted just as they had been told to, and followed Syco. Only Magill and Cutter immediately noticed their early departure. Magill, ignoring his briefing from Syco, continued driving behind the main group of bikers, deciding that the instructions he had received from Cutter were more important.

Syco came to a standstill, and the other two bikers pulled up alongside him. Reckon looked at Syco, and shouted, "What's wrong, bro?"

Syco held up his hand, asking the other two to hold on, as he watched Fixit complete the three-point turn in the road.

Nobody had noticed what Syco had seen just a few metres after heading out on the main road. Parked up on their right-hand side, was a dark blue Ford Escort. Syco could not make out the identity of the passenger, who had lowered his head to conceal his face as the bikers appeared around the corner.

Patrick Armstrong was not as quick to react. Syco recognised him sitting behind the steering wheel, in the few seconds before Patrick pretended to type something into his phone, an excuse he used to also lower his head, in an effort to hide his face from the unexpected ride past The Nameless Ones.

Syco explained what he had seen to the two other bikers, and momentarily left his bike on the side stand to quickly speak with Fixit. Returning to his bike, he led the way back down the road, with Chalky and Reckon only a wheel's-length behind him, and one each side of him, so they were almost riding down the road three abreast.

Patrick Armstrong had watched the bike gang disappear almost out of sight in his wing mirror, and was about to start the car engine, when he saw three of the bikers and one of the vans turn around in the road in the distance.

He watched the activity and movement of one of the bikers, as he got off and back on to his bike. As they began to return down the road toward them, he knew that he and his cousin, Alfie, had been spotted. Spotted meant recognised, and recognised suggested to Patrick that, for some reason, the Armstrong family had become targets of this biker gang. He started the car and began to drive away. He had no intention to hang around to find out what that reason was.

* * *

Grant took his phone from his pocket and pressed the buttons to call the local police station. His call was answered quickly.

"Staffordshire police, how I can help?"

"DS Richard Bradley, please," Grant replied.

"Can I ask who is calling, please?" asked the operator, while clicking the mobile number that came up on her screen to record it into the system.

"Just tell him that I am Nameless," Grant replied.

"I do need a name, before I can put you through," the operator said.

"Why don't you speak to him, and I bet you a beer that he will want to speak to me," Grant replied patiently.

"One moment, sir," came the professional reply, followed by silence.

A few moments later, DS Bradley spoke.

"To say that I am surprised would be the understatement of the year. What do you want?"

"I want to talk to you about David Warriner," Grant replied.

"Sure, come to the station," the detective said.

Grant was surprised how easily his request had been accepted.

"Why don't we meet on neutral ground?" Grant suggested. "There's a café close to the Fortunates clubhouse. Do you know it?"

"Shall we say in an hour or so?" Bradley asked.

"See you there," Grant replied.

"I'm guessing your visit went as bad as mine?" Bradley asked.

263

Grant touched his sore ear and ended the call, without saying another word.

* * *

The Armstrong cousins raced down the road, the driver watching the bikers behind them, closing the gap rapidly.

"Go left!" Alfie shouted.

His cousin didn't respond, so he screamed.

"Take the next fucking left!"

Whether it was the stress of the situation, or the fact that Patrick didn't know his left from his right, he turned the steering wheel sharply to the right, and turned the car into the side road immediately to his right.

"What the fuck are you doing?" Alfie screamed. "This is a fucking dead end."

Patrick Armstrong raced up to the end of the short road that came to an abrupt end, the factory enclosure wall bringing his escape to an unexpected halt. He slammed on the brakes, stopping a few feet short of the wall, and looked into the wing mirror. Two bikes had come to a stop a few yards beyond the entrance to the side road. He watched, as they began to move slowly toward them.

Chalky and Reckon slowly approached the car down the narrow road that was approximately a car-and-a-half wide. They both saw the reverse lights shine, as the car was put into reverse gear and began to head toward them, increasing in speed with every second.

The two bikers simultaneously came up with different

evasion tactics. Reckon went with the approach of moving his bike as close to the side of the road as possible, while Chalky attempted to do a sharp U-turn, so he could ride away from the reversing vehicle. As the car sped past Reckon's bike, missing him by a few inches, the biker knew that his idea had been the better of the two available options. This was confirmed seconds later, when the car slammed into Chalky and his bike with the rear of the car, which was halfway through his U-turn.

Reckon looked down the road to see two things. The reversing car had come to a stop, prevented from going farther, because of the fact that Chalky and his bike were now wedged under the rear axle of the car. The second thing he saw was Syco at the bottom of the side road, and just behind him, was the van driven by Fixit. He was surprised when he saw Syco kick out the side stand of his bike and lean it over to the left.

Syco had turned into the side road, just in time to see the car crash into Chalky's bike, and watched the bike and rider get crunched under the back of the car. The rear wheels of the car were lifted off the surface of the road as the bike went underneath it, and Syco could just about see the limp body of Chalky. The angle of his neck and head suggested things were not going to be good for him.

Syco kicked the side of his boot against the side of his right foot plate. A small button was pressed, which released the cover of the personally designed footrest. He reached down and retrieved the hidden pistol that sat inside the cavity now exposed by the opened lid.

The Kahr Arms P380 was less than five inches in length and weighed less than ten ounces, and while it was not pretty, it was renowned for functioning every time.

He held the pistol in his right hand and ran toward the vehicle that was now being revved by the driver, who was clearly panicking and attempting to get some kind of traction, which was just not possible, considering the situation of the rear-wheel drive vehicle.

Calmly and coldly, he opened the driver's door and placed the barrel of the pistol against the temple of Patrick Armstrong. He clicked off the safety catch, a noise that Armstrong heard, making him freeze, his foot remaining fully pressed down on the accelerator pedal.

"Turn the engine off, lock your fingers behind your head, tell your cousin to stop pissing himself and to do the same, and then both of you get out of the car, very slowly," Syco told the two occupants of the car.

Patrick Armstrong looked to his left, where his cousin, Alfie, was leaking from both ends. Tears streamed from his eyes, and the dark stain spreading out over the seat, was a clear sign that piss was leaking out, too.

Reckon had turned around in the road, and was now only a few feet from where Syco was stood.

He hit the red emergency cut off switch of his bike, and not wanting to cause any reaction from Syco, quietly said, "Syco, just easy on the trigger, brother."

Without looking at his fellow biker, Syco allowed his finger to ease slightly off the pressure he was applying to the pistol trigger. He tapped the end of the barrel against Patrick Armstrong's head, and said, "Out, now." His voice was almost menacing.

The driver swung his legs to his right, and felt the barrel of the pistol pressed hard against the side of this head.

"Slowly, you prick," Syco ordered. "Do not make me kill you, because trust me, right now, I want to put a bullet through the void where a brain should sit."

"I can't open my door if my hands are behind my head," Alfie Armstrong said in a snivelly voice.

Reckon dismounted and walked to the passenger side of the car, and opened the door.

"Get out," he told the still crying Alfie. "And don't get close to me," he instructed, as the smell of urine hit his nose.

Unseen by everyone, Fixit had reversed his van out of the side road, and then reversed it back into it, so the back of the van now faced the tense scene. He had opened the rear doors and watched the Armstrong cousins walking toward him, Alfie leading the way, with Reckon adjacent to him, while Syco was at the back of the group of four people, with Patrick Armstrong directly in front of him. With every step they took, Syco tapped the muzzle of the pistol against the back of Patrick's head, saying with every tap, "Give me a reason to kill you." He repeated the sentence right to the point of reaching the van.

Reckon placed his large hands into Alfie's back, and shoved him into the van. So petrified was Alfie, that he didn't attempt to remove his hands from the back of his head, resulting in his knees slamming into the van, making him topple forward and slamming his face into the interior floor.

Syco applied permanent pressure against the back of Patrick's head with the pistol.

"In," he instructed.

Patrick Armstrong stepped up into the van, bending forward, so as not to bang his head against the top of the van. As he did so, he felt the muzzle of the pistol slide down from his head to the middle of his back.

Syco followed him into the van, not wanting to relieve the pressure of the gun against the body of Armstrong.

"Kneel down," he instructed. This was the last thing that Patrick Armstrong heard for a while as, before he could do as he was told, he felt the sharp pain caused by the pistol being slammed into his head. His unconscious body fell on top of his cousin, pinning down the weeping man.

Syco left the vehicle, walking backwards, the pistol still firmly aimed in the direction of the Armstrong boys. As he stepped back onto the road, Reckon slowly approached him, and even more slowly, reached out his hand toward the pistol and clicked the safety catch back into its safe position.

Syco did not lower the pistol, its aim still directed at the two bodies in the back of the van. Reckon placed his hand gently on top of the gun, and lowered it and the arm of Syco, until they were both next to Syco's thigh.

"Stand down, Syco," Reckon said quietly.

Syco turned his head and looked into the eyes of Reckon. Reckon felt like there was no recognition in the eyes of his biker friend.

"Syco, stand easy, brother," said Reckon, this time a bit more firmly.

The intense look in the eyes of the man holding gun slowly began to soften.

"I'm okay," Syco eventually said.

"Mate, I don't think you have been okay for a long time," a relieved Reckon replied.

Both men nervously laughed, and Fixit slammed the van doors firmly shut.

"What now?" Fixit asked.

"Return to the clubhouse and have a beer I think," Reckon replied.

"I think he is referring to Chalky," Syco said, his voice remained cold, almost detached from the reality of the situation.

Without saying a word, Reckon walked to the car and lowered himself to the floor. He crawled under the car, as far as he dared, hoping that the bike would continue to take the weight above him. He reached his arm out and began to pat around Chalky's jacket. The biker didn't move or respond in any way. He felt something and unzipping the jacket pocket, reached inside with his gloved hand, and pulled out Chalky's mobile phone. For reasons unknown to him, he zipped the pocket closed again, before crawling back out from under the car.

As he stood back up to his feet, Fixit asked, "How is he?"

Reckon looked over at both of his fellow bikers, saying, "Well, if that was one of us under there and Chalky was stood here, I think he would be doing his best to draw a chalk outline around our body."

"Shouldn't we remove his cut?" Fixit asked.

Syco looked at him, and then back at the body of Chalky.

"Good luck doing that," he replied, before focusing back on the phone.

He pressed the number nine button three times on the mobile, and waited for the call to be answered.

"Emergency services, which services do you require?"

"Biker hit by a car, doesn't look good," Reckon replied.

"What is your location, sir?" the operator asked.

"Use this phone to get that information," Reckon replied, and without saying another word, he placed the phone onto the floor next to the mangled bike, leaving the call open.

"He looked at the two men stood by the van, and placed his finger against his lips, signalling the fact that he wanted them to remain silent. He then rotated his finger in a circular motion in the air, and after three rotations, pointed his finger toward the exit from the side road.

All three men knew it was time to leave.

* * *

Grant sat opposite to Stacker and Mr. Deception in the clubhouse.

"Right, Will," Grant said.

"Please call me Mr. Deception," Will replied.

"Fuck off, you moron," Grant replied, making Stacker laugh loudly.

"Right," he began again. "Everything is set up for you, thanks to Stacker. You know what you are here to do, so start doing it."

"Err, I have no idea what he is here to do," Stacker said.

"To put it simply, mate, Will here will make the limited damage we cause to the Armstrong family look much worse than it actually is. He is a master at making images look entirely different," Grant replied.

"I assume that you are describing what we have done to that young girl downstairs as limited damage?" Stacker asked.

"She ain't dead, brother, but Will is going to make it look like she is," Grant answered.

"Which is why they call me Mr. Deception," Will quickly

added.

"Mate, the only person who refers to you as Mr. Deception is yourself," Grant said smiling. "Now, go and do your stuff and create some deception. Your first subject awaits you. Stacker introduce you to her."

"Okay, but where are you going?" he asked.

"I feel the need to interrogate a copper," Grant replied.

* * *

As Grant left Stacker to show Will the Armstrong girl, Cutter slowed down to allow Magill to pull up alongside him. Looking at the driver of the van, he simply nodded his head.

Texting and driving, Magill typed out a message that said:

> *They are on their way, full colours. Cutter says make them feel welcome!!*

He pressed the send button and threw his mobile onto the dashboard, giving Cutter the thumbs up, and then pulled in behind the biker once again.

* * *

Grant parked his bike, unknowingly, in the same place as Cutter had done when he had visited the same café where he had arranged to meet DS Bradley. He had arrived early, in the hope of enjoying a coffee in peace, before the detective arrived. He was disappointed to see Bradley sat at one of the outside tables.

"Hi, I took the liberty of ordering you a coffee," said the detective. "I see you as a coffee, no milk type of guy."

Grant tapped the glass in the café door and took a seat. A few moments later, a waitress appeared.

"Can I get you anything else?"

"Yes, love, you can take this coffee away, and replace it with a flat white, please," Grant said pleasantly.

"Got you, wrong again," Bradley said as the waitress took the black coffee away.

Grant simply smiled at the detective, the smile hiding the fact that he loved to drink a strong black coffee, and had only ordered a flat white, because it was the most opposite to a black coffee that he could immediately think of.

The roar of bike engines rumbled through the air, delaying Grant's response. Both he and Bradley looked in the direction of the Fortunates' clubhouse entrance, watching the bikers park their bikes out front. Bradley noticed that the bikers were wearing the colours of The Nameless Ones, whereas Grant noticed that a number of bikers and one van were missing, and then saw Magill manoeuvre his van down the side street at the far side of the clubhouse building.

"Your boys looking for trouble?" Bradley asked Grant.

"No, just reaching out in an effort to merge," Grant lied.

"Merge?" Bradley replied, surprised by Grant's answer.

"Yeah, we think that The Nameless Fortunates has a certain ring to it," Grant replied, the smile returning to his face, as he played with the detective's mind.

Bradley briefly considered continuing this conversation,

but wanted to get to the real reason for Grant wanting to speak with him.

"So, what do you want to talk about? I assume that it is connected to your visit with David Warriner? What's your connection to him?" he asked.

"You assume correctly, and he's an old school friend," Grant said honestly.

"So the arrival of you and your biker friends is no coincidence?" Bradley responded.

"Pure coincidence," Grant replied, doing his best to keep his responses short and sweet.

"Why don't we start to be honest with each other?" the detective asked, now bored with Grant's games. "Let me start with the facts, as I know them. David Warriner, guilty of the attempted murder of a member of a family he blamed for the death of his wife and daughters. A new lot of bikers suddenly arrive in the area. The word on the street is that a female member of said Armstrong family hasn't been seen for a few days. You visit David Warriner, and now tell me that he is an old school friend. Now you don't have to be a detective to start placing some pieces into the jigsaw puzzle."

Grant waited for a few seconds, before responding. He looked over his shoulder to see the last of the bikers disappearing through the Fortunates' clubhouse door. He returned his attention to the detective.

"Let me start by correcting some of your facts. We turned up way after the attempted murder of Kelvin Armstrong. The fact that a member of that family hasn't been seen for a while, cannot be connected to us, so that is just another jigsaw puzzle for you to put together. I did visit David, as I say, he is an old school friend," Grant intentionally emphasised the word

273

old. "Nothing strange there. What is strange, is that you also visited him, suggesting that you were speaking with him about something other than the solved case of the attempted murder of Kelvin Armstrong. You still working on the murder of David's family, detective?"

"Your ear looks tender, anything to do with David?" Bradley asked.

"He plays rough, what did he do to you? You looked at bit out of sorts when I last saw you," Grant responded.

"The man plays being mad very well, don't you think?" the detective asked.

"Why do you believe he is playing at it?" Grant asked, remembering how Warriner had attacked him.

"Now, I don't have much to go on, but I would describe it as a gut feeling. We know from talking to neighbours that the Warriner marriage had been strained for a long time. Rachel Warriner was frustrated with her husband, because of his failure to better himself, support his family better and generally, his failure as a man. She had told quite a few friends of her intention to leave David and take the three girls with her. She had said that his behaviour had become erratic, ever since the Armstrong family had moved next door to them—mood swings, foul temper and heavy drinking sessions. Personally, if you really want to know, I don't think the Armstrongs had anything to do with the killings, although, I will admit that their behaviour did not help the situation. I believe that it was David who killed his daughters and probably had something to do with his wife's death, too." Detective Bradley watched Grant closely, looking for any kind of reaction to what he had just disclosed.

Grant took a while to process what he had just been told,

274

before responding.

"No evidence though, no proof. Just a copper's intuition. You can't take that to the CPS can you?"

"There is one piece of evidence," Bradley replied. "Experts can say, without any doubt, that the words drawn in blood on the walls of the bedroom, where the girl's bodies were found, were written by someone who is left-handed. Now, every member of the Armstrong family is right-handed, whereas David Warriner is left-handed. No doubt another coincidence!"

"What did you say?" Grant asked, responding very quickly.

"That Warriner is left," the detective started to reply, before being interrupted by Grant.

"No, not that. What did you say about the blood?"

"That it was written by a left-handed person," Bradley answered, unsure where Grant was going with this.

"You said the words were drawn in blood, not written in blood," Grant replied.

"Drawn, written ... what's the difference? I only described it that way, because during one interview with Warriner, he said that they had drawn the words in blood. I guess it just stuck with me," Bradley answered.

"Drawn in blood, not drawing blood," Grant said out loud. He said it to himself, as a vocalised thought, rather than a response to the detective.

DS Bradley could clearly see that something had Grant rattled. He had suddenly gone very pale, and there was a look of almost confusion on his face.

"I have to stop this," Grant said, once again to himself.

* * *

MadDog was surprised at the lack of surprise shown by the Fortunates, as The Nameless Ones strolled into their clubhouse. The only people present were the bikers themselves—no other visitors, no women either. It was as if they were expected. He was even more surprised by the almost warm welcome.

"Welcome, brothers. Grab yourself a free drink from the bar, or if you would prefer, a cold 'un. There is a barrel of bottles resting in cold water out back," Skull said, the toothy grin of his face tattoo stretching as he smiled.

"Where's your president?" MadDog asked.

"Stretch? Why he's out back in the yard enjoying a cold one himself," Skull replied, still smiling.

MadDog headed toward the far end of the room, assuming that he would eventually find a backdoor that would lead outside. The rest of The Nameless Ones followed him, making their way through the throng of other bikers, who appeared very comfortable in their home environment.

MadDog found the door he was looking for, pushed it open, and was briefly blinded, as the sunlight shone into the building contrasted harshly with the dark interior.

Stretch was sat on an old sofa, one leg stretched out on the item of furniture. The small yard was split into two halves. The first half comprising of badly constructed wooden shelter sitting on a rickety wooden floor made from railway sleepers. It was in this area that the sofa was located, along with a few metal framed chairs and two matching tables, as well as two high tables with circular tops, accompanied by two tall stools at each of these tables.

The rest of the yard was concrete laid, and surrounded by a high wooden fence that had suffered from many years of being attacked by the elements of the weather, combined with a lack of maintenance. A couple of partially constructed bikes stood in the far corner of this part of the yard. Compared to their own clubhouse area, this was a poor cousin, MadDog thought.

The Nameless Ones bikers stood in a tight and much smaller group than they had when they started the journey, behind MadDog, in the small wooden floor area.

"Welcome to the home of Satan's Fortunates, brothers. Are you here to pay your dues?" Stretch asked the ensemble of bikers stood in front of him.

"We're here to tell you how it is and how it's going to be," Chaos replied aggressively.

Stretch laughed derisively and turned his head to look directly at the biker who had spoken.

"A collection of veterans who happen to ride bikes," he said, adding a hint of disrespect when saying the word veterans. "And suddenly, you believe you are bikers. You don't understand the term. You have no idea or experience of the lifestyle, the commitment. What it actually means to hand over your life to the world of being a biker. We use the term one-percent to declare our disrespect of social acceptance and public laws. You use it to describe how much of your pay packet is left."

"You are not our masters," Chaos replied, already losing the battle of words with the rival gang's president, who was more intelligent than many gave him credit for.

"And you, brother, are not our slaves. You are not worthy

of even that title. You come here wearing your colours, as if they mean something. I have heard your leader talk about respect and honour, and yet here you are, showing no respect and demonstrating no honour. It is also worth mentioning that I see your leader is not with you."

MadDog could sense that the regular instigator of trouble was about to notch up the tension already building to an uncomfortable level. He held out a calming hand in the direction of Chaos.

"Nameless is tending to other business," he said to Stretch.

Stretch looked at him, and the smile had disappeared.

"I have already referred to two of your standards. Let us take a closer look at the third. Honesty!"

There was no response from MadDog or any other of The Nameless Ones, who were now clearly and uneasily on edge. This was not going how any of them had expected.

"Honesty," Stretch continued. "You are the least honest collection of men I have ever come across. Let me first get rid of the mask that your leader hides behind. Grant is not Nameless."

MadDog could not hide the look of surprise on his face, upon hearing the real name of the man who had brought them all together being used by a man who should not have been aware of it.

"Did you think that I am not connected? Did you believe that I am not capable of finding information about my enemies? Information is power, and as you are about to find out, you are totally powerless. The second part of your dishonesty lies in the area of why you are here. To get away from a civilian life you neither understand, nor are able to survive in. This is what Grant told me, but you and I know the truth. Now, I have no interest or real connection to the Armstrong family, other than a few of my brethren have screwed the hell out of a couple of their ladies." The last word he used was said in a way that suggested the last thing he thought the Armstrong women were, would be described as ladies.

"So, now that I have dealt with your lack of honesty, the fact that you have no honour, and you demonstrate no respect to anyone, most of all yourselves, let us now find out if you have two other traits that you are all going to have in abundance, just to get out of here alive. Bravery and fighting skills. I really do hope you have come equipped." Stretch stood for the first time since had begun to speak, and gestured with his hand the way back to the door that led back into the clubhouse.

At the back of the group, Shovel opened the door a couple of inches and peeked inside. Satan's Fortunates were spread around the room, covering every potential path between them and the freedom of the front doors. He allowed the door to slowly close, knowing that that escape route was not an option. The collection of knives, machetes, an axe, and a number of baseball bats, being brandished by the bikers inside the clubhouse, made that abundantly clear.

"Over the fucking fence," he shouted.

Confused, the other Nameless Ones did not immediately react, until the door burst open and the biker wielding the axe swung it in a downward arch, burying its metal head into the shoulder of Shovel. Almost as one, they began to scatter into the open area of the yard, looking for the easiest route to get out of this situation. Only three people did not react in this way.

Shovel collapsed to his knees, and the axe wielding biker

pulled up on the handle of his weapon of choice, ripping the axe head out of Shovel's shoulder. Shovel stared at the open wound left behind, almost transfixed by the flow of blood that began to coat his leather jacket.

MadDog, who upon hearing the shouted warning, had momentarily looked over his shoulder, taking his attention away from Stretch. He did not see the attack that came his way, but he did feel it as the knife sunk into the side of his neck. Stretch pulled the knife out and was hit by a huge spurt of blood. It hit him at chin level, and immediately began to slide down his neck and drip onto the deck's wooden floor. MadDog covered the wound with both hands, his wide open eyes staring at his attacker, as the life quickly began to leave his body.

The third member of The Nameless Ones not to head into the yard, had been standing just to the left of Shovel. As the wounded biker fell to the ground, he stepped behind him and into the clubhouse. As he entered the building, he came face-to-face with a biker holding a wooden baseball bat, both hands on the handle, above his head. He held both arms high into the air and screamed at the top of his voice, "I'm Cutter!"

The biker lowered the baseball bat and made his way past the surrendering figure in front of him.

"Today you live, you fucking traitor," he said to Cutter, as he made his way outside.

Many more of The Nameless One may have been injured, if it had not been for the actions of Ordnance, who, as the growing numbers of Satan's Fortunates' bikers poured out into the yard, launched his huge bulk at the wooden fence that surrounded the yard enclosure. Thankfully, the fencing had not received much attention, and so was weak and rotting, aiding Ordnance's ease with which he burst through the fence, sending shards of wood panels flying into the air. The force he had used to take on the fence, caused him to fall to the floor as he burst through it. For some reason, as he stood back up, he felt like he had been punched in the back of his thigh. In the confusion and chaos of the flight process, his senses had been dulled. It was a second after feeling the punch to his leg, that he heard the gunshot.

He looked down at the back of his leg and saw the small hole in his jeans. At first a small trickle of blood appeared from the hole, which slowly began to transform into a darkening of the denim material of his jeans around the bullet hole.

"Fuck, that's gonna sting tomorrow," he said, as he began to limp as fast as his wounded leg would allow him, down the alleyway that stood on the other side of the fencing.

* * *

Simultaneously, Grant and Bradley thought they had heard a voice shouting something, and both looked in the direction of the Fortunates' clubhouse. Moments later, when they heard the gunshot, they realised something very serious was occurring. Their reactive thoughts were, however, completely different to their physical reactions. Grant's first thoughts were for the safety of the men he had sent into a dangerous situation—a situation he had given very little thought to, as his mind sank further into a revengeful obsession. Bradley's first thought was one honed by years of being a copper—public safety.

DS Bradley reached into his jacket's inside pocket and retrieved his police issued personal radio, pressing the orange emergency button, allowing his radio transmission to override all other transmissions. He spoke as clearly and calmly as he could, given the situation. In his entire career, he had only been involved in a situation involving a firearm being discharged once before now.

"Control, this is Charlie-Delta-One-Six, bikers' clubhouse on Queens Street, gunfire heard, all available officers required on scene, over." His voice sounded calm, but inside, he was a ball of tense nervousness. He had used the ten seconds that the emergency button gave him well. He waited for the control operator to respond, before pressing the PTT button to talk again.

The police control operator responded immediately to Bradley's radio transmission.

"All available units, I say again, all available units. Emergency assistance required at 56 Queens Street, firearm discharged. DS Bradley is on scene. All responding units acknowledge on route with ETA."

Happy that reinforcements were en route, Bradley turned to speak to Grant. There was no sign of him. He looked around the immediate area, eventually turning his focus to the direction of the Fortunates clubhouse frontage, but he could not spot the biker.

The second after hearing the gunshot, Grant had not hung around. He saw that Bradley's attention was momentarily interrupted, as he struggled to get something out of the inside of his jacket. He ran, heading across the road, moving around the back of a single-decker bus that unbeknownst to Grant at the time, was in the perfect position to block Bradley's view and hide Grant's progress across the main road. He just about avoided being hit by two cars, before disappearing down the side road that he had watched The Nameless Ones' bikes ride down not that long ago.

He had only just turned the corner, when he came face-to-face with a pale-skinned and limping Ordnance.

"What the hell is happening, mate?" he asked the injured biker.

"It's gone totally pear-shaped, bro, absolutely FUBAR. It was like they were ready for us coming," Ordnance replied.

Grant held out his hand, and said firmly, "Give me your keys now, and follow me."

Ordnance did as he was told, handing his bike keys over to Grant, and did his best to keep up with him, as Grant turned on his heels and headed back onto the main road.

DS Bradley knew that it was pointless shouting, or trying to chase the fleeing biker and his comrade, as he spotted Grant mounting a bike parked almost directly outside the front door of the clubhouse. He continued to watch, as he saw the second, much larger figure, position himself on the back seat of the bike, behind Grant. He observed the dark stain on the back of this man's jeans and suspected it was a bloodstain straightaway.

The bike roared away and Bradley made his way, cautiously, across the road. He positioned himself outside and to the side of the clubhouse door, gently pushing it open, so it did not bounce back to its closed position. He quickly peeked into the open doorway for a second or two.

Standing with his back flat to the brick wall, his mind raced. He had spotted nothing, no immediate threat during his quick glance into the building. All of his training and experience told him to stand-fast and await the support that he knew was en route, but for some unfathomable reason, he ignored all of that and entered the building, stooping down slightly to keep himself low and making a smaller target for any ensuing assailant.

He ducked his head quickly into and out of the next doorway. The room was empty, except for an eclectic mix of sofas and chairs.

"Police, lay on the floor," he shouted, lost of any other ideas about what to say.

There was no response, no noise whatsoever.

He quickly looked into the room once again, completed a quick assessment of the area, before rushing into the room, and diving behind the cover of an old green sofa. Adjusting his position, he looked around the side of the sofa, deciding that it was a better option than raising his head above the top of it.

At the far end of the room, he could see a door, slightly open, and without daylight streaming through the narrow gap between the door and its frame.

"This is the police," he called out. "The building is surrounded."

He returned to the cover of the piece of furniture, and rested his head against it, realising how pathetic his words sounded, he thought to himself.

What the hell are you doing, Richard Bradley, trying to get yourself killed this close to drawing your pension?

He waited for no more than a minute, listening out for any kind of noise. From outside, still some distance away, he heard the faint wailing of police sirens.

Bravado took the place of professional caution, as DS

Bradley slowly stood up. The room was silent. From outside the back door … more silence. Staying constantly alert for any movement around the room, he made his way to the door, through whose opening shone the daylight. As he got close, he turned sideways and pushed it farther open with his foot. It stopped against an unseen obstacle. For the first time since he had entered the building, he heard a noise—the familiar sound of a human being in agony—one he had heard on too many occasions. Carefully, moving his head side to side to gain as much sight of the outdoor area, he squeezed himself through the narrow gap. As he did so, he called out, "This is the police. Do not shoot. I am here to help."

The first thing he saw was a biker he knew well sat on a sofa at the far end of the sheltered, wooden floor area.

"Thank heavens you are here, officer," Stretch said. "There has been a right old shindig going on. I am lucky to be alive, I can tell thee."

DS Bradley looked down and to his left. A body lay on the floor, and was clearly the source of the groaning noise. The man's shoulder was a bloody gaping mess of sliced flesh, shattered bone and deep claret blood. In the hand of his uninjured arm sat a small pistol. Bradley guessed it was no more than a .40 calibre, and thought he recognised it as being similar to a Beretta style pistol he had come across at the scene of shooting a couple of years earlier.

"What's been going on, Stretch?" Bradley asked the lounging biker, his eyes still on the moaning body lying to his left.

"Well, officer, that fella right there, came rushing, all aggressive like, with a few other leather clad blokes, and started to make all kinds of threats," Stretch replied, his face serious and hard to read. "Well, some of my boys had to take

285

action like, defend themselves, so to speak."

"Looks like one of your boys took a machete to this man. A bit over the top, wouldn't you say?" Bradley asked in response.

"He had a gun, Mr, Bradley. What can I say?" Stretch's face remained as before. "It was like, how would you lot say? Reasonable force, proportionate to the circumstances. Isn't that how you describe it?"

Bradley turned to look at Stretch and studied his face. He had no idea why he was bothering, because he already knew the man was lying through his back teeth.

"A machete … reasonable force. Really?" he asked.

"Well, actually it was an axe. We use it to chop wood. Luckily, it was at hand, if you think about it," Stretch replied, allowing a small smile to form.

"And where is the axe wielding maniac?" Bradley asked.

"Gave chase, Mr. Bradley. Performing his civic duties. A brave and honourable man wouldn't you say?"

"And the rest of the alleged attackers?" Bradley enquired.

"Ran away like the cowards they are, with a few of my brothers giving chase, Mr. Bradley. That one over there," he said as he pointed toward the broken fence where the body of MadDog lay. "He got himself hurt in all the action and fell where he lies."

DS Bradley looked over at the body, a pool of blood was congealing adjacent to his neck and head. Before Bradley could get his next sentence out, which was to ask Stretch to accompany him to the police station so he could assist with enquiries, the sound of a high-powered weapon pierced the relative silence.

"Sounds like the cavalry have arrived, Mr. Bradley," Stretch said, the small smile now transformed into a huge grin.

A Change of Mind

The minute of time that passed, before the shot that Bradley heard was fired, passed slowly, both for the police marksman and the recipient of the bullet.

As Ordnance had rushed toward the fence, Chaos surveyed the scene of carnage around him. Shovel was on the floor behind him, yelling out in pain and doing his best to stem the flow of blood coming from the wound at the top of his shoulder. His hand had almost disappeared into the large open wound caused by the axe attack. In front of him, MadDog was crawling on his knees and one hand, the other being used to apply pressure to the knife wound in the side of his neck, out of which his blood was gushing. He was making his way toward the fence panel that Ordnance has just launched himself through, even at this early stage, he knew that MadDog was not going to get very far.

One of the Fortunates grabbed his arm and Chaos swung around, his trailing arm arced toward the face of his attacker, and the heel of his open hand slammed into the biker's chin. He fell to the floor like a felled tree, but not before Chaos heard the crunching sound of a jawbone being dislocated. This action gave him the few seconds he needed to start his escape. As he passed MadDog, he briefly dropped to one knee and placed his hand on the head of his fallen colleague.

"Sleep well, brother," he said, before standing back up and disappearing through the hole in the fence.

Looking to his right, he was surprised to see an empty alleyway. There was no sign of Ordnance. He made his way to the end of the short alleyway, and onto the side road. From there, he could see the van that Magill had been driving, but the driver's seat was empty. Once again, there was no sign of Ordnance, so headed up the road toward the main road, where he knew his bike was parked. He heard the roar of a bike and looked up, just in time to see two people on a bike. One was clearly Ordnance, and the other, he thought he recognised as Grant. Neither of the two men were wearing helmets, and for some reason, Ordnance was riding pillion.

With a head full of confusion and questions, he continued to the main road, and turning right once again, he saw his bike parked alongside two others that he recognised. He reached his bike at the same time as the screeching tyres under the pressure of heavily applied brakes, brought the police car to an abrupt halt, about thirty metres from where he stood.

The doors of the police car flew open, and Chaos saw two men climb out of the vehicle and stoop down behind the doors—the windows of both were fully open. He sensed, more than actually saw, movement from behind the vehicle's doors, and then saw the boot lid open. Moments later, both in the space where car windows had been, the recognisable sight of the muzzles of two rifles appeared, behind which were the heads of the two police marksmen, both taking aim through the weapons sights directly at him.

"On the floor! Get on the floor, now!" came the shouted order from behind one of the police car doors.

"On the floor, and place your hands on the back of your head," the second order was shouted from behind the other car door.

Chaos did not lie on the floor, nor did he place his hands behind his head. This was a man who had always been known as an instigator of action, normally the violent type of action.

"Hold on, boys. I have something for you," he shouted back at the police. He reached into the inside of his bike jacket. His intention of withdrawing his hand with the middle finger raised in the direction of the police, was not allowed to happen. The bullet hit him in the chest and spun his already dying body one-hundred-and-eighty degrees. Now, with his back to the police car, he fell forward, his hand finally falling from inside his jacket, with the middle finger almost fully raised, and as his head arched backward, he finally hit the ground. His chest slammed against the tarmac covered road, a millisecond before his chin smashed into it. His dying words were, "Thanks for looking after my seat, now move over, because I'm on my way back to Hell."

* * *

Arriving at the gates of their clubhouse, Ordnance climbed off the back of his bike, and with some considerable effort, accompanied by a substantial amount of pain, he limped to the gate and slammed a large clenched fist against it several times.

The gate was eventually opened, to Grant's surprise, by Double D. He rode past her, glaring at her as he did so. She ignored him, and closed the gate behind the bike and the limping Ordnance.

Grant stopped the bike just inside the compound, he killed the engine and walked angrily toward the woman.

"What the hell are you doing here?" he yelled.

"I went to my room and decided to stay here," she replied matter-of-factly.

"When I tell you to do something, you fucking do it, do you hear me?" Grant yelled once again.

"I'm the type of medic who likes to save lives, not stretcher them off the battlefield," she replied. "And the day I follow the orders of a madman, will be the day I yes to a rapist."

She looked at the limping Ordnance, who, deciding he would rather be somewhere else, was making his way toward the garages.

"Where do you think you are going, you fucking big idiot?" she shouted at him. "Get in the clubhouse and I will fix that leg of yours."

She glared at Grant, and said, "And then I am out of here, for good."

"The only thing good about you, is your ability to suck cock," Grant retorted viciously.

Double D glanced down in the general direction of Grant's crotch. "You call that a cock?"

Meanwhile, Ordnance limped his way, like a scolded child, to the rear door of the clubhouse. Every time the foot of his injured leg came into contact with the floor, he repeated the word, "Ow."

Double D stormed past him, saying, "You are a fucking cock. Come on, get in here, limpy."

Grant headed to the garage and entered the corridor that

led to the basement of the clubhouse. His arrival was met by Stacker, Hammer, Fixit, Reckon and Syco.

"Wow, you look a bit ruffled around the edges, bro," Stacker said.

At that moment, Will, or Mr. Deception, as he preferred to be called, appeared from the room that had been rapidly constructed for him by Stacker. Before he could get a word out, Grant pointed at him, and said, "Pack your stuff and go. Your services are no longer required."

"Do I still get paid?" Will enquired.

Grant spun on his heels and stared angrily at Will. His face was becoming redder with each passing second, and his hands were clenched so tightly that his fingers began to turn white, due to the lack of circulation.

Hammer walked over to the young man, who was not rooted to the spot, fearfully looking back at Grant. He placed his arm around the shoulders of Will, and said quietly, "I think you should do as he says. It doesn't look like he is having a good day."

Will returned briefly to his workstation and retrieved his laptop and the other few electronic items he used for his work. Returning into the larger basement room, he thought twice about mentioning the money again, deciding eventually just to leave.

Grant waited until Will was far enough down the corridor to be out of earshot, before beginning to explain what had happened.

"So, who do we have left?" Syco asked.

Grant mentally worked out the numbers in his head before speaking.

"Six or seven, I reckon—us four, plus Double D and Ordnance, who are somewhere upstairs."

"So, what do we do now?" Hammer enquired.

"We dump the three Armstrongs we have into the back of Fixit's van. He drops them off somewhere in the vicinity of the Armstrong home. As for you lot, just go," Grant replied.

"Go where?" Stacker asked.

"Go home," Grant replied. "Your real identities are unknown by the police. I don't think they will be interested in anyone other than me."

"But why aren't we doing what we set out to do?" Hammer asked, confused with the overload of information.

"Because they didn't do it," Grant replied, frustrated that he had just explained everything. "It is now obvious to me that my friend killed his own kids, and probably had something to do with the death of his wife, too. Basically, I think I have been set up."

Stacker was about to add something to the conversation, but was prevented from doing so, by the ringtone of Grant's phone.

Grant walked a few feet from the main group, and answered the call.

Despite not being able to see his face, the four men could see that something wasn't right about the phone conversation Grant was involved in.

"When?" Grant asked the person who had called.

There were a few unheard words, and then Grant asked again, "Who did it?"

His question was answered by more words that the group of men standing just a few feet away could not hear.

"How bad?" Grant finally asked.

The answer he received must have been short, because

seconds later, he ended the call. He turned to face the group of men, his face was pale.

"Change of plan," he said. "All of you just get out of here, and get as far away from here as possible. Forget all about your involvement with The Nameless Ones."

His breathing had increased, his shoulders dropped, and despite the paleness of his facial skin, there was a look of pure madness in his eyes.

Stacker asked the question that they all wanted the answer to.

"Grant, what's happened, bro?"

"They've killed Shuffler," Grant responded coldly.

* * *

Through a small gap between the two doors, Cutter watched as DS Bradley walked out of the clubhouse, following the crack of a weapon being fired from out front.

He slipped out of the room he had been hiding in, making his way to the rear door and out into the daylight.

"Job done as requested, Cutter," Stretch said upon seeing Cutter appear through the door. "Now, make sure your friend reaches out with the money he promised."

"Our mutual friend won't be contacting you directly, but you will get the money agreed upon," Cutter replied, knowing there was no chance of Fox speaking directly with the likes of Stretch or the Fortunates.

Without another word being said between them, Cutter made his way out of the bikers' yard, using the gap in the broken fence, kindly provided by one of the men he had helped to set up. He took off his bike jacket and slung it over his shoulder, casually walking down the alley and onto the side road. He immediately spotted the van, walked over to it, and climbed into the cab on the passenger seat side.

Behind the driver's seat sat Magill, his legs bent so his knees sat under his chin, his arms hugging his legs close to him.

"Get behind the wheel and fucking drive," Cutter told him.

"The police are going to be all over that main road," Magill replied, visibly shaking with fear.

"Then we won't head that way, you cowardly piece of shit. I will tell you what route to take," Cutter responded, his mind now thinking of how to cleanly get rid of Magill and start the tidying up process.

"Can I ask where we are heading?" Magill asked, starting up the van.

"To make Grant permanently nameless," he replied, a cruel smile on his face.

* * *

"What about you?" Stacker asked, looking at a man whose mind he had watched travel deeper into a state of madness for some time.

"Don't worry yourself about me," Grant replied, his voice almost feeling detached from everything and everyone around him.

"Come with us, bro," Hammer said. "You can hide out with Ordnance or something."

"No, I have one last job to do," Grant replied.

"And what would that be?" Hammer asked.

"Slaughter the fucking lot of them," Grant replied. His journey to total madness was almost complete.

It was, inevitably, Stacker who broke the silence that had followed Grant's statement.

"Grant, leave them and walk away, my friend."

"Can't do it, Stacker," Grant responded.

"Look, the girl is dead already," Stacker replied, much to the surprise of everyone in the room who was not aware. "She died an hour or so ago. Double D gave her a heavy dose of drugs to ease the pain, as her suffering came to an end."

"The pain she felt will be nothing, compared to what I have planned for those two," Grant said, looking at the limp bodies of Patrick and Alfie Armstrong.

Surprisingly, it was Syco who was the first to make a move. He handed his pistol to Grant, saying, "Make the slaughter quick and clean. I am out of here. Thanks for the break from monotony."

Grant took the handgun, nodded his head respectively at Syco, and replied, "It wouldn't be a slaughter if it was quick and clean."

Syco began to walk down the corridor, followed soon after by Hammer, who didn't say a word. He simply gripped the top of Grant's shoulder as he walked past him.

Reckon was the next to move. He shook Grant's hand and hugged him, before saying, "You know how to reach me, bro. I will help you hide, if Ordnance can't help." He hung his head as he walked away, internally feeling shame and guilt for effectively leaving a brother behind.

Stacker stood firm.

"I'm going nowhere," he said, pure determination in his tone.

Grant looked down at the pistol. He released the magazine from its housing, and after checking its contents, returned it back from where it had come from. Pulling back the slide, he loaded a round into the chamber and clicked the safety catch. He pointed the loaded pistol at Stacker's head.

"Then let the slaughter begin with you, brother," Grant said ominously.

"You wouldn't shoot me, Grant," Stacker said, maintaining eye contact with his friend.

"Yes, he would," a voice called out from behind Grant.

Stacker broke his eye contact with Grant. Looking beyond him, he saw Double D and Ordnance standing at the end of the corridor. Ordnance had his injured thigh heavily bandaged around the outside of his jeans.

Grant did not bother looking back. He knew the voice and guessed that Double D probably had Ordnance with her.

"The woman speaks sense for once," Grant said to Stacker.

Stacker shook his head with dismay. Of all the possible outcomes he had imagined, this had never been one of them. He walked slowly, and very reluctantly, toward the two figures at the far end of the basement. As he passed Grant, pistol now lowered to the side of his leg, he came to a stop.

He turned his head, looking at the side of Grant's face.

"Do what you feel you have to do, friend, then get some help, and get yourself cared for," he said quietly.

He joined Double D and Ordnance. Grant did not turn around until way after the three people had long exited the corridor. In fact, by the time he looked down the corridor and realised that, with the exception of three members of the

Armstrong family, he was alone, the three had already ridden away from the clubhouse. So good was the soundproofing of this very well-constructed basement, he had not heard the bike engines roar into life and ride out of his life for good.

Grant clicked the safety catch, once again making it safe, and pushed the pistol into his belt so it sat over his hip. He checked that the two Armstrong men were securely restrained, before walking over to where he knew the now dead body of Courtney Armstrong lay.

He pulled back the heavy sheeting and walked inside. He scanned his eyes up and down the body of the woman lying in front of him.

Underneath the corpse, thick shoots of bamboo covered in congealed blood could be seen. In places, some of the bamboo canes had grown strong enough to fully penetrate the body, the blood soaked tips of which could be seen poking out.

Whatever drug she had been given to sedate her, had not worked that well. Her dead face was etched with the pain she had experienced. Grant noticed that her arms were no longer restrained, guessing that Double D had removed them when she had administered the drugs. He also noticed that the fingers of the hand he could see were curled and contorted, further evidence of the unimaginable pain suffered.

Leaving the basement, he returned to the clubhouse via the garage. He collected two jerry cans of fuel, which he carried into the clubhouse building. Walking around the clubhouse, he entered every room, pouring petrol about as he did so. As hard as he tried, he could not summon any feeling of guilt as he walked into, and subsequently exited, each bedroom of those people who he knew to be dead. Dead because of him.

With every room liberally doused with fuel, he threw the

297

empty petrol containers into the bar area and returned to the garage, where once again, he picked up two more full jerry cans.

Pouring a trail of petrol behind him as he walked down the underground corridor, he finished off by covering the floor and walls of the basement with what petrol was left. The final fuel can had a small amount of petrol left in it, and he poured it over the bodies of the two Armstrong cousins. Patrick Armstrong started to regain consciousness as Grant shook out the final drops of the flammable liquid over his head.

"Who the hell are you, and what the fuck do you think you are doing?" Patrick asked, still groggy from the bang on the head from Syco.

"I am your nightmare, and you are going to burn," Grant responded. "But not before you suffer like your family made my brother suffer," His voice was filled with menace and hatred.

"I don't have a clue what you are talking about," Patrick replied, struggling against his restraints as he spoke.

Grant lowered his head so his face was a few inches from the face of Patrick Armstrong.

"Good luck finding someone who cares less than I do," he said smiling. He took a large inward sniff and added. "I do love the smell of petrol. It must be a biker thing, but I love the stench of a burning body even more."

Patrick Armstrong spat into Grant's face. Grant did nothing more than wipe away the spittle with his hand, and spread it over the face of the man who had produced it.

Grant started to walk away, when Patrick asked him, "Where are you going?" The fear in his voice could almost be tasted.

"I need a few tools to work with. Don't worry yourself. It will give you time to think about what awaits you, and allow for your cousin to come around. Please feel free to share with him how little time he has left." Grant continued to walk away from the two men as he spoke.

Pulling out his mobile phone, he waved it in air.

"Any messages you would like me to send to dear Kelvin?" The laugh that exited Grant's body was manic.

* * *

The nurse stood next to the hospital bed, in which lay the still body of the newest patient in the critical care unit. She was checking the monitors and equipment that were keeping him alive. Monitoring screens, a ventilator, lines and tubes leading from the machines to the body of Shuffler, all accompanied by the mechanical breathing noises caused by the ventilator, were things that the nurse was accustomed to. The very things so necessary to keep the patients alive were, more often than not, the things that unnerved visitors the most.

There had been no visitors for this poor man, though. The nurse pondered over this for a few moments. She had never known a CCU patient to not have someone enquiring about them. Even the two prison staff members who had arrived with him had now left. All the hospital had was the paperwork discharging a man, known only as Shuffler, from prison. No prison wanted a death in custody, especially one they could easily be rid of with a simple document.

"We will care for you, Shuffler, whoever you are," the nurse said with real compassion. She stroked his forehead, before leaving the room.

"I'll be back later," she said, ensuring the door closed gently behind her.

The mechanical breathing sound was the only companion Shuffler had.

* * *

Standing behind the bar inside the clubhouse, Grant poured himself a whisky. It had been some years since he last tasted this particular drink.

Grant had always had a tendency to become violent after drinking whisky. It had been Julia who had issued the ultimatum of "it goes, or I go," many years ago. Grant had decided that his wife was needed in his life more than whisky was, and anyway, brandy made for a more than adequate replacement for the amber liquid he now poured down his throat.

He would have probably poured himself a second, and possibly a third, if it had not been for the sudden and unexpected sounding of a horn from outside.

He reluctantly left the bar and walked outside. Not bothering to look who was now persistently beeping the horn on the other side of the gate, he opened it up. He looked at the van, and in particular, the driver. Magill was waving his hands frantically, in an effort to let Grant know that he wanted him to open both gates.

Grant ignored the waving motions and walked to the passenger door of the van. Magill lowered the window.

"Open the goddamn gates and let me in, will you?" Magill asked.

Grant looked at him, confused by the arrival of this unexpected visitor.

"Magill, do yourself a favour and fuck off," he said impatiently.

"You have to let me in. The coppers are all over the place," Magill replied just as impatiently.

"Well the last place you want to be is here," Grant responded.

"Where else can I go?" Magill asked pleadingly.

"Back to your pathetic little life, I guess," Grant said.

Unseen by Grant, at the very back of the van, Cutter slowly opened one of the rear doors, just wide enough to allow him to get out of the van. The high powered pistol in his hand, which he had retrieved from one of the internal compartments within the bodywork panelling, was all ready to fire, should the need suddenly arise.

He left the door open, not wanting it to make a noise in the process of closing it and attracting the attention of the man leaning against the open door window. He slowly walked down the side of the van, approaching Grant with the black handled, silver bodied Desert Eagle .50 calibre handgun, now raised and pointed at his target. He made it to within a few feet, before Grant realised he was not alone on the outside of the vehicle.

"Do as the man is asking, Grant," Cutter ordered.

Grant didn't move, and didn't turn his head to look at the gunman. He spoke slowly and calmly.

"So, you are calling me Grant now. Interesting."

"Would you prefer me to call you, John?" Cutter asked. "You were once called John, weren't you"?

"Hey, you are the one holding the gun, so you can call me whatever you like," Grant replied.

"Open the gates, let the van through, and then we can all have a drink, and I will answer all your questions," Cutter responded, his voice as calm as Grant's.

Grant did as he told, leaving the gates open after Cutter had told him to do so when he had tried to close them behind the passing van.

"Just walk into the clubhouse and sit down at the bar," Cutter had said to him.

As they both entered the clubhouse door, Cutter shouted over to Magill, telling him to close the gates and then join them at the bar. Magill waved in response, a large grin on his face. He was so happy to see Grant being ordered around and not in control for once.

Grant sat at the bar as he had been told. He waited for Cutter to walk around the other side of the bar, before saying anything. Cutter stopped him.

"Wait for a moment," he said.

With the gun in one hand, still pointed at Grant, he first placed a bottle of brandy on the bar top, and then placed two glasses next to it.

"Pour us a couple of drinks, then we can talk."

Grant once again did as he was told. As he finished pouring the second drink, Magill burst into the room.

"Do I get one, too?" he asked as he walked, a bounce in his step, toward the two men.

Cutter momentarily moved the aim of the weapon away from Grant. As its muzzle came into direct alignment with

Magill, he pulled the trigger. The impact of the bullet, entering into Magill's brain via his forehead, took him off his feet and simultaneously blew his brains out of the back of his skull. Bits of bone, blood, flesh and brain matter splattered onto the floor, seconds before Magill's body joined them.

Grant flinched as the gun was fired and the bullet flew past his head, missing him by inches. The ringing in his ears left every other sound muffled and difficult to hear.

"Grant, Grant," Cutter shouted repeatedly, until the partially deaf and fully shocked man looked at him.

"That was a sign of my intentions," he said, "just in case you had any doubts."

Grant lifted one of the glasses to his mouth, tilted it slightly toward Cutter, and downed the warming liquid in one gulp.

Cutter replicated Grant's actions.

With both glasses returned to the bar, Grant asked, "Who are you?"

"Is that it?" Cutter responded. "After everything that has happened, that is the only question you have?"

"I think it's a good starting point," Grant replied.

"Well," Cutter began, "let me tell you who I am."

Grant listened intently to every word, as the man on the other side of the bar not only answered his question, but many others in the process.

"I want you to cast your mind back, to the point in your life when your military training had ended and you were facing a posting to Northern Ireland. You returned to your hometown for a week's annual leave, and spent the majority of that leave in the company of a young lady. As far as I am told, the pair of you spent most of your time together in bed. Now, I can only assume that, for you, those few days and nights were just

303

a bit of fun, but I can tell you that for that woman, they meant so much more. In fact, she fell in love with you. Now, I am sure you remember her name, but let me remind you. Karen, fell head over heels in love with you, and one week later, you left her bed and her life, forever. It, of course, wasn't the first Warriner's life you had walked out on though, was it, John? You had walked out of her brother David's life a couple of years earlier, when you first joined the Army. My mother did not tell Uncle David that you were my father until she was dying. That was a few months before his wife killed herself, and a short time later, as I am sure you have worked out by now, he murdered my three young cousins."

Cutter paused for a few seconds, allowing Grant to take it all in. There was no response from Grant, so he continued.

"Throughout my childhood, I listened to my mother, telling me about this mysterious man who was my father. She never said a bad word about you. And so I waited, waited for this hero to return and be my dad, but as we both know, that never happened. As time passed by, I grew to hate you, and my Uncle David unknowingly helped to increase that hate. He would tell me about his school friend, this lad named John, who he admired and looked up to. Someone who would leave him alone, to live a life longing for his friend to eventually return, but he never did. Of course, I made the link by listening to both sets of memories. I was about thirteen, when I came to realise that both my mother and uncle were talking about the same person, the same cocksure man who would return to his hometown flashing his money about in the pubs, and impressing the ladies. So, now I have another name I can call you. So what shall it be? Nameless, Grant, John, or shall we agree on Dad?"

Grant raised his eyebrows and sighed.

"Thanks for the trip down your highway of memories. Now, when do you send me down the highway to hell?" Grant did not seem phased or affected by anything he had just listened to. It was as if his dark heart had finally shrivelled to nothing.

"Oh, trust me, from the very beginning that was my intention, but as time has passed by, I have come to understand you more. I now realise that death is something you would embrace lovingly. Of course, I know that by not killing you, I will be hugely upsetting a mutual friend of ours. After all, that is what agent Fox paid good money for," Cutter said, still waiting for the reaction he longed for, but once again, he was disappointed.

"Fox, I should have known he was somewhere lurking in the background," Grant replied.

"Yeah, he tracked me down and told me all about your successful working relationship," Cutter said sarcastically. "He said I would be the perfect weapon against you."

"You and Fox are very much alike. You both want that dramatic impact. It eats you up when you don't get it, doesn't it, son?" Grant responded, also looking for a reaction.

He stood up and stretched his arms outwards to their full length.

"So, here I am, after all these years of disappointment and hate. Do what you were sent to do, be the serving dog of war that you clearly are." Grant awaited the searing heat of a bullet to enter his chest or head. He closed his eyes and waited some more.

"A god-like ego, just as Fox described you," Cutter said. Grant opened his eyes, really disappointed that his antagonising approach had not delivered the desired end result.

"As I said," Cutter continued, "I have worked you out. You don't fear death—you fear not being in control, so I intend to take all control away from you."

"Oh, do explain. I am dying of fucking boredom here," Grant replied, still working on the approach that winding up his newly discovered offspring, would make him pull the trigger of the weapon still firmly aimed at him.

Cutter smiled and began talking again.

He spent just a few minutes spelling out exactly what Grant had to do. He ended with the words, "Your worst nightmare, I would imagine."

"Really?" Grant replied. "And exactly what makes you think I am going to go along with your little plan?"

Cutter did not respond. He pulled his mobile from the front pocket of his jeans, unlocked it and opened up the favourite's page on his contacts. He pressed the contact name he wanted to call and, placing the phone on top of the bar, he pressed the loudspeaker button.

They both listened to the call ringing out. Four times it rang, before being answered.

"Hello, Cutter," said the voice.

"Hello, Mr. Pheasant," Cutter replied. "You are on speaker phone, please ask the lady to speak."

"Talk, you bitch," Grant heard Agent Pheasant say to someone.

A familiar voice responded, and Grant knew that he was beaten.

"Fuck off, you prick," said the voice of Emma in the background.

"Emma," Cutter said into the phone. "I have a good friend of yours here with me. Do me a favour, darling, and speak to

306

Grant, would you?"

There was a short period of silence, before Emma eventually spoke one solitary word. "Grant?"

"Emma, are you okay?" Grant asked her. The sound of defeat in his voice was all that Cutter had been waiting for.

"This arsehole has just produced a knife, and has placed it against my throat," Emma replied, her ballsy approach to dealing with conflict still her preferred plan.

"Emma, everything will be okay," Grant told her, and then speaking to the man holding the knife against her throat, he said, "Pheasant, put the knife away and leave her safe, and you won't have to spend the rest of your life looking over your shoulder." Grant pressed the red button on the screen of Cutter's mobile phone, and ended the call without another word.

Cutter looked at Grant with a smile of satisfaction.

"I need twenty-four hours, just to tie up some loose ends," Grant said.

"You don't deserve it, but okay. Look at it as a long overdue gift for all your birthdays that I missed," Cutter replied.

"Call off your gopher," Grant said.

"I will, the moment I am confident that you have done what you have to do. And trust me, I will be watching you for the next twenty-four hours," Cutter replied, still smiling.

"I will do exactly what you want, just promise me that the girl will not be harmed," Grant pleaded.

"It's not nice having no control over your future, is it, father?"

The End of the Vengeful Road

I t was a few minutes before seven o'clock the following morning, when Grant eventually emerged from the hedgerow, behind which he had been hiding. He had been there for around two hours, surveying the area around the hospital building, looking for any sign of the police. He was satisfied that they were not outside the building, but remained unsure about whether or not they had a presence inside.

At about the same time, Ordnance was sitting on his bike that he had parked behind his caravan, somewhere in South Wales, during the very late hours of the night before. He placed a couple of the painkillers, given to him by Double D, into his mouth and crunched down on them, chewing and swallowing them dry. He wondered what had happened at the clubhouse after he had left. He couldn't help thinking he should have done more to change the outcome.

Double D was sat on the doorstep of the backdoor of her house, a cup of hot coffee in her hand. Her mind was also full of thoughts about Grant, about the man she had briefly had feelings for, but knowing that walking away from a man with dark and mental intentions, was without any doubt, the best thing she could have done.

Syco rode his bike off the early morning Dover to Calais ferry. A few months riding around Europe was just what was needed, he thought to himself, as he mentally enjoyed the long winding roads of Europe that lay ahead of him. Those were the only thoughts he had.

Stacker sat in front of his laptop. He moved the cursor over the green submit button and pressed the enter key on the keyboard. He wondered how long he would have to wait, before receiving some interest in the advert he had just posted, the advert selling his beloved motorbike. He no longer wanted any connection with the biker world. He knew it would be painful and he would miss it like hell. He also knew that it would be more painful to remember the people and things he had experienced of late, and getting on a bike again would just rekindle those memories. He made the decision that his biking days were over, and would forever blame Grant for that decision.

* * *

DS Richard Bradley had arrived at the clubhouse of The Nameless Ones a few hours after Cutter had walked out of the compound gates, which had been around thirty minutes after Grant had left.

He had not gone there expecting to find anyone, neither was he expecting to see the place surrounded by firefighters and their vehicles trying to put out the raging fire that had now consumed the building.

He carried on driving past the building, having no doubt

that he would be called upon to return there at some later date. For now, he decided that the best place he could be, was in the warmth and comfort of his own bed.

He was confident that one day soon, he would come face-to-face with the man who called himself Nameless, he just didn't know how quickly that moment would come around.

He spent the rest of the journey home, unconsciously scanning the pavements and roads for that very man.

* * *

Grant entered the hospital via an entrance less busy than that of the main one, or that to the accident and emergency department. He walked along corridors, constantly on the lookout for any sign of the police. He read the hospital signs, following them to the second floor, to where the ICU was located. He used the stairs to reach the second floor. He had learned from many visits to hospitals over the years, that most visitors and hospital staff tended to use the lifts to make their way between floors. He almost smiled at the irony of this, a place to improve your health, where most people decided to stand still in a mechanical box and allow it to do all the work for them.

It took him about fifteen minutes to find the ICU, and as he expected, after pushing and then pulling the door, he discovered entry into the ward was controlled. He placed one hand on the door and leaned against it. He did not want to use the buzzer and intercom system to announce his arrival. He felt the door open toward him and stepped back to get out of the way, as a nurse appeared in the doorway.

"Can I help you?" she asked.

Caught out slightly, Grant paused before answering. He didn't really know if Shuffler had been admitted to this unit or not. He had made an assumption, following a short conversation with Jenny Wolstenholme, about seven hours earlier. During that conversation, she had explained that Shuffler had left the prison alive, and had since been officially released from custody. Grant had enough prison experience to understand the meaning of that course of action by the prison authorities—it meant they expected the person to die.

"Yes, I hope so," he said to the nurse. "I believe someone I know has been admitted to this ward."

"And the name of this person would be?" the nurse asked him.

"Shuffler," Grant replied. "He's just known as Shuffler."

"What is your relationship to this person?" the nurse asked suspiciously.

"He's my brother," Grant replied, comfortable that he wasn't totally lying to the nurse.

"I'm sorry, sir, I cannot let you in to see your brother," the nurse told him. "Visiting is strictly controlled, as I am sure you can appreciate."

Grant saw no point in arguing. At least he now knew that Shuffler was still alive.

"Yes, I understand, nurse," Grant replied. "Thank you anyway."

The nurse watched as the sad and tired looking man started to walk away.

"Sir, I can tell you that I have been tending to your brother throughout the night," she said. Grant stopped walking and turned to look at the nurse.

"He is in extremely critical condition. I'm afraid he may not survive the trauma he has sustained."

"I am sure that you and your colleagues will do your best for him," Grant said back to her.

"We will, sir. You have my word on that," the nurse replied.

Grant gave her a weak, but well-intended smile, and continued to walk away.

The nurse watched his progress, until he turned right into another corridor and was out of her sight. As a nurse working in the ICU, she had experienced pain and sorrow, so she knew all too well that the man she had just met was breaking under the sorrow he was currently feeling.

* * *

Cutter sat in the dark BMW in the hospital car park, watching Grant enter the building, and about thirty minutes later, leave through the same entrance. He watched the man, shoulders dropped and head sunk, walk across the narrow road, and disappear into the surrounding shrubbery. He waited about ten minutes, before starting the engine. He drove out of the car park and toward the exit of the hospital grounds.

He reached the T-junction where the hospital exit road met with the busy main road. The amount of traffic gave him the time he needed to look left and right down both sides of the road. He saw Grant almost immediately, walking slowly along the pavement in the general direction of the police station, which was about a forty-minute walk away.

He steered the BMW right onto the main road and drove past Grant, who was too preoccupied to have seen him, even if he had known what type of car Cutter was driving.

Fifty minutes after leaving the hospital, Grant stood looking across a road at the police station, and briefly wondered if he was doing the right thing. Surely, he thought, death was a better option than this. Unfortunately for him, it was not his life at stake, and the final realisation of the situation hit him. He had no control over what was happening, other than to do what Cutter had told him to do, and for that, he had respect for the man, even if it was reluctant respect.

He pulled his jacket forward so it sat properly on his shoulders, his final feeble effort to make himself presentable. It was a futile effort, his unshaven, tired face showed him to be the sleep deprived and beaten man that he was.

Two police officers walked passed him on the steps of the police station as he approached the front door. They both eyed him with the suspicion of two inexperienced coppers. He ignored them and walked into the station. He positioned himself at the front desk and waited for the police sergeant to acknowledge his arrival.

"Take a seat, sir," the officer said, only briefly casting his eyes upward. "I'll be with you in a minute or so."

"DS Bradley, please," Grant replied.

"As I said, sir, take a seat for a moment," the police sergeant responded firmly.

"I don't want to take a seat, I want to speak to DS Richard Bradley," Grant replied just as firmly. "And I want to speak to him now."

The police officer resisted the urge to slam his pen down on the reception desk, instead placing it down firmly and precisely. He stood up straight and looked at the man, who was bringing about a bad start to his shift.

"And what, may I ask, would make me disturb a very busy detective?" he asked.

One word, said bluntly, changed the attitude of the police sergeant.

"Murder," Grant answered.

* * *

Richard Bradley was at home, just finishing his breakfast porridge, when his mobile rang. His wife gave him the look that she always gave when she heard the ringtone. Richard smiled at her and let the phone ring for a few more seconds, allowing a few more bars of the song "Breaking the Law" to play.

"That is your work mobile, Richard. I really don't think that ringtone is appropriate," his wife said as he took the call.

"DS Bradley, this had better be good, because it's damn early," he said into the phone.

"Sir," the police sergeant said in response. "I have a man here at the station, insisting that he needs to speak to you now."

"Really, a crazy this early in the day? Does this person have a name?" Bradley asked.

"He says he is nameless and that you would understand that," the slightly confused officer replied.

DS Bradley's response was immediate. "Do not let that man out of the station," he ordered. "I don't care what you have to do, but that man goes nowhere. Do you understand?"

"Yes sir," the sergeant replied, now looking at Grant with a totally different attitude.

* * *

As Cutter watched the car screech to a halt outside the station, and saw DS Bradley running up the small number of steps at the front of the police station, he made a quick phone call.

"It's done," he said. "You can restore his data."

Cutter could almost feel the smile on Fox's face as he spoke back to him.

"It has already been done. The correct personal information files are available again. Not just for him, but for them all. The Nameless Ones are no longer nameless," agent Fox replied.

Cutter ended the call, closed his eyes and spoke quietly. "Rest in peace, Mum. He will now begin to experience the loneliness that he caused for you and Uncle David."

* * *

Richard Bradley sat in the interview room. Across the table from him, sat a pathetic looking version of the man he knew only as Nameless.

"I am going to record this interview," he told Grant, who nodded his head in response.

DS Bradley unwrapped a cassette tape, placed into the

315

recording machine and pressed down on two red buttons.

"The time is zero-nine-forty-seven. Present in the room are DS Richard Bradley and ...," he looked at the man sat opposite him. "You need to state your name for the purpose of the tape."

"Grant, also previously known as John Richardson," Grant said quietly.

DS Bradley jotted down the two names on the page of the notebook in front of him.

"So, do I call you Grant or John?" Bradley asked.

"Legally, it would be Grant," Grant replied.

"And would that be Grant Richardson?" Bradley asked again.

"No, it's just Grant," he replied.

"Would I be correct in saying that you have come to the station of your own accord and have specifically asked to speak with me?" Bradley asked.

"Yes, that is correct," Grant replied, his responses sounding more tired than the one before.

"And what would you like to talk to me about, Grant?"

"Murder. I am here to hold my hands up and admit responsibility for the murder of at least four people, and the indirect responsibility for the deaths of countless others." Grant's response was given without any emotion.

Bradley could hardly believe what he was hearing, but continued to approach the interview professionally. This needed to be handled precisely, because he had no idea, at the moment, what angle this man was coming from.

"You state at least four murders. Could you be more specific about that number?" he asked Grant.

"No, not really," Grant replied.

"Considering the seriousness of what you have said, I would advise that you seek legal representation, Grant," Bradley said.

"I don't need to waste the time of a solicitor, just to say the word guilty in a courtroom," Grant replied coldly.

"Well, I do need to pause this interview and seek advice," Bradley responded.

"No, Bradley, you don't," Grant said. For the first time since the interview had begun, Grant showed some emotion. Not surprisingly, it was anger.

"What you need to do is, keep that tape rolling and listen to what I have to tell you. This is your one and only opportunity. You walk out of the door, and I clam up tighter than a Yorkshire man with the generosity kicked out of him."

Bradley stayed seated.

"Talk away, Grant. It's your life," Bradley told him.

"Yeah, exactly, my life and my life sentence," Grant replied. "The one bit of control I have left."

The detective listened for almost two hours, as Grant spoke almost nonstop. It was either an outpouring of grief and guilt, an unloading of demons in the man's heart, or a complete load of bullshit. Whatever it was, he couldn't stop listening.

Names such as Cowboy, One a Year and Tankslapper were thrown into the inane chatter like they were supposed to mean something to him. Someone known as The Priest ebbed and waned throughout the verbal onslaught, although Bradley couldn't work out if he was a biker, or a murderer, or even if it was a single person or several.

Twice during the one-way interview, he had to ask Grant to stop talking while he changed the tapes, but the verbal spillage continued. Bradley did his best to change the tapes and make notes as best as he could during those periods.

317

There were many mentions of a man named Ian, a name that provoked real agony within Grant, and the closest it came to Bradley sensing something resembling remorse. Secret organisations rolled into identity changes, and personal information being deleted, although Grant had mentioned several times that all that would be available now, as men known as Fox, Pheasant and Bloom would have seen to that.

By the time Grant eventually stopped talking, DS Bradley was exhausted.

He waited before speaking, not wanting to be the reason for stopping the flow of information, if that is what it actually was.

"Grant, or John, or whatever your name is," he said, "you have told me what, on the surface, seems like an unbelievable tale, and I need to go away and check this all out. However, the one thing missing is a reason, a motive."

"Evil," Grant replied.

"You believe you are evil?" Bradley asked.

"No," Grant replied, staring at the detective, his eyes unblinking. "I had to get rid of the evil."

Speaking into the recording machine, Bradley said, "The time is now eleven-fifty-six, and I am terminating this interview. Grant, John Robinson, I am detaining you while I look into the events you have spoken about this morning."

"Am I under arrest?" Grant asked.

"Yes, you are under arrest for suspicion of the murders of an unknown number of persons and involvement in the deaths, and or, disappearances of others," the detective replied.

Grant asked one more question. "Can I have my phone call now, please?"

"Yes you may, but first I need to take you to the custody

sergeant, who will read you your rights and process you for custody," Bradley replied.

The formal processing, which involved the taking of all Grant's personal details, photographing him and taking his fingerprints, took around another fifty minutes. Grant cooperated throughout. DS Bradley could not believe the change in the demeanour of the man since he had last seen him the day before.

"Cell number two, detective," the custody desk sergeant told Bradley.

"Phone call," Grant said immediately.

"The phone is on the wall behind you," the sergeant responded gruffly.

"Let him use the custody suite phone, please, sergeant," Bradley said. "And don't rush him."

The detective ushered the sergeant to the farthest point away from the desk. He wanted to give Grant as much privacy as possible to make his call.

"I can't remember the number," Grant called over to Bradley. "It's in my mobile."

Bradley walked over to the small clear property bag, now containing Grant's personal effects. Taking the phone out, he handed it to Grant, saying, "Use your mobile to make the call if you want."

"No, I just need to remind myself of the number," Grant replied, the contacts screen on his phone already open. He pretended to be searching for the number he wanted, a number he knew all too well, while all the time, pressing the edit button, followed by select all, and finally, delete.

"Thanks," he said to Bradley, handing him his mobile back.

He called the number and waited for it to be answered,

praying that it would be answered.

"Hello," a female voice finally said.

"You alone now?" Grant asked.

"Grant, is that you?" Emma asked.

"No, it's, John," he replied. "Are you alone now?"

"Yes, I'm alone. I promise you, I am all right," Emma replied, confused as to why Grant was referring to himself as John.

"Where are you, Grant?" she asked.

"I am in the best place now," he replied vaguely.

"Grant, are you okay?" Emma asked, unable to hide the worry she now felt.

"I don't think I have ever been okay," he replied, and put the phone down to end the call.

* * *

DS Bradley, ably assisted by DC Pete "Woody" Wood, spent the majority of the next forty-eight hours investigating the things that his newly acquired suspect had admitted to. He found nothing—no reports of missing persons, no open murder investigations, and no information about a Bloom Foundation or government department named CORT.

Phone calls to other police stations, special branches, the anti-terrorist squad, and as many of the intelligence services as would speak to him, all came up with nothing.

He was at the point of realising that he had been the victim of a hoax, and the most he would be able to do was charge the man downstairs in the cells with wasting police time, until the phone on Woody's desk rang and Woody held it toward him, saying, "I think you will want to take this call, boss."

Bradley took the phone from Woody.

"Hello, Detective Bradley speaking. Who am I talking to, please?"

"Detective Bradley," replied a woman's voice," "I am Sister Renshaw. I work at the general hospital in Shrewsbury."

"And how may I be of assistance, sister?" Bradley replied courteously.

"I understand that you have been enquiring about possible murder victims, or suspicious deaths reported over the past two years," she replied. "Especially any involving male victims with the first name of Ian. Is this correct?"

"That is correct, sister, yes," Bradley answered, his voice sounding tired. He fully expected this call to result in another dead end.

"Well, I was on duty some time ago, when a body of a man was dumped outside of our hospital. He died within a few hours of us finding him. Extremely bad injuries had been sustained, mainly blast and burn injuries, as far as I can recollect. I remember this one in particular, because in the emergency room, while removing as much of the man's clothing as we could, I noticed a rather unique tattoo."

Bradley had no idea where this conversation was going, so he attempted to hurry along a bit.

"What information do you think you have for me, sister?" he asked impatiently.

"Well, the tattoo was just above the victim's penis, and it said, 'Hi, my name is Ian.'"

Bradley quickly became a bit more engaged in the telephone call.

"And what did you find out about this Ian?" he asked.

"At the time, absolutely nothing," the sister replied. "Obviously, the local police became involved, but the man could not be identified, neither from fingerprints or dental records. It was like he did not exist."

"You said, at the time, sister. Has something changed?" Bradley asked.

"Well, yes, it has actually, all a bit strangely, really," the nurse replied.

"In what way, please, sister?" Bradley asked, his patience now stretched to its absolute limits.

"When I heard about the enquiry, I did another search of our records database. Obviously, with it being a suspicious death, we kept records of dental imprints and blood type, etcetera," she explained.

"Yes, yes, I understand all of that, but you said that you were unable to identify this person," Bradley said bluntly.

"I did indeed," the sister replied. "But this time, it came up with a name, which is very strange indeed, don't you think?"

"And what was that name?" Bradley asked.

"An Ian Churchill. Is that the man you are looking for?" she asked.

"I have no idea, but thanks for your call, sister." DS Bradley handed the phone back to DC Wood.

* * *

DS Bradley stood outside of cell number two in the custody area, and opened up the panel that covered the observation window. Grant was in the exactly the same position as he had been on every occasion he had had reason to speak to him over the past two days—lying on his bed.

"Grant," he called through the cell door. "Does the name Ian Churchill mean anything to you?"

Grant held up his right hand and raised his thumb, without looking in the direction of the cell door.

He slid the observation panel cover back into place.

"Got you," he said and returned to his office.

Grant continued to lay on his bed. His mind began to contemplate what life would be like back in a prison, this time, on the other side of the bars.

Epilogue

IN MEMORY OF
Mark Ray
1970 ~ 2018
A friend, a colleague, who wanted to be an author.

About the Author

Eddie was born in Stoke-on-Trent, England. He joined the British Army at the age of sixteen, serving in Northern Ireland, Germany and London, before joining the Prison Service. After twenty-five years as a Prison Officer, he took a completely different career path, and began working for the NHS, where he currently works as a department manager. Eddie started to write in 2015, after hitting rock bottom and eventually being diagnosed with concealed depression. He has written three books thus far, and is currently working on books four and five in the "Take it for *Grant*ed" series of thriller novels.

You can connect with me on:
- 𝕏 https://www.twitter.com/eddie_author
- f https://www.facebook.com/EddieMannAuthor

Also by Eddie Mann

Ordinarily Unthinkable

"Ordinarily Unthinkable," by Eddie Mann, is a tale of Grant, a man with a mysterious past.

After the senseless deaths of his wife and daughter, Grant seeks revenge on those responsible for this abhorrent act.

Who is responsible, and will Grant exact revenge for those who he loved and lost?

Ordinarily Unthinkable is a fast-paced, exciting novel which will have the reader gripped.

Messenger

GRANT IS BACK!

Left for dead, he awakens to find himself in the clutches of an organisation secretly funded by the British government, forced to work for them by a revelation that rocks him to his very core.

Grant is determined to break away from the clutches of this secretive agency, while still completing the task of finding and stopping an horrific serial killer and getting back what he thought he had lost forever.

CPSIA information can be obtained
at www.ICGtesting.com
Printed in the USA
BVHW041829080419
544942BV00019B/248/P